The Exigent Shadow
and Other Strange Obsessions

BY THE SAME AUTHOR

The Little Fays in the Air
Don Juan in Paradise

The Exigent Shadow
and Other Strange Obsessions

by
Catulle Mendès

Translated, annotated and introduced by
Brian Stableford

A Black Coat Press Book

English adaptation and introduction Copyright © 2019 by Brian Stableford.

Cover illustration Copyright © 2019 illustration by Daniele Serra.

Visit our website at www.blackcoatpress.com

ISBN 978-1-61227-849-0. First Printing. April 2019. Published by Black Coat Press, an imprint of Hollywood Comics.com, LLC, P.O. Box 17270, Encino, CA 91416. All rights reserved. Except for review purposes, no part of this book may be reproduced or transmitted in any form or by any means, electronic or mechanical, including photocopying, recording, or by any information storage and retrieval system, without permission in writing from the publisher. The stories and characters depicted in this novel are entirely fictional. Printed in the United States of America.

TABLE OF CONTENTS

Introduction	7
The Man in the Green Caravan	13
The Pond	41
The Amorous Child	52
The Bouquet of Forget-Me-Nots	83
The Unexpected	88
Wedding Night	94
The Guest	99
Possessed	105
The Arsonist	110
The Flute-Player	116
The Tearful Day	124
The Chaste Town	129
56 Rue des Filles-Dieu; Or, The Heautonparateroumene	134
A Village, Near the Road	190
The Exigent Shadow	208
Fear on the Island	222
The Reflection, the Odor, the Flame and the Image	229
The Portrait on the Empty Wall	235
Effects Without Causes	239
The Curious Adventure of a Hat	245
The Gratitude of a Trumpet	247
Official Record of an Interrogation	249
The Tears That Do Not Know What To Mourn	255

Introduction

The present volume is one of a set of three collections assembling a substantial fraction of the short fantastic fiction of Catulle Mendès (1841-1909). It assembles tales of the *fantastique* dealing with anomalous events and altered states of consciousness that might or might not have supernatural causes. One of the other two collections, *The Little Fays in the Air and Other Tales of Faerie*, is an addendum to the series of collections and anthologies produced in association with *Tales of Enchantment and Disenchantment: A History of Faerie, with an Exemplary Anthology of Tales*, and collects more than twenty tales of fays and some associational items. The third volume, *Don Juan in Paradise and Other Amorous Fantasie*s assembles more than eighty *contes*, fables and apologues employing supernatural motifs other than the apparatus of faerie.

The first three stories in the present collection come from the first phase of Mendès' career, when he was heavily influenced by the work of Edgar Poe—his translation of "The Premature Burial" was reprinted in an 1889 collection, *Le Cruel berceau*, with no indication that it was a translation and not an original work—and that influence shows in both their style and subject-matter. The three stories were reprinted in his first collection, *Histoires d'Amour* (1868). Mendès had begun writing short stories in 1860, and the works he produced during the next decade were aimed at periodicals that frequently used substantial articles and stories. He was the founder in 1861 of the *Revue fantaisiste*, which followed the then-standard practice of using relatively long feature articles and stories, but as the editor of the periodical, required to fill a fixed number of pages on a regular basis, he routinely had to supply "fillers" of various sorts. Most periodicals employed reviews and short items of non-fiction for that purpose, but Mendès immediately began deploying fictional "character sketches" of a kind that were later to supply the bulk of three collections entitled *Monstres parisiens*, published in the 1880s.

That marketplace was devastated by the economic upheavals following France's catastrophic defeat in the Franco-Prussian War of 1870, and the bulk of Mendes' literary effort in the 1870s went into poetry and work for the theater, but the situation changed drastically in the early 1880s when advances in the technologies of printing and paper production made newspapers and periodicals much cheaper to produce, resulting in a rapid and prodigal proliferation, and consequent fierce competition between them. French newspapers already had a long tradition of "feuilleton fiction," by which a section of one page was ruled off, and the space below it used for serial fiction. Convention had established that the space below a standard feuilleton could accommodate between 1400 and 1700 words of text, and although much of the short fiction published by newspapers in the 1880s and 1890s was not actually placed beneath the feuilleton, that remained the standard expectation of word-length. Mendès frequently reduced the wordage even further, however, in order that his work could be more easily slotted into the limited space available in newspapers that were only four pages long, with the back page mostly taken up by advertisements.

When that boom began, Mendès was ready and prepared to take advantage of it. He soon became an editor again, for the short-lived geographical periodical *Le Monde Inconnu* and the longer-lasting bi-weekly *Revue Populaire*, both launched in 1882. The latter's chief stock-in-trade was reprinted serial novels, but in both periodicals Mendès employed his expertise in supplying fillers, initially under the pseudonyms Jean-qui-Passe and René Maugéant. Many were brief anecdotal sketches of contemporary Parisian life, often featuring Jean-qui-Passe's friend Valentin, who remained the hero of many of Mendès short stories long after the author had abandoned the pseudonym. Mendès soon quit both periodicals, but continued supplying material in the same vein to other periodicals, broadening the scope of his fiction vastly in an urgent quest for variation and originality.

One of the threads of concern that Mendès carried forward into that new work, and tried to develop further, was the fascination with abnormal states of consciousness and visionary experience developed in the three stories from the 1860s reprinted here: the strangely phantasmagorical "L'Homme à la Voiture Verte" (tr. as "The Man in the Green Caravan" reprinted in an abridged form as "La Momie" in *Le Rose et le noir*, 1885); a relatively conventional account of a vision of a revenant, "L'Étang" (tr. as "The Pond"; reprinted in *L'Enfant amoureux* in 1896 as "Madeleine, ou L'Ombre de l'étang"); and an extremely unconventional account of doomed precocious amour, "Elias, étude" (tr. as "The Amorous Child"; "L'Enfant amoureux" was the replacement title attached to the story when it was reprinted in *L'Amour qui pleure et l'amour qui rit* in 1883, and as the title story of the 1896 collection).

Three of the early stories in which Mendès tried to adapt such materials to the length favored by newspaper stories were tales of revenants, although "Touffe de myosotis" (reprinted in *L'Amour qui pleure et l'amour qui rit*; tr. as "The Bouquet of Forget-me-Nots") lends itself more readily to interpretation as an account of delusional madness. "Inattendue" (tr. as "The Unexpected") and "La Robe de noces" (tr. as "Wedding Night"), two of the several items herein reprinted from *Le Rose et le noir*, do not permit any ambiguity, but the second could easily have been interpreted as a guilt-inducted hallucination had the final twist not confirmed the unusually gruesome reality. After penning those stories, however, Mendès seems to have abandoned conventional ghost stories in favor of much more surreal accounts of subjective hauntings such as "L'Hôte" (tr. as "The Guest"), "Le Possédé" (tr. as "The Possessed") and "L'Incendiaire" (tr. as "The Arsonist"), and straightforward tales of odd obsessions, such as "La Joueuse de flûte" (tr. as "The Flute Player").

Such material became scarcer in subsequent collections. "Le jour des pleurs" (tr. as "The Tearful Day") is the only example in *Pour les belles personnes* (1886) and such material remained very thin on the ground in the subsequent decade, save for stories describing perverse erotic obsessions in an entirely naturalistic fashion, such as the "La Ville chaste" (tr. as "The Chaste Town") in *La Messe rose*. Having largely given up on that interest for a while in the context of very short fiction, however, he went back to it in intense fashion in the four original stories assembled—along with a translation of a story by Heinrich von Kleist that had previously been reprinted, its source unacknowledged, *in Le Cruel Berceau*—in the most atypical of his collections, *Rue des Filles-Dieu, 56, ou L'Heautonparateroumène* (1895).

The title novella that begins the collection (tr. as "56 Rue des Filles-Dieu; or, The Heautonparateroumene") is an engagingly perverse account of an amnesiac being forced by a strange compulsion to play amateur detective in order to "solve" the mystery that will bring him to justice. Far more peculiar, however is "Un Village, près de la route..." (tr. as "A Village near the Road") in which the notional author gives details of the abnormal states of consciousness apparently induced by a supernatural will intent on inhibiting him from recording an incident that happened more than twenty years earlier to himself, Villiers de l'Isle-Adam, and several other people, some of whom, although unnamed, are identifiable as individuals who companied Mendès and Villiers to the première of a Wagner opera in Munich in 1870.

In addition to its peculiar self-referential narrative, "Un Village, près de la route..." is also unusual in its depiction of the principal reaction of the witnesses to the apparition as one of hilarity rather than fear, reflecting a certain deliberate nonsensicality on the part of the supernatural force or entity seemingly responsible for the abnormal experience. When the story was serialized as a short feuilleton in the *Écho de Paris*, of which Mendès was then the literary editor, some readers apparently complained that it was improper to leave the apparition so resolutely unexplained (they were missing the point of the story) and Mendès reacted by producing another equally inconsequential count of a haunting disguised as an autobiographical anecdote, "La Peur dans l'île" (tr. as "Fear on the Island"). In between the two stores, he produced by far the most flamboyant of his "madman's manuscript" stories in the brilliantly bizarre "L'Exigence de l'Ombre" (tr. as "The Exigent Shadow"), but it was the supposed whimsical nonsensicality of the supernatural that became something of a bee in his bonnet thereafter, and which he eventually adapted effectively to some of his shorter fiction.

Although "Le Reflet, l'odeur, la flame et l'image" (tr. as "The Reflection, the Odor, the Flame and the Image") and "Le Portrait du mur vide" (tr. as "The Portrait on the Empty Wall" in *L'Homme orchestre* (1896) are only slightly-surrealized fantasies of erotic nostalgia, the stories collected some years thereafter in *Le Carnaval fleuri* (1904), after an atypically long gap in his production—the boom in newspaper proliferation having run out of steam—show a very marked shift in his narrative methods, graphically illustrated by "Effets sans causes" (tr. as "Effects without Causes"), which picks up the threads of "Un Village, près de la route..." and extrapolates its inconsequentiality almost to the extent of a theory of the supernaturally absurd, further exemplified in "Curieuse aventure d'un chapeau" (tr as "The Curious Adventure of a Hat") and "La Reconnaissance du cornet à piston (tr. as "The Gratitude of a Trumpet"). Those three stories, with other exercises in surrealist fantasy, are grouped in a subsection of *Le Carnaval fleuri* entitled "Les Farces du Mystère," tacitly arguing the that the supernatural not only has a strong sense of humor but a very distinctive species of jocularity. The humor in question takes on a macabre black edge, however, in "Procès-verbal d'un interrogatoire" (tr. as "Official Record of an Interrogation.")

The last story in the present collection, "Les Larmes qui ne savant quoi pleurer" (tr. as "The Tears that do not know what to Mourn"), a companion-piece to "Le Jour des pleurs," comes from the final section of *Le Carnaval fleuri*, subtitled "Le Petit jardin des rêves," placed there not so much because it is more obviously a dream-fantasy than some of those in the previous section, but because it is entirely sober—lachrymose, in fact—rather than farcical, in spite of the peculiarity of the affliction featured therein. It does, however, serve to round out the collection of accounts of strange obsessions assembled here, which undoubtedly gain something from being brought together, in order to show not merely the scope and range of the author's fascination with eccentric states of mind but also the development of that imagery within the overall consistency.

Many other writers have written stories of the same general sort as those reproduced here—there is a whole subgenre of "madman's manuscript" stories, including several graphic examples by Mendès' immediate successor as literary editor of the *Écho de Paris*, Marcel Schwob—but Mendès' work in that vein is particularly interesting, not merely by virtue of its profusion and its uncommon imaginative range, but also because of the scrupulous attention that it attempts to devote to "Les Farces du Mystère," in tandem with its more straightforwardly disturbing aspect. That combination of effects makes the present collection unique with in the field of weird fiction, and quite fascinating.

All the translations were made from the versions of Catulle Mendès' collections reproduced on the Bibliothèque Nationale's *gallica* website.

Brian Stableford

The Man in the Green Caravan

I'm going to tell you about an adventure that happened to me two years ago. I ought to say right away that nervous individuals who rejoice in being impressed by the rapidity of events and unexpected complications will not find their expectations met here. I shall explain with simplicity, as they happened and were said, the things that I saw and heard; the sagacious reader will excuse me if the demands of my story oblige me to talk about myself first.

On the day when my father deemed that I was equipped with a sufficient number of diplomas, he summoned me to his study—my father was a notary in Dijon—and said to me with a benevolent smile:

"My son you're twenty-one years old; I've never had any reason to complain of you; you're an honest young man. Your intelligence isn't above average, perhaps it's a little below, but your professors have always given good reports of your assiduity and your mores. Here's five hundred francs. You'll quit Dijon tomorrow, to go wherever you like; I'm not one of those fathers who oppose their son's vocation."

With that, my father showed me the door. I wasn't astonished by his conduct, In spite to the remarkable lack of perspicacity that everyone agreed in recognizing in me, I wasn't unaware that, widowed a few years before, he lived in concubinage with a maidservant to whom he had give several children. It was only natural that he thought of getting me away from the house; my presence prevented him from accomplishing the long-caressed project of marrying that young woman. He gave me five hundred francs—that was very little since he was rich, but a great deal, since he was miserly.

The next day, I left Dijon, and since then, I haven't seen my father again. In the early days, I suffered somewhat from our separation;[1] now, I no longer think about it.

The day of my arrival in Paris was a day of celebration. There were flags at a great number of windows and colored glass lanterns destined to be illuminated in the evening. The streets were full of strollers; the largest streets were impracticable because of the accumulation of vehicles and pedestrians. I was annoyed rather than surprised by the spectacle, which was new to me. The whole day went by in insignificant promenades.

In the morning I had had breakfast in a place of mediocre appearance; I had paid a great deal to eat very little. I dined in the same place in the evening, for fear that if I went elsewhere I would pay even more dearly to eat even less. Meanwhile, the crowd became increasingly compact; I wondered how it was possible that there were enough houses in Paris to lodge all those people. I also calculated the infinite number of tables and chairs that must be contained in the public establishments that provided food, in order for so many people to be able to sit down.

Supposing, in sum, I said to myself, *that each of the men passing alongside me has a mistress, which isn't improbable, there must be a great many women in Paris dishabituated to virtue.* Since then, I've accustomed myself somewhat to Parisian life. The difficulties, which appeared to me at first to be insoluble, have been considerably simplified in my eyes; I've learned from experience that many people eat at the same table and love the same woman.

By eight o'clock in the evening it was impossible to walk without stepping on the ankle-boot of a female stroller or without the heel of a man flattening your shoes It happened to

---

[1] It is at this point that the revised version entitled "Le Momie" in *Le Rose et le noir* (1885) begins to vary from the original version, almost all of the following text being cut.

me several times to be both victim and executioner; my left foot suffered the weight of a heavy idler white my right foot made the leather of a foreign boot squeak. At a certain moment the crowd, like a tide, carried me away; I found myself in a more spacious place and I experienced a great relief, although, to tell the truth, the situation would have been intolerable for a man who had not been subjected previously to even worse inconveniences.

I was in the Champs-Élysées. I saw open-air theaters in which women were singing, clad in scintillating dresses with very low necklines. Others, who weren't singing, were sitting in a semicircle in a décor that represented a drawing-room full of decorations. That spectacle, I don't know why, reminded me of the attitude of certain women in provincial drawing-rooms, whom my habits had always prevented me from frequenting much.

In addition to the café-concerts there were a multitude of stalls that were only there temporarily for the occasion of the fête. I also remarked public amusements such as frog games, Chinese billiards and spinning tops. Finally, at certain street-corners, there were huge vehicles, vehicles as tall as houses, stationed without horses, which one might have thought abandoned; they were the vagabond domiciles of fairground performers whom the hope of a few good receipts had brought to Paris.

I took pleasure in listening to the patter of the poor devils who were trying to attract the indifferent people toward their stalls. I visited a menagerie and a wax museum. Then I saw fireworks; then the crowd flowed away, and then I was alone.

I went to walk under the great trees, thinking about the probable future and ruminating things of the past. I had left in Dijon a great-uncle whose heir I was to be and a young cousin who was to be my wife. For a year, I had not heard mention of my cousin; when my father gave me the order to quit Dijon I had returned to college, and had not had the leisure of embracing Dorothée—her name was Dorothée—before my departure.

Now I thought I saw both of them, my uncle and my cousin, passing along the ramparts, where the people of the town had the custom of strolling; she was laughing madly and provocatively, not disdaining to attract the attention of cavalry officers who made their sabers clink; he was grave and debonair. Dorothée was wearing a jaconet dress with a floral pattern, which she had put on for the first time at Pentecost; my uncle had his large maroon coat and his heavy gold chain. Oh, my uncle's gold chain! How many times I had dreamed of making it a necklace for my cousin Dorothée![2]

While walking, my eyes half-closed, in the declining light of the illuminations, I collided with the foot of a bizarrely-dressed young boy who was lying on the ground at the foot of a tree. Abruptly woken up, he performed, with a great deal of grace, an acrobatic operation known in gymnastic terminology as a somersault and then, falling back on his feet, he bowed and said: "What can I do for your service?"

"Absolutely nothing. You were asleep, I woke you up; I'm going away, go back to sleep."

I continued on my way and resumed my reverie. I had scarcely rejoined the characters in my interrupted dream when I heard: "Monsieur! Monsieur! Monsieur!" The voice that pronounced the words appeared to emerge from underground. I turned round. The boy was walking on his hands behind me, his head down and his legs in the air.

"Monsieur! Monsieur!" he repeated. This time, I feared momentarily the appearance of a gnome, an inhabitant of subterranean depths, the voice seemed to come from so far away. I was dealing with a distinguished ventriloquist.

When he supposed me to be sufficiently interested by these various ramblings, the child began walking alongside me with a resolute attitude.

"What do you want with me?" I asked, smiling.

---

[2] This paragraph is retained in the revised version, prior to the text substituted for the cut.

"Oh, almost nothing," he said. "Do you see that green vehicle parked over there at the corner of the Avenue Marigny? It's my master's house. I'm both his domestic and his clown: cook by day, showman by night. My master has a singular métier. He's very knowledgeable. He sent me away this evening because he's drunk. I haven't eaten and I don't know where I'll sleep. Give me shelter, and if you need a domestic, take me."

At that moment we were passing a yew tree whose colored glass lanterns were still illuminated. I took pleasure in considering the companion of my promenade. He appeared to be thirteen or fourteen years of age. His forehead, mild and sad, was bowed down by melancholy, but oh, his mischievous little eyes! Those eyes had no melancholy; at first sight, at least, one would have thought so. They were agitating in their orbits with an incredible volubility; nevertheless, a vague gaze sometimes emanated from them like that of a calf; then, their fixity permitted their color to be recognized; they were pale blue. But they soon resumed their initial agility and the color became ungraspable through a thousand rapid jets of light.

I mentioned that the child's costume had surprised me. As regards form and fabric, it was the ordinary attire of fairground clowns, but the color differed. Instead of composing a regular mixture of white and red sections, the little geometric figures, adapted exactly to one another, were either a lugubrious black or a mat white; in the middle of each white patch there was a cross designed in ink, and the center of each black patch was occupied by a silver paper tear. Thus accommodated, the costume had a sort of lugubrious gaiety; it provoked antithesis. It was very droll and very sinister. The involuntary joy inspired by the livery of every public entertainer was complicated very considerably here, and the two colors that, juxtaposed with one another, trouble the most indifferent soul, employed in that manner, produced a more forceful sadness. The joy was reinforced in a very particular fashion by the effect of the contrast, and the sadness was also redoubled by the effect of the contrast.

If a Parisian gamin, always on the lookout for the distractions of the street, had chanced to be there, the little fellow in question, accustomed by taste to laughing at the drolleries of street performers and following coffins, out of idleness, would have been diverted for a long time considering that clown, whose garment mocked mortuary things; and a melancholy would also have gripped him at the sight of the somber emblems mocked by the costume. He would have experienced the pleasure first, or the melancholy, depending on whether he first envisaged the garment or the ornaments that distinguished it; in the former case, the pleasure would be redoubled by the aspect of the lugubrious decorations; in the latter, the melancholy would be increased by the contemplation of the garment itself. Imagine a large cup half-full of wine; add to it a glass of pure water; the wine would not appear to change color, but the volume would be greater.

For myself, I allowed myself to be invaded by a certain languor at the sight of the lugubrious undersized individual; my natural tenderness for children prevented me from seeing the ridiculous side that he might present, and, involuntarily, I could not help feeling some compassion for the joker who, asleep a moment ago, was simulating a cadaver wrapped in a sinister cloth, for that scrap of a shroud performing a somersault and following me walking on his hands.

The boy's coiffure was in harmony with his garment; it was reminiscent of the little hat worn by Louis XI. Brightly colored religious images like those that amuse children in the days of their first communion, could be seen in the pleats of an ample round cap without a peak, and among the images, a crucifix of double cardboard, black and white, loomed up.

While I observed him, the child smiled with a humble expression and appeared to be waiting for a response.

However, I was prey to a curiosity that simple people will find sufficiently motivated. By what caprice was the little acrobat wearing a costume in such scant conformity with the tastes of his age? I had supposed right away that a sinister industry, practiced by his master, had constrained him to choose it.

I interrogated the little man.

His response confirmed my initial suspicions; his master had constrained him to don that costume. With what objective? The child did not deign to inform me.

"There are reasons for that," he said.

"What reasons?"

He remained silent.

Then I consented to give him a shelter, hoping that with a little time and patience I might arrive at knowing the truth.

We headed toward a hotel in the Rue Montmartre where I had taken care, during my wanderings, to retain a room. Scarcely had we entered my room, however, than my guest threw himself on an armchair, where he went to sleep profoundly. I shook him, gently at first, but soon with violence; nothing had any effect; a slight snore was the only response I obtained.

I went to bed in my turn, not without some chagrin. On the floor above, a piano was playing a waltz, and soon, slumber having weighed upon my eyelids, I dreamed that my cousin Dorothée, in a ballroom that resembled simultaneously a fairground tent and a village cemetery, under the radiance of three fantastic moons, was executing monstrous dances with delirious clowns and unkempt undertakers.

When I woke up, there was a further disappointment. I rubbed my eyes; the armchair was empty. I searched the smallest corners: no one. The wily youth had taken advantage of my slumber to run away. I recognized that I had been duped, and that thought caused me to enter into a great fury. One thing calmed me down, however; my clothes had been carefully brushed and my boots were resplendent, freshly waxed. Those were delicate attentions to which a well-born man could not be insensible. It would not have taken much for my rancor to give way to a profound gratitude.

In sum, I had better things to do than think any longer about my adventure of the previous evening; I had no chance of finding the escaped child, and if I had found him, he would undoubtedly have escaped again. In any case, I thought, the curiosity he had inspired in me would probably have been disappointed; there was no appearance that I was really on the track of some marvel; a fairground performer, running out of expedients, must have composed that costume in order to attract idlers. There are such bizarre imaginations! Then again, supposing that the accoutrement were demanded by a profession, it followed from the very fact that it was a profession that it must be something well-known, and hence uninteresting.

That reasoning was destined to have an effect diametrically opposite to the one I expected; the humiliation of not knowing something that everyone might know redoubled my desire to learn it, in such a fashion that, although I had resolved to occupy myself with other matters, I thought about nothing except the young clown, and toward midday, having neglected breakfast, I found myself at the corner of the avenue where the large green vehicle had been stationed.

The avenue was deserted; the vehicle had disappeared. In the neighboring streets, stalls still subsisted, some in the process of demolition, others open to the curious. On the exterior platform of one of the latter I spotted a robust man dressed in a flesh-colored leotard; he was eating bacon and plums, sitting on a big drum destined to astonish the ears of the crowd. I went toward him resolutely, for I had finally repudiated all shame. I confessed to myself my violent desire to find the funereal joker, and my curiosity, immoderately increased, rendered me comparable to a baby playfully distanced from the breast of his nurse or a dog deprived of a half-gnawed bone.

"Monsieur," I said to the performer, "do you know a young boy thirteen or fourteen years of age, who is doubtless employed by one of your colleagues and is dressed in this fashion..."

I described the fugitive's costume briefly.

"Monsieur," the strong man replied, "the savage woman is the seventh wonder of the world; as for those who do not recognize that the calf with five legs and two heads really possesses five legs and two legs, they are impudent imbeciles."

Having made that fine response, he continued eating, without paying any further heed to me.

I resumed my route, and my desire was exasperated.

Two well-dressed strollers were walking ahead of me. One of them, the younger, was talking with a great volubility. Every time he passed a fairground spectacle, he did not fail to address a few amicable words to the master of the vagabond maisonette; the latter responded with a respect that did not exclude familiarity, and they parted the best friends in the world.

That man, who had courteous manners, might, I thought, thanks to his acquaintances, be in a position to furnish me with information. Having approached him, I repeated the question I had posed to the strong man.

He replied: "Monsieur, the traveling players and merchants of the fair form a class of individuals that has never been studied sufficiently. Poets have sometimes, and novelists often, gleaned inspiration therefrom and selected characters, but the former only dress vain imaginations in fantastic costumes, while the latter make the grave error of mingling their heroes with improbable adventures. A special, true book has never been attempted; that book, I am writing. Unexpected revelations will be found there, and moving anecdotes; it will be seen there that the father and mother of a young human monster, remarkable by virtue of the prodigious quantity of meat that he swallowed every day, were reduced by poverty to letting him die of hunger.

"People will learn that at Montrouge, during the fair, for two days, the animals of the menagerie had not eaten for two days, so poor was the exhibitor of ferocious beasts, and so mediocre were his receipts. Inexorable butchers refused any credit. However, there were five or six persons in the tent, impatient for the promised spectacle; clients only paid when they left. How could the beasts have been sated, how could he have avoided dying of hunger himself, if the performance had not taken place? Then, that man of base profession, who, the evening before, I would willingly have called an idler and a coward, penetrated without shuddering, with nothing in his hand but a frail stick, into the cage of roaring lions and famished hyenas!

"You see, Monsieur, that my book will not lack some interest, and you will certainly find the information you desire therein."

With that, the friend of the traveling performers saluted me fraternally and took his companion's arm again.

Burning lovers whom distance or fatality separates from your good friends; poets whom rhyme has resolved to flee; mothers who, in a bed damp with the sweat of your death-throes, await, shivering, the return of your son; spoiled stars who deplore the disappearance of a sister plunged in obscure annihilation; green birds of America with long bifurcated tails who regret your inseparable companion flown away; all of you who bear in your soul the impatience of death or the ungraspable joy; you who nourish that implacable vulture, the desire for denouement, I have understood your dolors and I have had my fill of your anguish. And you, centuple ancestor of my lover, adorable mother Eve, I excuse your fault so fortunately expiated! And you, miraculous Psyche, eternal bride of the eternal Eros, I understand the desire that made you draw aside your lover's nocturnal veil, and I feel sorry for you, beautiful languishing soul, for not having been able to realize your curious dream entirely. Alas, alas, something always opposes the satisfaction of great curiosities! Sometimes it is a lamp imprudently inclined, sometimes the surly response of some fairground performer. Oh, the accursed drop of oil!

Suddenly—I was sure of not being mistaken—suddenly, behind me, I saw him. It was him, him, oh, really him, with his black and white costume with the little crosses and the silver tears, and the holy images and the crucifix in double cardboard, black and white. He was alone, all alone, and he was walking on his hands and performing somersaults. For whom? For what? For nothing, for pleasure. Oh, lightning is slow and the wind is a tortoise. Nothing more. A voice laughed, which emerged from under the ground.

Where is he? I shall go mad.

Then I was on the point of weeping.

That confession will undoubtedly seem ridiculous to those who have not found themselves in a situation analogous to mine; but it is well-known that the most futile desire, when its accomplishment seems to become impossible, produces frightful impatience, and, in consequence, heavy sadness.

I resigned myself to not seeing the little acrobat, but I made every effort to continue hearing him. At times, sounds reached my ear, easily recognized; I dared not follow them, knowing that they emerged from the voice of a ventriloquist; nevertheless I turned round. Oh, double brute that I was, not to have turned round sooner. A few paces away, stationed behind a row of large trees, was the enormous green vehicle, and leaning over the wooden gallery that formed the front of the seat, the ungraspable undersized individual, trumpet in hand, was leaping around and crying out, to the great satisfaction of three or four idlers.

I felt an immense joy, and you will not hesitate to believe that I hastened to take my place among the listeners. Alas, the show was over, and the clown contented himself with repeating: "Enter! Everything can be seen for four sous, for next to nothing!"

One after another, the idlers drifted away, some with a gesture of indifference, others a gesture of horror. Only I set foot on the wobbling stairway that led to the entrance of the booth; but the boy, having gone ahead of me, shut the door in my face, abruptly.

The adventure was becoming inexplicable. That child, whose métier was to show himself to everyone, avoided me alone; that vehicle, open to everyone, was closed to me alone.

I was about to make long reflections in that regard when I felt a hand on my right shoulder. I turned round. I was facing a little man, very old.

"Monsieur," he said, "will you excuse the stupidities of my domestic? He's a child in whom a bizarre way of life also inspires bizarre ideas; I offer you my apologies for his conduct."

"You're the proprietor of this vehicle?" I exclaimed.

"Yes, Monsieur. What do you desire?"

"I desire to see your spectacle."[3]

---

[3] It is at this point that the original text is resumed in the revised version, with numerous piecemeal cuts and amendments, many referring to the boy who has been excised from the story, after the interpolation of the following bridging text, subsequent to the brief memory of Dorothée on the ramparts:

However, I wasn't only occupied by those memories; although a minor position in an insurance company and some copying work permitted me not to eat excessively into the sum I owed to paternal munificence, I experienced anxieties on the subject of my future, and I had thought frequently of attempting some industrial enterprise with the funds at my disposal.

One morning, when I was having lunch at the creamery, plunged in those reflections, my eyes fell upon the advertisements in a newspaper. One of them struck me. A scientist who had made a discovery of capital importance was offering to share the profits with the person who entrusted him with a very small sum indispensable to his final experiments. I knew that many people distrusted offers of a fortune inserted on the fourth page of public papers, but I had never understood the motives for that suspicion. I resolved immediately to enter into communication with the inventor, and when my meal was finished—it was Sunday—I went to the address indicated by the newspaper.

To tell the truth, I had reason to be surprised when I arrived outside number 26, Rue Saint-Ferdinand; there was, in fact, a number painted on the planks of a fence, but there was no

"What! You take me for an exhibitor of curious beasts or waxworks?"

The old man seemed so profoundly indignant, as he pronounced those words, that I was utterly nonplused. He went on:

"I am a member of several Academies in Germany and three scientific societies in Norway. I haven't devoted my entire life to solving the most elevated scientific problems to be insulted in that fashion, at my age, by a man of yours. However"—he suddenly calmed down—"I agree that appearances are against me, and in the interests of my glory, I'd like to explain things to you.

"The labor to which I devote myself demands complicated cares, and my great age forbids me to suffer them; I have been obliged to take on an assistant; the boy that you met fulfills that office in my regard with the rarest devotion. In order to satisfy the necessities of life I have been obliged to create a small industry; from the debris of my experiments and the rejects of my cabinet I have composed a sufficiently curious collection, which passers-by can visit for a modest sum. We go from town to town in the season of public fairs.

"The traveling isn't importunate to me, and I shall live thus until a little money, earned or lent by a generous hand, furnishes me with the means to become rich, and glorious among men, As for the spectacle that Peter Klein—that's the name of my domestic—puts on. I don't believe that it is of a nature to interest you. In any case, Peter has conceived an an-

---

house. I had before me a plot of waste ground on which stood a few fairground stalls, and among them, an enormous green caravan, unhitched. I was about to turn away, thinking that the newspaper was in error, when a little man, very old and stiff, clad in a black frock-coat buttoned up to the chin, got down from the vehicle—a sort of house on wheels—and approached, a smile on his lips.

"Isn't it me, Monsieur, to whom you desire to speak?"

tipathy toward you that renders your person quite intolerable to him."

My surprise was at its peak; the thousand termites of impatience were swarming in my head and nibbling away at my brain in all directions.

"Monsieur," I suddenly said, "I'm not rich, but if fifteen or twenty louis would suffice for you and it would please you to associate me with your enterprise, I'm ready to offer them to you."

It was all I possessed, but at that moment, of what sacrifice would I not have been capable in order to satisfy my curiosity?

"You'll excuse my suspicion," the little old man replied, "but I've been duped by similar proposals more than once. Are you speaking seriously?"

I raised my had to my pocket as if I were going to take out a wallet; he stopped me with a gesture.

"That's all right; I believe you. Come."

Having said that he headed for the large green vehicle; I followed him toward the rear of the vehicle. On the way I observed him rapidly. His was a jaundiced and earthen face; you might have thought it made of parchment. That faced was decorated with little holes and bumps, like an uncultivated field full of mounds and potholes; in the center of each hollow, and at the summit of each swelling, a horrible hairy scab was visible. He had yellow eyes devoid of gleam, a wide mouth with green lips, and he was bald. His costume, which was very severe, was composed of a black coat, worn but obviously maintained with the utmost care, and excessively narrow trousers of the same color, with no apparent waistcoat or shirt, the coat being buttoned all the way to the top.

What was truly remarkable in the aspect of the man, however, was his gait and his movements; he might have been made of wood, and his gesture seemed to be the result of some ingenious mechanism. Maentzel's chess-player had never appeared to me to be possible, but I was on the point of adding faith to such a surprising mechanical phenomenon.[4]

Every time my guide raised his foot in order to walk, the movement stiffened the calf and bent the knee with an abrupt jerk; that first measure accomplished, the thigh rose to a mediocre height and the hip jutted out like that of a cardboard polchinelle when the string is pulled. When the foot returned to the ground, an analogous dislocation took place. The arms and the rest of the body had no more spontaneity in their evolutions. All of that was accomplished with a regularity that was simultaneously solemn and risible. Even the voice appeared to be the effect of a machine designed to modulate sounds: short sentences, dry words; no inflection, no slowness, no quickening. Just as the notes follow one another, inevitably and predictably, in a barrel-organ, the words followed one another in that mouth.

Thanks to the automaton that was walking ahead of me, it took rather a long time to reach the vehicle; at brief intervals he stopped, not to recover his breath—he was devoid of a pulse—but as if to reset some dislocated spring We arrived, however. He opened a door and lowered a footstep, and we entered a place where the most complete obscurity reigned.

"You're going to see very surprising things," said my host.

With those words, a great light invaded the room: a bloody, sinister light. I could scarcely retain a cry, for I saw terrible things: a woman would have fainted, a child would have died. Numerous cadavers surrounded me, their backs to the wall: singular, yellow, frightening cadavers. Some were laughing, others writhing as if in agony; some were naked, others richly clad. There were heads crowned with abundant

---

[4] I have left the name Maentzel as it appears in the original; Edgar Poe called the exhibitor who toured the United States with the alleged chess-playing automaton, known as the Turk, Maelzel in his essay exposing the fraud, which is probably correct.

hair, and headless victims of execution. One, a newborn, was trailing in the rags of a shroud like a slug; semi-naked witches were astride the skeletons of goats; larvae and stryges were crouched in the corners of the walls, and on their skulls, filthy vampires were agitating their fantastic wings. Frightful rictuses! Terrible dislocations! Impossible torsions! Ugliness and horror!

All of that appeared to be alive and agitating, ready to cry out and ready to take flight, and yet it was dead; nothing was speaking, nothing was budging. It even seemed to me that the beings I saw were less than cadavers; one might have thought that a sabbat had been petrified at the moment of its most frantic joy; I was in the presence of an annihilation grimmer and more profound than that of death. And in every toothless mouth, in every eyeless orbit, something was illuminated that radiated outside the body; hence the light that had abruptly invaded the room; hence the red hearth in the belly of every specter and the flames that, like blood, circulated beneath the skin, and, toward the tips of the nails or claws, sprang forth in flashes. Never had a human mind conceived a more horrible and terrible hellish debauchery. My teeth were chattering; I nearly died.

"Enough!" I cried. "Enough! Enough!"

Everything was extinguished; everything vanished; obscurity enveloped me.

"This," said the old man who had introduced me into that funereal place, "is merely an innocent phantasmagoria. Now you're going to see the reality of things."

He lit a lamp; I distinguished thirty or forty mummies in a good state of conservation.

"You see," my host went on, "that there's nothing here that isn't very simple and quite normal; but a few fragments of phosphorus ignited in those mouths and those eyes are sufficient to produce fantastic effects. The cadavers arranged to your left are natural mummies—which is to say that they've attained that degree of desiccation without the slightest human aid.

"Natural mummies owe their conservation to heat or cold. A traveler succumbs while traversing a sandy desert; the hot sun finishes up extracting in miasmas all the moisture in his body; a mummy results of a singular lightness. Take note of this shrunken monster whose beard in intact and whose wrist is disappearing into his wide open mouth; this is a desert mummy. For a Libyan people whose name I've forgotten, it was the object of a particular cult. I stole it at the peril of my life. I was young when I carried out that escapade.

"I mentioned the lightness of these mummies; a breath was sufficient to knock that one over. But it's necessary not to believe that mummification by heat, favored by sandy terrain, is impossible in other conditions. In Mexico, a few leagues from Mexico City, in the stony plain, a battle took place in the sixteenth century between the Mexicans and the Spaniards; the dead were numerous. Today the battlefield is covered with petrified cadavers; I brought back from there two moustached Spaniards whose proud attitude reveals their nationality. I'll only mention the caves of Saint-Michel in Bordeaux, the subterrains of the Cordeliers and Jacobins in Toulouse; they're things that everyone has seen. The conservation of the cadavers there is due to the special quality of the soil and a constant temperature of eighteen degrees centigrade.

"Snow produces effects analogous to those of sand. Perhaps you've visited the morgue of Mont Saint-Bernard. It's a grotto with two openings; the mummies are sat against the rock and perpetual currents of air favor the evaporation of corrupting miasmas. Personally, in traveling the icy mountains of Norway with a knapsack, I discovered a large number of mummies. You can see here those that appeared to me to be the most interesting.

"To tell the truth, mummification by cold can't be as complete as that resulting from heat. Heat desiccates permanently; once the degree of dryness necessary to the conservation is attained in that manner, the mummy remains incorruptible no matter where it is transported. It isn't the same in the other case; the cadaver deteriorates as soon as it ceases to be in contact with the conserving refrigerant.

"Before attacking the great problem that I dreamed of resolving, before imagining my own method of embalming, I had to observe the processes of nature; they're utterly insufficient. The mummies that result—as you can judge—would be objects of horror and disgust even for those who would have been the people most dear to the living individuals. I renounced imitating nature, therefore, and studied the means of conservation employed by primitive peoples.

"Three sorts of embalming were practiced in ancient Egypt. Mummification by desiccation or a certain degree of combustion was abandoned to people of inferior rank. Persons of the middle class proceeded by the immersion of cadavers for several months in concentrated solutions of natron; withdrawn from the desiccating liquid, the body was filed with myrrh, aloes and cinnamon. Families of high rank observed more complicated rites; first the cadaver was carefully stripped of interior parts that are very susceptible to corruption; the entrails, interlaced with herbs and bathed aromatics, filed a wooden coffer in cedar-wood, which custom required to be thrown into the Nile. The brain was extracted through the occipital hole or the nostrils. When those preparations were complete, the human carcass took a bath in bitumen; when supersaturated with bitumen it was enveloped in gold leaf; linen strips coated with gum or other balsamic substances covered the gold leaf; and the remains of a man who had been powerful reposed, accommodated to fate, in a cypress or sycamore case.

"If I were to make a complete list of methods of embalming among ancient peoples I would not omit the Guanches, inhabitants of the Fortunate Isles.[5] There the mummies are called xaxos. In the same way that the Carthusians dig their graves a little every morning before breakfast, every Guanche

---

[5] The Fortunate Isles are nowadays known as the Canary Islands; the Guanches were their original inhabitants.

prepared every day, by drying it in the sun, the goatskin in which he would later be buried.

"The day after a death, the relatives transported the body of the deceased solemnly to the house of the embalmer. A white marble table, bearing some resemblance to the tables used in our modern amphitheaters, was destined to receive the cadaver. Prayers were said, and then everyone withdrew. Then the embalmer made use of a stone named *taboua* to make a large opening in the belly of the subject. Flux of black blood, vomiting of intestines, sacrilege and stink! The interior of the cadaver was cleaned like a cooking utensil, then filled with powerful aromatics. A hot stove received the remains thus dishonored, and a fortnight later, the burial took place, in an inaccessible grotto. The dead man hid in the depths, oblivion in oblivion.

"There are grottoes of that sort in Tenerife; the most celebrated is that of Baranco de Herque, between Ario and Gulmar, in the region of Abona. It was discovered in the time when Clavijo wrote his *Noticias*.[6] More than a thousand xaxos were counted there, and all had beards and hair! A few had fingernails. An agreeable odor was exhaled therefrom.

"I won't talk to you about the Persians, who conserved the dead in honey or wax, or the Romans, who employed pickling salt, as for lobsters. The Jews alone seem to have disdained embalming. Scorn for the body, an indication of strength, distinguishes peoples of courage from those penetrated by the hope of a vengeful or remunerative eternality.

"Now I could describe to you the methods of mummification used in the Middle Ages, and bring you up to date with modern discoveries. I'm not unaware that Tranchina,[7] a physician of Palermo, had the idea of injecting a preservative liquid into the body by means of an incision of the carotid; nor Bils, who employed trickery, nor Charles de Maïto, who invented

---

[6] *Noticias de la historia de Canarias* (1776) by José de Viera y Clavijo.
[7] Giuseppe Tranchina (1797-1837).

salty solution of clear oil and turpentine; nor the Dutchmen Swammerdam and Ruysch,[8] whose method has been lost; nor other celebrated embalmers of yesterday and today; but I ought to reduce the length of my speech in order to arrive more rapidly at things that will doubtless interest you more intimately."

The proprietor of the green vehicle collected himself momentarily.

"What are all these methods?" he went on. "More or less ingenious imaginations. With what do they end? A delay of a few days, a few years, or a few centuries, at the most in the annihilation of the cadaver. Is that the goal? No. The mummy ought to remain a mummy eternally. On the Day of Judgment, it is necessary that it stands up as a mummy. That result, no one has obtained, and even if it had been attained, at what cost would that be, great God! Sacrilegious excavations of the abdomen, odious incisions of carotid—those are the least frightful things that have been found. I'd rather be dissected by the scalpel of a medical student than embalmed in than fashion. And they are, in verity, fine mummies. Look"—he designated the corpses placed to my right—"look, I tell you: no more eyes, rarely any hair, not always any fingernails, worse than a cadaver. Perpetuity in conservation, respect for the deceased,

---

[8] Schwammerdam and Ruysch manufactured anatomical specimens for educational purposes at the end of the seventeenth century. Their work was mentioned in a historical study by the French physiologist and philosopher Pierre Cabanis (1757-1808), from which Mendès might well have borrowed other data, although he probably obtained the inspiration for this story from Léon Gozlan, one of the authors whose work he published in his *Revue Fantaisiste* in 1861, whose *Le Vampire du Val-de-Grace* (tr. as *The Vampire of the Val-de-Grace*), published in that year, features a physician who develops a new technique for preserving bodies very similar to the one claimed by the character in the present story, written in 1863; Gozlan gives a similar account of the history of such practices.

the beauty of the mummy: that is the triple problem. No one has dared to attempt it! I have solved it."

The little man was moving back and forth tumultuously. His movements followed one after another with a very precipitate regularity. He pauses were almost imperceptible, so brief were they. The mechanism was at its paroxysm. The voice still had the same stiffness, but the words, still with the same lack of the unexpected, followed one another impetuously, as the notes follow one another when an organ-grinder, impatient to get away, turns the wooden handle furiously. However, having calmed down, he said: "Follow me. You'll see."

I went behind him into little cabinet hung with yellow chintz. A bull's-eye allowed feeble daylight to penetrate. On a bed of silk with scarlet fringes, the cadaver of a woman reposed, clad in the Oriental fashion. Golden spangles, agitated by the slightest breath of air, decorated her skirt and bodice. Her face was veiled.

"Eight months have gone by," said the old man, "since I experimented my discovery on this body. The conservation is perfect. The forms have remained intact. The suppleness of the skin is only comparable to that of living skin. The flesh is firm; no perfume; natural odor. A certain warmth is maintained in the limbs. Is it not true that this is the exact resemblance of life, and that the vicinity of his xaxos would be dangerous for anyone but a child or an old man? According to all appearances, the problem is solved."

I stood there, stupefied. That mummy was a miraculous thing. Only the immobility of the breast, the stiffness of the fingers and a certain rigidity in the pose revealed that it was a cadaver. I had a desire to touch it. The man of the green caravan permitted that. On applying my hand to a shoulder, I perceived that he had gone a little far with regard to the warmth that he affirmed to be maintained in the limbs; the body was enveloped by the chill that indicates the absence of life.

"It's certain," I said, after a few moments of contemplation, "that you've made a singular discovery. Why don't you submit this mummy to the appreciation of scientific bodies?"

"Alas," replied the old man, "This xaxos isn't absolutely perfect. A yellow tint, which you might have remarked, covers the skin of the cadaver and becomes more apparent with every passing day. That slight fault would appear very grave in the eyes of certain people. I know where the imperfection originates; my next mummy won't be tainted by it. I'm waiting, before exposing my method to competent men, to have made a new experiment."

"And it's for that experiment that you need a little money."

"For that very reason."

I thought for a few moments. There was no doubting the large profits to be made from the old man's invention, once it was known and approved by the Academies, but I scarcely desired to owe my fortune to an industry—after a few years, it would be nothing but an industry—touching the religious matters of the tomb. The man of the green caravan fixed his strangely illuminated eyes upon me.

"I know where to find a fine human cadaver," he said. "Today, I'll have it transported to your home in a trunk, and tonight, I'll reveal my secret to you."

He fell silent for a few seconds, and then added: "Would you like to give me the money?"

I gave him four hundred francs, and I was about to go away, having left him my name and address, when a suspicion struck me. I had not seen the face of the mummy. I made that observation to him.

"Oh! Haven't I shown it to you? It's the most admirably conserved part of the body."

The veil was removed. I leaned over curiously.

Here, I have to say something strangely terrible, so cruelly implausible, that I fear being accused of artifice by the majority of my readers.

The cadaver lying before me was that of my cousin Dorothée.

At the sight of my cousin Dorothée dead and embalmed I did not utter a cry, or shed a tear. The surprise overcame the dolor. My facial features must only had testified to a profound amazement, in such a fashion that the old man said to me: "It's admirable isn't it?"

"Admirable, indeed," I replied. Then I added, in a slightly tremulous voice: "Where did you get this cadaver?"

"I found it on the bank of a little river as I was going to Dijon for the fair. In all probability, it's the body of a drowned young woman, which the current had pushed to the bank.

This time, the emotion seized me by the throat. I could not have added a single word. I had no pulse. The man of the green caravan led me out of the door, and said: "Until this evening."

I nodded my head in acquiescence.

I launched myself out of the pitch. I started running aimlessly along the Champs-Élysées. It was the hour when rich people go to the Bois. People must have taken me for a madman, and in fact, I was one. A thousand various thoughts were clawing my brain. Tears were tearing my heart. I was still running. I had no idea where I would have gone, if I hadn't encountered a bench, against which, without seeing it, I bumped my knees violently. I hurt myself badly, and the pain constrained me to sit down. Then I dissolved in abundant tears.

Once again, I saw my cousin dressed as a bayadere, on the silken bed, in the little cabinet hung with yellow chintz. The man of the green caravan was lying next to her, taking amorously to her. Who knows? Perhaps inexpressible bonds existed between the child submissive to infernal incantations and the magician who had buried her forever in that death similar to life?

I could not explain why, at that moment, my jealousy was complicated by jealousy and hatred. In sum, such as she was—a cadaver, a mummy—my cousin was beautiful. That man was not so old and so decrepit that one would not have thought that immediately; I had seen him animated in a singular fashion. It was not because of the yellow tint that had invaded her that the mummy did not seem suitable to be confided to strange hands; he did not want to be separated from it because he loved it.

Then I saw again, through the somber resplendence formed by my eyelashes, brought together and gleaming with tears, the phantasmagorias of the black chamber. The witches were sitting familiarly on my shoulders; they were pressing my mouth with their mouths, illuminated by phosphorus, while the goats were tugging the tails of my frock-coat. The vampire was fanning me with its sinister wings. I witnessed the encounter of the Mexicans and the Spaniards. I was a Spaniard. I fell dead. For a long time I remained motionless, for a very long time; the days passed, and then the years, and then the centuries. I despaired of getting up again before the Last Judgment.

A great stiffness immobilized my limbs; I could not touch my body, but I sensed that I was drying out. I no longer had eyes, but I could still see. A bird of prey landed on my abdomen, which it tried to tear apart, but it wore away its beak against my stony flesh without even being able to tear away a shred of my solidified hide. A little old man came, following a clown dressed in black and white. He examined me at length, sniffed me, turned me in all directions, and said: "That's good." With the aid of his companions I was loaded on to his shoulders and transported to a large vehicle stationed some distance away, and while we were going, infernal circles of specters and mummies, snowmen and stuffed animals, whirled around us in the darkness.

The depression that had taken possession of me had procured me a strange slumber, akin to somnambulism and fecund in nightmares. How long my dream lasted, I don't know; it was horrible. When I woke up, I had hanks of hair in my hands that I had torn out, and pieces of torn cloth. I had ripped my shirt, bitten the sleeves of my coat and scorched my face. I was bleeding abundantly from the nose. I went toward the fountain at the round-point and rubbed my face with fresh water. That restored me somewhat. One singular thing: I was perfectly sure of having sat down on a bench, but I had awakened standing up, leaning against a tree. What had I done during my sleep? The daylight that was penetrating my brain was obscure, and I could not perceive anything in a clear fashion.

Night had fallen and the street-lights were being illuminated.

In sum, I had never been profoundly in love with my cousin. It had been a childhood romance, futile and very superficial, of which I would certainly have lost the memory rapidly in Paris. I would soon have forgotten our little conversations after dinner on the doorstep, while my father and my uncle took coffee in the garden. The dreams that we had formed together would have vanished sooner or later. I had written verses for her for which she scarcely cared. The letters that she had written in reply, on pink paper, peppered with spelling mistakes, I had gathered into a little packet tied up with a blue ribbon. That was all.

Notified in vulgar circumstances, by a letter or a relative charged at the same time with other messages, her death would only have caused me a moderate sorrow. Such is the human heart. I would have said: "Poor child!" and then I would have remembered that my cousin was rather flighty, and a little too docile to my advice. Admitting that, by some miracle, I had followed through with my childhood projects, I might well have repented of it one day or another. My uncle had been so weak, and little Dorothée had been so badly brought up! But in the present circumstances, I envisaged things from a very different point of view. The smallest trifle would have taken on a marvelous importance in my eyes; and it seemed to me that the death of my cousin left me as alone and miserable as the death of a wife or an adored mistress would have done.

In the morning, you will recall, I had not had breakfast. The hour for dinner had passed without me thinking about eating. Having not taken account of that disturbance of my habits, I considered as an effect of despair the sharp pangs that I was experiencing in my stomach, and thus I judged my chagrin to be greater than it really was.

I resolved to seek some distraction in order to escape a possible recurrence of a crisis. I headed for the boulevard and obtained a place in the stalls of I know not what little theater. A *féerie* was being performed. The affluence of spectators was considerable.

I scarcely recall what the play was about; it had beautiful sets and very diverting changes of scene.

After the first act, all that remained to me of the day's emotions was a numbness that was less and less noticeable.

I consulted my watch. I had time to see a few more tableaux without surpassing the time arranged to meet the old man. That rendezvous was, after all, my great affair; my fortune depended on it. Already, I was glimpsing the death of my cousin in less lugubrious colors. Alive, she would not have been embalmed and the man of the green caravan would not have been able to convince me of the excellence of his method. He had promised to bring me a fine cadaver. I was doing a good deed in favoring an enterprise whose success could not fail to be agreeable to society. I was quite satisfied with myself.

In the second act of the *féerie* there was an extraordinarily ingenious ballet. Flora goddess of gardens, wants to offer the most beautiful of flowers to Miranda, the most beautiful of women. The Rose, the Violet and the Lily are disputing the prize for beauty, and dancing in turn before the throne of their queen. Flora, equally delighted by the charms of the three subjects, finds herself in a great embarrassment. She ends up by linking the rival flowers together by means of a garland of ivy, and the living bouquet kneels down with languid poses before the glorious young woman. Then the entire flower-garden is animated; dancers in flower costumes surge forth from all directions; it is the entrance of the *corps de ballet*.

And suddenly I utter a terrible cry: my cousin Dorothée is there, in the costume of a dancer, figuring the Immortelle, the pale flower of the dead!

Abruptly, I quit the theater, and I felt very emotional. I had anxieties regarding my reason. People have been known to go mad after less singular adventures. A seller of licorice water went past; I drank three glasses of lemonade one after another. I recovered a certain calm, and prepared to go home. The time of the rendezvous could not be far off. Not being familiar with Paris, however, I went astray. I had to ask for directions several times. Finally, after an hour of detours, I tugged the bell-cord at my house.

"My key?" I asked the concierge.

"There's someone in your apartment," replied a surly voice.

I'm late, I thought, and ran up the stairs. My apartment—I still live there—is on the fourth floor I arrived at my door out of breath. A dread—I could not have said what—prevented me from opening it myself; I made a noise to announce my presence.

"Come in!" said a familiar voice.

I went in.

"Bonjour, cousin!" cried Dorothée, throwing her arms around my neck: my cousin Dorothée, alive, full of life, in the costume of a dancer figuring the Immortelle!

Dorothée explained everything to me. The man of the green caravan had taken advantage of my credulity to trick me out of a few louis. As for my cousin, she had quit Dijon ten months ago on the arm of a cavalry officer, who had brought her to Paris. He had abandoned her; she had loved another; then others. Having become poor, she played bit parts for very modest sums in the little theaters on the boulevards. For six weeks she had posed in painters' studios. Later, she had played a somnambulist for a fairground trickster. Eventually, she had arrived at playing the role of an artificial mummy for the man of the green caravan.

"This morning," she said, "I didn't recognize your voice, but after you'd gone, I discovered your name and address. I had to appear at the theater this evening, and I didn't even take the time to change; I've come to console you for your misadventure."

To tell the truth, I experienced a great humiliation in allowing myself to be deceived; in addition, I was very sensible to the loss of my money.

"Bah!" cried my cousin. "You had almost nothing, now you have nothing at all. Don't give it another thought, and let me say one thing to you: My dear René, I love you!"

The Pond

Toward the end of a rainy day in summer, having reached—slowly, because my horse was weary—the summit of a hill wooded with young pines, I finally perceived the gables and the woods of the domain of Les Aulnes,[9] which occupied the misty floor of the valley.

I had come to take possession, as the titular heir, of that vast domain, abandoned for forty years to the insufficient care of a steward by virtue of the reprehensible neglect of the previous owner, my father, who had died recently.

I hastened the pace of my mount with a slap of my riding-crop and commenced the descent of the hill. The slope of the path was steep; the four horseshoes clattered perilously over pebbles coated with a greasy mud. Under the low and heavy sky, the verdure of the pines to the right and left was dismal; below me, in the misty depths of the valley, the château loomed up, square and somber mass surrounded, as far as the eye could see, by a great wild forest, intercut by fields of heather and ponds covered with frightfully green reeds.

I remembered that my father had always testified a great aversion of the domain of Les Aulnes; he shivered at the name alone. I don't know why I thought about that at that moment.

A fine cold drizzle began, by which I felt very inconvenienced, for, the morning having been rather fine, I had omitted to bring a cloak or any traveling garment. In reality, I would have liked to have arrived.

Having reached the bottom of the hill, I had nothing more to do than traverse a small village of a hundred or a hundred and fifty hearths, of which the last thatched cottages extended as far as the main entrance of the château. The sound of my horse's hoof-beats brought eight or ten peasants in rags

---

[9] The Alders.

running, who considered me curiously without saluting me. I was obliged to attribute to the prolonged contemplation of the young pines through which I had just passed the singular coloration that certain objects took on in my eyes; the arms and faces of the wretched villagers, who were staring at me with a bestial and fearful persistence, appeared to be very pale, almost green. Women slid their heads and hands amid the groups of men. It seemed to me that those heads and those hands were oscillating restlessly, also wan and green.

The gate of the château was closed. Through the bars, leprous with rust, the great seigneurial courtyard could be seen, encumbered by long grass, and, further away, the ancient abandoned dwelling. The rain, becoming heavy, chilled me veritably.

I got down from the horse, and tethered the animal, whose neck was curbed by fatigue, to a ring sealed in the wall. I was fortunate enough to discover quite quickly the bell-pull dissimulated in the confused ironwork of the gate. Instead of the sustained and joyful ding-a-ling that any being endowed with reason would have expected, however, two slow, somber, lugubrious belfry clangs resounded frightfully in the distance and in the shadow, for dusk was already falling.

From a little low house adjacent to the right flank of the château, an old woman emerged, who was carrying a lamp. Very tall, very thin, enveloped rather than clad in a gray dress of coarse cloth that resembled a dirty shroud, she headed for the gate at a spectral pace, slow and light. The lamp, which illuminated her face clearly, enabled me to see haggard and dull eyes beneath gray hair; her cheeks were very pale.

"Be welcome to your home, Monsieur," she said, while a large key screeched in the lock.

She was the steward's wife.

"Thank you, Madame Chartier," I replied, "but I've arrived in rather bad weather."

"Bad weather, indeed."

She guided me toward the little house; the damp long grass came up to my knees.

"Who will take care of my horse?" I asked

"I will," she said.

"You have no domestics, Madame?"

"No."

"Who takes care of the château and cultivates the fields, then?"

She looked at me with an expression of astonishment.

"There are no fields here," she said.

We went into a damp room on the ground floor, poorly heated and poorly lighted by a small peat fire; there was doubtless only one lamp in the house, which Madame Chartier had taken in order to come to meet me.

"Chartier," said the steward's wife, touching the shoulder of an old man who seemed to be asleep by the fireside, "get up, the new master is here."

The old man turned toward me, his face wan, his eyes haggard and dull.

"Be welcome in your home, Monsieur," he said.

He stood up, offered me a chair, and added: "Warm yourself, Monsieur, in order not to catch cold."

Madame Chartier, who had doubtless gone out in order to take my horse to the stable, came back laden with plates and glasses; silently, she began setting an oblong table, which she pulled alongside the fireplace.

These are surly folk, I thought, and secretly formed the project of soon dismissing the lugubrious couple; but the moment had not come to reveal my intentions.

"Well, Monsieur Chartier," I said, in order to break a silence that was becoming disagreeable to me, "are you happy in my home, and can I hope to see you here for a long time?"

"You won't see me for very long," he said.

"Why is that? Are you going to quit Les Aulnes?"

"Oh, I'll never quit it, Monsieur, but you'll soon be leaving again."

I smiled, for my formal intention was to establish myself definitively in my new property.

"Oh, Monsieur," said the voice of Madame Chartier behind me, "you'll leave soon."

I was about to protest against that singular affirmation when the old woman added: "Dinner is served."

We sat down at table. "Are you waiting for someone?" I asked, having noticed that four places were set.

"Yes, Monsieur, we're waiting for my daughter," said the steward, serving the soup.

"Ah! You have a daughter?" I hope that a young face might spread some gaiety here and there.

"We don't have a daughter," said Madame Chartier.

The dinner was not copious; nevertheless, I was able to satisfy amply the appetite that I owed to my long day's journey, for my hosts did not eat.

I asked Monsieur Chartier whether he was ill.

"Everyone is ill here," he said, "because of the pond."

"In fact, I thought I noticed that the inhabitants of the village are singularly pale."

"They have fevers, but they suffer less than us because they're not as close o the pond."

"Ah! Truly?" I said, with a slight shiver, for I have always had a particular fear of fever."

After dinner, Madame Chartier withdrew in order to prepare a room, not in the château, which a long abandonment had rendered uninhabitable, but in the house, on the first floor. The steward and I drew near to the hearth.

"Monsieur," said the old man, "excuse us for receiving you so poorly; people are sad hereabouts; the fever takes the children in the cradle and only quits the people who resist it in the cemetery." He extended his hand toward the window and added: "It's because of the pond, which it's necessary to drain; and we're sadder than the others, Monsieur, because we lost our daughter a month ago."

"Your daughter is dead, my dear Monsieur Chartier?" I said, with a barely exaggerated tenderness.

"God knows, Monsieur. As for us, we don't know what has become of her." He continued in a low voice: "Madeleine was very sad, very ill; she was as we are, my good Monsieur. But the birds still sing when they're ill, and Madeleine sang next to us, who didn't talk. I hoped that she would resist the scourge, and I said to myself: *Later, if it pleases God, I'll take her to live in a city*. To see her with rosy cheeks, we'd have given our lives, my wife and I, but she was very pale. She went too often to the water's edge. I don't know why, but she loved that water, which made her ill.

"Often, when her mother called her for dinner, she was sitting in the wet grass beside the pond. We scolded her, but it didn't do any good. It pleased her, she said, to hear the sound of the wind in the rushes of the marsh. She had nothing else to distract her, the dear child. In other places, the daughters of poor people can pick flowers, take birds from the nest, raise doves and play with them, as in those images I've seen in the shops in towns; here, Monsieur, there are no other flowers than the nenuphars in the pond; the little birds are afraid to nest in our great somber trees, and the doves one might catch are crows.

"My poor daughter loved the pond very much. In the evening, sometimes, I heard her open her window, in the room where you'll be sleeping tonight, my good Monsieur. 'Come back in, Madeleine,' I shouted. 'Go to bed. You'll catch cold.'

"'No, no,' she said to me.

"And when I asked her what she as looking at, she said: 'There's a star in the pond.'

"One morning, at breakfast time, Madeleine didn't come downstairs. Her mother went up to her room. 'Madeleine's gone out!' she shouted. That was a month ago, on a Sunday morning,. Madeleine hasn't come back yet."

Monsieur Chartier had spoken slowly, in a very monotonous tone. He fell silent, weeping. The disappearance of their daughter was a more than sufficient explanation of the sullen appearance of my hosts; I repented of having judged them badly, and it was with a plausibly sincere commiseration that I pressed the sad old man's hands when I retired.

My bedroom was a small room with walls covered in damp paper; there was an iron bed in one corner, two bare chairs to the right and left of a walnut chest of drawers, a portrait of a young woman—doubtless Madeleine—facing the only window, and that was all.

I went to bed and went to sleep, but not without difficulty, for the steward's story had predisposed my mind to lugubrious thoughts; then I thought about the fever, of which I was particularly apprehensive.

After a few hours of agitated sleep I awoke with a start.

"Hey! Who goes there?" I exclaimed.

Where do the bizarre states of physical and mental malaise originate into which nervous individuals sometimes fall by night? One is cold, one is hot, one is astonished, one is alarmed; something terrible might be happening that one cannot see.

The lamp, which I had not extinguished, permitted me to convince myself that I was alone, absolutely alone, with the portrait.

From my bed, where I was no longer asleep, I observed that painting at length. It was a very pale young woman, clad in white, in a languid pose; she was contemplating the window with a strange ardor. As I lay down, I had not paid any heed to the excessively vivid expression of that inanimate face. As one follows the gaze of someone next to you involuntarily, I directed my eyes parallel to those of the portrait. The casement had no curtains; beyond the window-panes the formless silhouettes of the forest appeared, and in the shadow, there was only one star.

As I turned back toward Madeleine I noticed that her gaze had become more ardent, but it was easy for me to explain to myself why it appeared thus; plunged momentarily into the darkness, my eyes must have seen those of the portrait, on which the lamp cast its light directly, more vividly.

What I could not explain, and still do not understand, was the absurd idea—doubtless the result of my nervous overexcitement—that counseled me to open the window, as if to obey the will of the portrait, and, when the window was open, to turn back toward it in order to collect an expression of thanks. To tell the truth, I was quite certain of rediscovering in the painting the aspect it had had before, and which it had pleased the artist to impose upon it, for I was not yet absolutely unreasonable.

A gust of wind that came into the room extinguished the lamp, and the portrait disappeared. Outside, the darkness was profound; beneath the low, black sky, vast trees were outlined, frighteningly, against the night, around a large pale extent in which furtive glimmers of steel shuddered and the somber reflection of a single star: that was the pond.

Shivering—why? I don't know—I gazed at the sky, the trees and the pond.

It was asleep, but it was alive. I divined that there was a relentless agitation within it, revealed externally by the quivering of the rushes; strange visions haunted it internally, tenebrous dreams of the dormant water, the respiration of which, amid the rushes, was gasping dolorously. Something disquieting and fascinating lay in that pool; my soul followed the reflection of its own darkness in the depths of that black mirror.

Near the edge closest to the house, the rushes were very dense; their tips inclined and rose again in unison, as if under the same breath, forming a black moving surface that darkened further the darkness of the nearby trees.

Was it really possible, though, that the thing that I could now see swaying at the top of the reeds was only the reflection of a tree? I could distinguish perfectly a body and a gigantic head, slowly stirred like those of a sleeping giant by the rocking of the tenebrous water; and two terrible arms extended a long way in the direction of my window.

I made vain efforts to draw away from the casement; more powerful than mine, a mysterious will nailed me to the spot. I was very attentive. To what? I didn't know; to something that was going to happen. Something was certainly going to happen.

I heard a little sound below the window and I lowered my head. Something was moving along the wall, white, furtive and rapid, like a flying sheet of linen, heading for the pond. It was a woman, or her specter. For an instant, the vague form stopped, and turned round, under the pale light of a single star, I perceived a face, and I recognized it.

Was I going mad? I recognized the face in the portrait. That form was Madeleine.

While she approached the pond, the wind must have changed direction, for the rushes, which had been inclined toward my window a moment before, lowered now to meet the young woman, and it was toward her that the long arms extended, of the Shadow cradled by the summit of the reeds.

Madeleine seemed to hesitate, prey to a violent emotion. Sometimes she launched herself toward the phantom of the pool, sometimes she remained motionless, and one might have thought that she was about to retrace her steps; but soon she resumed her interrupted course, and already she had reached the obscure and dolorous point in the tangle of trees where the ground was about to become the water. On the edge of the pond, although within range of the fantastic arms that were striving toward her as if to embrace her, she halted, all white. In the heavens there was only a single star; there was also a single star in the pond.

However, I was not dreaming, and I saw that.

For a long, long time she remained indecisive, and sometimes she tried to flee toward the house; but more often, bewildered, shivering in the breeze, in the garments of the dead or a bride, she extended her arms toward the Shadow that was calling to her silently.

Finally, she launched herself into the pond, the frightful pond. She must have had water up to her hips, because I could only see the whiteness of her upper body; she was still advancing toward the Shadow, and the Shadow was also advancing toward her. Then I could no longer see anything but her head, appearing from time to time in the thickness of the reeds. Then I no longer saw anything.

But the rushes were gasping more dolorously, crumpled, curbed and parted; the phantom that was following the movement of their tips was split in such a fashion that its torso was often carried in one direction while the legs drew away in the other; and its arms, as if they were embracing some prey finally grasped, in the pond, suddenly disappeared in a large scission of the reeds.

It was evident that Madeleine had drowned. In that black, frightful, abject water she had drowned. I could no longer see her, but surely I would have heard her cry out, if the frightful water had not filled her mouth. Oh, the horrible death! The feet sinking into the wet mud of the marsh and the hand clinging in vain to the fugitive support of the reds! Gradually, the movements became sparse, jerky, less prolonged; Madeleine was doubtless expiring. Again the wind alone agitated the sonorous long grass and I saw the phantom slowly reform on the surface of the black vegetation.

The next morning, at breakfast, I ate little and did not speak at all. The steward asked me when it would be convenient for me to visit the domain.

"This very moment," I replied, "for I'm leaving this evening."

As we headed toward the pond I noticed a section of an old ruined wall in the forest.

"What's that?" I asked.

"That's all that remains of an old chapel," relied Monsieur Chartier. "Your father greatly admired the stained glass window that represents an apostle extending his arms toward the heavens." The steward added: "When the moon rises behind the window, it projects the image of the apostle at prayer over the reeds of the pond; sometimes, by night, it's terrible."

As Monsieur Chartier finished speaking I felt my knees brushed by something furtive, light and soft. I thought it was a cat passing between my legs. It was a napkin, still wet, detached by the wind from a washing-line where linen was drying, a few paces away from us in the direction of the house, between two trees.

Oh, damn it! I exclaimed, silently. *It's necessary to agree that fever and insomnia have made a great fool of me! I've mistaken for a woman clad in white some sheet or skirt carried away by the wind, and the reflection of a stained glass window on the grass for a phantom!*

And I started to laugh, in order to reassure myself. I had never laughed so wholeheartedly—at myself, at least. In reality, I was tranquil. However, because of some business that I remembered then, I left for Paris the same day, before nightfall.

Three years went by. I had sold the domain of Les Aulnes to an industrial company, which was attempting to sanitize the land by draining the marshes. I gave no further thought to my sojourn in that sad house, except at night, very rarely, during the bad hours when one would like to be asleep. Then, one day, in a newspaper opened at random, I read the following article:

In the unhealthy region of , whose inhabitants are beginning to enjoy better health thanks to the draining of the marshes undertaken by a celebrated philanthropic society, a large pond is still found that forms part of a domain known by the name of Les Aulnes.

That pond is famous in local superstition. Every night, it is said, a gigantic phantom appears there, which sways slowly at the summit of the reeds. A few enlightened individuals having supposed that the pretended phantom was nothing but the reflection of an old stained glass window contained in a nearby wall, the wall was demolished, but according to the local people, the phantom has not ceased to appear every night.

"It has not ceased to appear!" I repeated, shivering, and, picking up the newspaper, which I had dropped in my disturbance, I continued reading with feverish eyes:

What is certain is that recently, during the routine work of the sanitization of the marsh, one of the workmen, who was turning over stones near the edge nearest to the house of Monsieur Chartier, the steward of the domain, discovered among the reeds, profoundly buried in the mud, an absolutely fleshless skeleton. It was recognized as the skeleton of a young woman, whose death must date back three or four years.

Oh, into what fear my anterior convictions disappeared on reading that! It was not a sheet of linen flying away under the wind, the white and hesitant form that I had seen from my window; it was Madeleine herself, dragged into the pond by a real phantom.

But Madeleine's death had undoubtedly occurred a month before my arrival in the funereal dwelling. Some obscure will, therefore, had accorded me for a few hours a detestable power of retrospective vision; or perhaps the dead sometimes emerge from their darkness by night in order to come to replay on earth the lamentable scene of their agony.

The Amorous Child

To Madame Juliette Chardin

Madame,

   I dare to dedicate to you this study based on your personal recollections and those of our dear and illustrious friend Doctor Delton, leaving in shadow, in accordance with your desire, but with regret, the part of the denouement in which your overly subtle conscience wants to see a fault on the part of Juliette, in which the reader would doubtless only have seen a duty accomplished; for the promise made to Elias ought not to have taken precedence over an anterior oath, and Juliette, for having been the consolation of a moribund, was not disengaged from making the happiness of a living man. Such as the advice of Monsieur Chardin, today your husband, and Doctor Delton; it is also that of your humble and respectful servant.

C.M.

May 1868

   In his remarkable treatise *Uber die Krankheite der Kinder und ihren Entwickelung der moralischen Kraefte*—which is to say: *On Maladies of Children and their Influence on the Development of the Moral Faculties*—Professor Spitzberg, vice-president of the Academy of Medical Sciences of Dusseldorf, brings to light several examples of truly extraordinary precocity in children seven or eight years of age ill since infancy, and believes that he is able to draw therefrom the conclusion that in cases where continual suffering does not obliterate absolutely the intelligence of young invalids, it can, on the contrary, precipitate its development.
   The innumerable reflections on which Dr. Spitzberg supports his theory might interest keenly the majority of my read-

ers, but it would be difficult for me to explain them, those reflections being, by their nature, very delicate and subtle, and, on the other hand, formulated in a language so scantly accommodated to the presumable range of ordinary minds that it would be quite impossible for me to make any of them comprehensible. I shall limit myself to adding that the life and death of young Baron Elias de Borg, who forms the subject of this study, seems to militate vigorously in favor of the above-mentioned theory.

Nevertheless, my desire being to write a story and not to furnish arms against the adversaries of the honorable vice-president of the Academy of Medical Sciences of Dusseldorf, I shall not prevent the persons who adhere to Professor Spitzermann in opposition to Professor Spitzberg from crying that an exception cannot affirm a law; and as for those of my readers whom not knowing anything about either one of those illustrious antagonists, will simply be shocked by the apparent implausibility of my story, they are begged to consider that real life sometimes presents to observation incidents and characters far superior in singularity to the most ludicrous imaginings of poets and novelists.

Toward the end of 1853, one of the important members of the Parliament of Christiana, Count Nils-Agrippa de Borg, whose illustrious origin and reputedly immense fortune had recommended him for a long time to the attention of the court in Stockholm, had the honor of being chosen to represent His Majesty King Charles XV in Berlin. Although he maintained, as was appropriate, the honor of the Swedish name in diplomatic relations, he compromised the dignity of his official character strangely by his liaison, secret at first, but soon scandalous, with the daughter of a Prussian colonel: conduct that earned him, on the part of this master the King, as well as severe criticism, the advice to repair his fault immediately by marrying the young woman. The latter being poor and of mediocre birth, the Count, who had other plans, only yielded with a great deal of reluctance.

His submission, too evidently constrained, did not enable to him to reenter grace, and he was recalled in the same year as his marriage. Deeply humiliated by his fall, he held it against Madame de Borg. The woman whom he had adored as a mistress became odious to him as a wife. Far from taking her to Stockholm, he constrained her to live in all seasons in a lugubrious castle, partly ruined, situated in Norway, in the unhealthy region of Dormsoë,[10] where the Countess, already suffering from a pulmonary ailment, according to all appearances, would not live for many more years. She could have resisted and complained to the king, but, weak and sad, she consented.

When she was taken to Norway, she was pregnant. Frail, she gave birth to a child who was even frailer. He was named Elias. The Count only came to Dormsoë once a year, in the hunting season. Then the ancient habitation filled up with guests and noise, the beaters singing in the courtyards and the horses whinnying in the stables. In the evening there were long, tumultuous meals at which Madame de Borg was not invited to appear. Her husband only visited her on the day of his arrival and the day of his departure. They were short conversations. When he perceived the pale, sickly Elias for the first time, his back arched and his legs bent, aiding himself with his hands in order to walk, with the consequence that he resembled a young animal, the Count asked: "What is that monster?"

"It's your son," replied the offended mother.

"Say yours, Madame," replied Borg, and left.

In that climate, and by virtue of her chagrins, the unhealthy condition of the Countess got worse by the hour. Soon, she no longer quit her room, an ancient, very profound room that had large windows. She remained there all day,

---

[10] Mendès employed this fictitious place-name in another story as that of a city that is obviously Tromsø, so the imaginary region is presumably in the far north, not far from the edge of the Arctic circle.

semi-recumbent in a large armchair, considering through the windows the vast melancholy ensemble of the somber forest and the tenebrous sky.

Elias, who was five years old, played alongside her, crawling. They were hours of frightful sadness. In the evening, she wept. The child, whose intelligence developed with a rare rapidity, strove to console his mother for a dolor of which he appeared to divine the cause. But the Countess dared not keep Elias with her for too long, fearing that it was not healthy for that poor being, already so delicate, to remain enclosed in what was almost a mortuary chamber, in which only the sickly odor of some potion mingled with the insipidly lukewarm atmosphere that emanates from consumptives nearing their end.

When a white northern sunbeam came to caress the windows, she showed the sun to Elias and said to him: "Go and play, Elias." The infant left. No domestic accompanied him, the disfavor of the master authorizing the repulsion that the wretched child inspired.

He ran through the forest, rolling in the ferns, becoming tangled in the branches. Often at the summit of a mound, he lost his footing, never sure, and he fell to the bottom of some gorge at the peril of his life, unkempt, his garments soiled, and his hands bloody. When he felt weary, he lay down prone in the heather, and the woodcutters who went forth in pairs, carrying enormous flexible fir trees over their coupled shoulders, sometimes thought, on hearing the sound of his respiration and the plaint of the oppressed branches, that it was a young wolf that was there.

Then he returned, and the Countess saw him arrive from her window, and shouted to him: "Come quickly!" He ran; he crossed the lawn in a few bounds like a wounded chamois; he ran upstairs, clinging to the banisters; finally, he fell, weary and out of breath, at his mother' feet, and the mother, joyful for a moment, kissed his sparse hair, mingled with brambles, recklessly, taking that deformed body between her knees and hiding it in her skirts, in order only to see the face of her son, so pale, so sad, and so similar to her own.

Thus the two neglected, unhappy beings lived, with no other consolation than their mutual love. Deprived of one, what would become of the other? One day, the Countess, her condition worse, had to remain in bed. Borg, summoned by a letter from his wife, did not come to Dormsoë. Elias was eight years old.

"Forgive your father," said the mother, as she died.

She was buried near the castle in the forest. No one saw the child weep. The number of servants, already very limited, was further reduced. Only an aged steward remained, almost as infirm as his young master. This, Elias was alone. He had been uncivilized; he became wild. He remained for entire days in a fir-wood not far from his mother's grave. Those who passed by heard strange words that he addressed to the mute stone. Sometimes, he did not come back at night, and slept on the glacial damp earth, shielded from the glacial wind by the wall of the sepulcher.

In the castle there was a library several hundred volumes rich; Elias spent in that gallery the rare moments left to him by his vagabondage through the forest. He read very little, however; he seemed to interrogate the books without daring to open them, spending entire hours staring at some worm-eaten binding. He was nine years old. He did not grow any taller; his deformities were more pronounced every day. He was a dwarf, lame and hunchbacked. He had conserved the pale and sad face of his early days, which his mother had loved. He was very somber. He rarely spoke.

One day, the old domestic said to him: "I've learned that the Count, your father, has just remarried."

Elias did not seem to have heard him, and went into the forest. He had fabricated crutches for himself in larch-wood, in order that they would last for a long time. It did not appear that he desired or hoped for a life different from the one that he led then, doubtless thinking that, the Count would have allowed the son to live there as he had allowed the mother to die there. That was probable, but it was not what happened. His second wife did not give him a child. Borg, who was no longer young, began to dread that his name and his fortune would remain devoid of an heir He remembered the little monster he had seen at Dormsoë.

One evening, Elias was in the gallery of books, silently absorbed in the contemplation of a voluminous folio, which the light of a hand-lamp traversed with a band of pale light. He heard an unfamiliar footfall behind him, and an almost harsh voice called him by his name. The Count had come to fetch his son, in order to take him to Paris, hoping that the science of French physicians might succeed in making a tolerable heir out of that ridiculous runt.

At the corner of the Avenue de Marigny and the Faubourg Saint-Honoré there is a town house, now uninhabited, of severe aspect. It was the dwelling of Monsieur de Borg. The first floor contained the reception rooms and the second the Count's personal apartment. The third was specially reserved for Baron Elias. After having traversed the antechamber, one entered a room upholstered in black velvet and ornamented with a few family portraits separated by panoplies, one of which—the one facing the principal door—was surmounted by a large knot of gold ribbon, on which was legible, in carmine letters, the ancient motto of the house of Borg: *Sumus qui fuimus*.[11]

After the drawing room came the library. The third room was a bedroom, as obscure as it was vast, singularized by heavy hangings of somber crimson satin overladen with armories in painted copper. At the back, in a bleak corner, there was a massive ebony bed, devoid of sculptures, very broad and very high, which resembled a black marble sepulcher. That room was as sad, and that bed as lugubrious, as if they had a presentiment of death-throes.

The apartments and the furniture sometimes testified to a sort of prescience of their destination. Beside the bed, a door-curtain, almost always partly raised, permitted the perception

---

[11] "We are who have been."

of a broad balcony that overlooked the interior courtyard of the house, and which the whim of the young baron had transformed into an opulent hothouse, with a crystal roof and walls. But the vicinity of that suspended garden, full of splendid florescences and delectable aromas, did not succeed in cheering up the somber chamber of repose: it was a tomb with flowers around it.

Eighteen months after his departure from Dormsoë, one morning in November. Elias was in that hothouse, his body enveloped in the density of the foliage, his head leaning on one of the transparent walls. He was eleven years old. He was pale, with the mummy-like pallor that the periodicity of fever gives the skin. His hair, long and straight, so blond that it was almost white, framed, as if between two plates of unpolished silver, a voluminous forehead that overhung the rest of the face, deepening the sad azure of the eyes and prolonging a shadow all the way to the excessively thin wings of the nose. The mouth tightened colorless lips, deformed by the habitude of a malicious torsion. There was something abnormal and constrained in the design of his features; here and there, a few wrinkles extended, and the face expressed a great lassitude: the lassitude of precocity.

Through the window on which the young baron's head as leaning one could perceive, beyond the interior buildings of the Hôtel de Borg, a part of the courtyard and the entire façade of a neighboring house. It was to a closed window of that house that Elias's gaze was attached: a fixed gaze, in which the disappointment of a long disappointment was legible. The child had been there for two hours, invisible, on watch.

Suddenly, the window that he was observing having opened, a young blonde woman leaned on the sill, distant and graceful. Elias's dazzled eyes closed; he withdrew his head swiftly, as a man lost in darkness recoils before the unexpected light of a torch; but soon, and slowly, in order to accustom himself to the splendor of the apparition, he drew nearer to the window again, gradually raising his eyelids, and finally remained motionless, his mouth open and his eyes wide. The malicious pleat of his lips had extended in an ecstatic smile; at times his nostrils flared, as if inhaling a distant perfume, and he seemed extraordinarily happy. He remained thus for a long time.

The young woman leaning on her window-sill had no suspicion of the joy that the sight of her gave to a poor sick child who was contemplating her from so far away. She seemed to be plunged in a pleasant and long dream. She might have been waiting for someone, for her gaze frequently interrogated the alley of a coaching entrance situated opposite her casement. It was from that direction that a man of elegant appearance soon appeared, who saluted her with a familiar gesture, traversed the courtyard and disappeared under the awning of a perron.

Instinctively, Elias had lowered his eyes; handsome momentarily with tenderness and joy, he had become hideous; his bulging eyes resembled two red balls; he bit his lips convulsively, and through a mobile window of the hothouse his grimacing head stretched toward the newcomer at the end of a neck as membranous and meager as that of a young vulture. When he looked up again, fearfully, the window had been closed; the vision had vanished.

Then, by virtue of an abrupt affluence of blood to the throat, Elias was seized by a hoarse coughing fit, sonorous and heart-rending. He did not quit his post however, hoping that a new incident might bring the idol back within range of his worship. He waited.

At times, he spoke. "Perhaps he's a relative." He coughed a little less forcefully, and added: "Yes, yes, doubtless her brother."

But suddenly, he shook his head furiously. "Her brother wouldn't come every day. It's not in that fashion that one waits for a brother." And his cough became more violent.

When the melancholy observer was certain that the young woman would not reappear again at the window, he recoiled slowly amid the confused branches of the shrubs, all the way to the middle of the balcony, and commenced to march back and forth, his head bowed and his mouth twisted, his hands clenched behind his back.

Marching, Elias was pitiable; his twisted spine, forming a hump in the interval between his shoulders, constrained him to drag himself along, painfully arched; he was a dwarf, moreover, and bandy-legged. His costume, which never varied, was composed of a coat of dark red velvet rather short and not very ample, garnished with fur, and tight trousers in black cloth. Thus clad, his sickly, prematurely aged, broken body, surmounted by a pale face with a sickly and grim expression, might have been mistaken for some Tom Thumb charged with representing Louis XIV, as understood by the actor Ligier, in a fairground spectacle.[12]

He dragged himself along silently, stopping sometimes to pick a flower, most often a white flower, consider it warmly, as if he found some analogy with a dear absent object, and then suddenly crumpled it, threw it on the floor and trampled it underfoot, and resumed his painful march, his head lower and his lip twisted more bitterly.

A domestic came in and said: "Will Monsieur le Baron consent to receive Monsieur le docteur Delton?"

Elias did not appear to have heard. Doubtless accustomed to the fashions of his young master, the valet did not repeat the question, but stood immobile in front of the door. The child continued his melancholy walk. Finally, after a long silence, he said, in the shrill voice particular to dwarfs: "That's all right." And, the domestic having stood aside respectfully, Elias went into the bedroom, to which Dr. Delton had just been introduced.

---

[12] Pierre-Mathieu Ligier (1796-1872) was a leading member of the company of the Comédie-Française from 1830-1851; the reference to "Tom Thumb" is not directly to the character in English folklore but rather to a generic term for performing dwarfs improvised from the stage-name of "General Tom Thumb" (Charles Stratton, 1838-1883) who became world famous by touring with P. T. Barnum's circus.

Dr. Delton is well known, if not for having seen him, at least by virtue of the magnificent portrait that Flandrin[13] has made of him, which was one of the great successes of the Salon of 1852. In that canvas, the savant specialist is not yet thirty. He has not changed since. Few men are endowed with such a handsome face. The slightly arrogant expression of his forehead does not contradict absolutely the familiarity of his smile, but the benevolence of his lip resembles clemency.

That smile has made Dr. Delton enemies. Furthermore, the strangeness of his doctrines, the often marvelous results of his treatments, recommend him in a sufficient fashion to the antipathy of a few less fortunate practitioners. It is well known that he attributes a large part to the influence of a healthy soul on a healthy body. With regard to a man known for being very dishonorable, who had daily indigestions, he said: "It's good consciences that make good stomachs, and one doesn't cure remorse with an emetic." Various circumstances in which he had given proof of a sensibility rather rare among his colleagues had earned him the qualification on the part of one of them of "Romantic physician."

Everyone remembers the generous conduct of the Comte de T , which became celebrated as the result of the indiscretion of a friend. The Comtesse de T*** died of a pulmonary malady, and, not unaware of her condition, she became frightfully depressed. It had been determined in the marriage contract of the two spouses that on the death of one of them, the objects of their personal usage, such as jewelry, garments and underwear, would belong, not to the surviving spouse, but to the collaterals of the deceased. In order to expel from his wife's mind any idea of imminent death, the Comte converted his fairly considerable fortune into adornments of every sort; every morning, the invalid received some present of enormous price. When she died, her husband was ruined, but she died believing herself to be saved and happy.

---

[13] Jean-Hippolyte Flandrin (1809-1864).

It was recounted that the counsels of Dr. Delton had directed the Comte. To persons who, recalling that adventure, alleged one day against him that the future of a healthy man doubtless destined for a long life ought not to have been sacrificed to the scarcely durable satisfactions of a dying woman, the physician replied that the last days of the moribund did not constitute in his eyes a future less respectable than the numerous future years of healthy individuals; that, in any case, it is not always laudable to reason very subtly; and that, for himself, he would gladly take the side of the sick, those being the weaker.

Elias came into the room without saluting, went directly to a chaise longue placed in a very dark corner of the vast room, sat down on it, drawing back his legs one beneath the other, and from there, finally, turned harsh and malevolent eyes toward the doctor. Delton, long accustomed to the ill humor of invalids, pretended not to pay any heed to that manifest hostility.

"Bonjour, Elias," he said, advancing a few paces.

The child did not move.

"Aren't you going to give me your hand today?" said the doctor, smiling.

"You want to have my hand in order to feel my pulse," Elias replied.

"I swear to you that I do not have the slightest desire to feel your pulse," replied Elton, sitting down near the chaise longue. "Is there any need, anyway? I know perfectly well that you have a fever. Would you like me to tell you how you slept? Very late, very little and very badly. You coughed frequently. You heard faint and innumerable buzzings in your ear, like the sounds of an army of ants on the march. Your temples were throbbing. You were very thirsty, especially as soon as you had drunk something. Scarcely had you become drowsy, in spite of the insipid and warm atmosphere by which you seemed to be enveloped, than you were agitated with a start, and, as well as being squeezed around the neck by the rope of an invisible executioner, you might have dreamed two or three times that a heavy animal was crouching on your chest."

"You're very knowledgeable," said Elias, bitterly.

"My word, yes. Knowledgeable enough to cure you."

As he said that, Delton took in his hand the small, warm and moist hands of the dwarf; he enveloped him with a benevolent paternal gaze and added: "Would you like me to cure you, my poor and dear child?"

There was such tenderness, such an evident sympathy, in the doctor's eyes and voice that Elias felt shaken in his resolution to be cold and hostile. His face cleared; but it was only a glimmer, and he replied in a sharp and rough voice: "Yes, you can cure me—which is to say that you can prevent me from dying. I've understood you, haven't I? Well, we can't reach an understanding.

"To be cured? Do you know what that word means to me? It's to be tall, it's to be straight; it's not to have a hump on my back, bow-legs and twisted feet; it's to resemble the people who go along the street and don't limp; it's to be able one day to be happy and unhappy in the fashion that other people are. There are men; I'd like them one day not to be disgusted merely by the sight of me. There are women; I'd like them to be able to love me. That's how I want to be cured.

"My ambition surpasses your power, isn't that true? What can you do for me? Deliver my forehead, my cheeks and my whole body from the incessant heat that envelops it? What's the point? I like the fever that puts my thought to sleep and isolates it from reality. To prolong my life for five or six years, perhaps even to destroy within me the germ of the hereditary phthisis that is gradually consuming me? In sum, to make me live, but to live deformed? I don't want that. You hear me: I tell you I don't want it."

In a softer voice, he added: "May my saintly and merciful mother be blessed; having been unable to give me the wherewithal to be happy, she bequeathed me the wherewithal to die."

Elias fell silent. He had very red cheeks and his forehead was shiny with a moisture that was almost cold.

The doctor considered him silently, and did not reply at first. "It's certain," he said, after a long pause, "that it is situated beyond all human power to render you upright and well made. Cure, for you, is perhaps only to live."

"Well then, let me die."

"No, you can be happy. Don't look at me with those melancholy and hostile eyes. I repeat to you that you can be happy. You're deformed? No matter; as an artist or scholar, do great things; the beauty of the work will redeem the deformity of the worker. In any case, you're powerfully rich; that is the wherewithal to make yourself respected, Monsieur le Baron. Let me cure you, and I'll answer for the rest."

"I shall not be loved," said the child.

"Women? You're eleven years old, and I doubt that you're amorous already."

Elias shivered. Delton did not appear to notice the movement, which the child attributed to his malady, saying: "I have a fever."

"Yes," said the doctor, "it's your condition." And he continued: "The fear of not being loved, therefore, doesn't constitute an obstacle to your immediate happiness. As for the future, don't be afraid. Why should you not love one day? One can speak to you about these things because suffering has made you a man before the age. The soul of young invalids is remarkable sensitive; their intelligence develops with a surprising precipitation, and that precocity exists in you to a degree that I've never encountered in the most…"

Delton hesitated

"The most rickety," Elias finished.

"So," said the doctor, "let's talk about women. I've seen a great many of them, and in a fashion entirely appropriate to acquire some knowledge of their character. Physicians learn many things and they have no need for that to be great observers; people don't hide anything from them. Well, I affirm to you that there are women in the world so adorably good that the name of woman, if they were all like the few, would be too laudatory a qualification if it were applied to the angels of heaven. Hope, my dear Elias; women have pity.

"Pity!" repeated the child, with a grimace.

"Yes. Let's suppose that at twenty, you encounter one of these women, doubtless exceptional, but less rare, in fact, than people in society imagine. The first sentiment she will experience for you will be pity. But you're noble, and you're rich; be good and be glorious, and above all, love her, the woman who will have had mercy. The tenderness that you inspire in her, for having been born of compassion, will be none the less amour, as you dream of it as a child, and as you will understand it as a man."

The doctor spoke for a long time with the communicative enthusiasm that distinguishes his eloquence. He did not take long to produce a sufficiently vivid impression on the soul of his patient. Before Delton had even finished, Elias stood up, marched rapidly back and forth in the room and, as if he were alone, spoke aloud to himself.

"Can it be possible? It could be that a woman would not reject a miserable cripple like me? Not being made like others, one could be loved like them? Oh, if it were possible..."

He cried thus, his hair flying, his eyes traversed by flames, and then, had he not had the jerky twists of his gait, he would have been handsome, so much does joy resemble a sun that sets shadow ablaze and makes a thatch roof golden.

"Now, Elias," said the doctor, who saw that the child had reached the degree of excitement that he judged it appropriate to attain, "do you want me to cure you?"

Elias came back to sit down on the chaise longue, looked fixedly at the physician and said: "Can you? Truly?"

"I believe so."

"Well, then, I want it. What is it necessary to do? Order; I'll obey."

Delton remained silent momentarily, then, playing with the invalid's pale cheeks, he said: "Since you're reasonable now, my dear Elias, listen to me. When your father brought you to Paris eighteen months ago, I saw immediately that it would be impossible to straighten your body. You were deformed; you would remain so; but I didn't conceive any serious anxiety with regard to your life; the malady that you seemed to have inherited from your mother had not yet affirmed its symptoms, and there was hope that it would be possible to prevent that.

"During the first weeks, no complications seemed to be on the point of emerging, and I would certainly have answered for you. But your condition was suddenly aggravated; your cheeks hollowed out; by virtue of a persistent insomnia, your eyes were bloodshot; your respiration ceased to be regular; sometimes it was hoarse and wheezy, as it is now. Finally, the fever arrived. That rapid explosion of an affection that I had not judged liable to manifest itself for several years surprised me greatly. I've searched for the cause of it; I haven't found it, but there must be one."

Elias frowned; the suspicion returned.

"That cause, it's necessary that I know, in order to cure you. You have some chagrin, my child. A violent dolor must have forced the latent malady to manifest itself. In sum, I believe, I'm sure, that you have a secret. Confide it to me, and I will cure you."

"Ah!" cried Elias, standing up angrily. "You've set a trap for me."

"In order to save you, Speak, I beg you. Am I not your friend?"

Elias was standing up, his face crimson.

"You're only my physician, Monsieur Delton," he said, with a viperine hiss in his throat, and I have no need of you, because I don't want to be cured."

As he finished that statement, with a disdainful gaze, Elias had raised the curtain that separated his bedroom from the balcony; he went into the hothouse, and, the curtain only falling back slowly, Delton was able to see the poor child pick, with a gesture in which a long contained passion burst forth, a magnificent white camellia, which he kissed and bit recklessly.

Elias had promised himself never to reveal his secret. There are souls that do not want to lay themselves bare. One can tear the ivy from the trunk of a tree, and a pearl-oyster from a rock, but not the confession of their joy or their dolor from those tenacious souls. Elias knew, in any case, that a revelation on his part could only be welcomed by smiles of pity. "You're a child," people would say, or "This isn't serious." And then, what words can serve to make comprehensible a sentiment so abnormal that even the person experiencing it can only explain its nature very imperfectly?

Was it amour, that strange idolatry for a distant figure, vaguely glimpsed? Although the intellectual faculties of the young baron had been powerfully developed by the malady, it did not appear that it had been the same for his physical temperament. Now, amour is a complex passion, which, in its entire manifestations, participates as much in the irritation of the nerves as the excitation of thought. It might be that, unfortunate since an early age because of his abandonment by his father, rather poorly treated by the domestics of the castle in Dormsoë, but admired and pampered by his dying mother, Elias had conserved for women in general a sort of grateful tenderness. However, if the sentiment that was drawing him to the young woman at the window was nothing but a filial piety transported to a person who reminded him of a vanished happiness, why was there so much unexplained desire? Why the tears? Why the jealousy?

Whatever it was, Elias was suffering. No one was there by whom he wanted to be consoled; he had been seen to reject the sympathetic entreaties of Dr. Delton; he had not forgiven his father for the melancholy demise of Madame de Borg. In any case, the Count, who went into society, was almost always absent from the house. Thus, the sad dwarf remained solitary, and he was dying slowly.

Once, he stayed in the hothouse until nightfall. It seemed to him that something unusual was happening in the neighboring house. He saw the windows of the façade light up one by one, and shadows passing in silhouette behind the closed curtains. Soon, carriages entered the courtyard. Elias watched women in brilliant costumes descend from them, their heads enveloped in gauze, their shoulders clad in white or blue mantles. Men who descended before them offered their arms to go up the perron, which was ornamented with magnificent flowers, and the stone steps of which had been covered by a carpet.

Two candelabra placed on the first step and the reflection of the illuminated windows cast such a bright light into the courtyard that the child could easily take account of what was happening there. He understood that it was a ball. With what rancor he considered all those men, especially the young men, who were not children, who were not hunchbacks, who were not going to die, and who were going to see her.

Like all abnormal passions, the young baron's amour—for it was, in fact, amour!—drew its strength from its very strangeness. If vulgar obstacles are sufficient to exasperate the sentiments of a lover placed in a common situation, to what degree of dolorous acuity must the passion of that deformed child, so evidently destined for despair, have been elevated?

Among the crowd descending from the carriages and climbing the steps he recognized the young man who came every day; he remarked that he was more handsome and much better dressed than the others. He detested them all, but that one he detested preferentially. At that moment, hatred and amour formed in Elias's heart such an equal balance that, given the alternative of taking the place of that man, who was perhaps the fiancé of the cherished unknown, or being able to kill him, he would have hesitated for a long time.

Gradually, the guests arrived in lesser numbers; the courtyard became almost silent; only a few groups of valets were visible, whispering in obscure corners; but the animation of the drawing rooms seemed to be extreme. Joyful music was audible; rapid couples were passing, dancing, behind the blazing casements. Elias thought about his twisted legs, his distorted knees, and smiled bitterly.

There was one window, although illuminated, where no fugitive forms were visible; that was the one at which the object of Elias's contemplation appeared every day. This evening, the child was still gazing at it tenderly; he deemed it fortunate that the room where his life was did not want to be distracted from its silence and its solitude, and he experienced a sensation analogous to that of a man who, on returning from a voyage, sees his house on fire, but remarks that the flames have not attained the part of the house where he prefers to work and dream.

But the room did not remain unoccupied for long. A form, light and white, palpitated in the curtains; the window opened, and the child uttered an exclamation of joy. Vaguely perceived in the penumbra formed by the ardent lighting of the drawing rooms mingled with the darkness, the daily apparition was leaning on the window sill. Elias's delight reached its peak. He had never experienced such happiness. He extended his arms; he called out; he would have liked to precipitate himself.

Is there not something frightfully melancholy in thinking that the young woman, beautiful and happy, and coming, wearied by a waltz, to breathe in the warm freshness of a autumn night at her window, was forever adored, hopelessly, by that paltry and deplorable child, whom great suffering had rendered capable of a great amour, and who was there, and who was weeping with joy, and whom she could not see weeping? Personally, it is moved by a sentiment of profound commiseration that I have undertaken to recount the story of the unfortunate son of the Countess de Borg.

The unknown woman seemed a soft white phantom in the night. Elis had a fever of intoxication. But suddenly, he uttered another exclamation, this time a cry of anguish. A man—oh, how rapidly the child recognized the quotidian visitor!—had come to lean on the sill beside her. He was speaking to her closely. What could he be saying to her? Eh! He was saying what Elias, he, Elias, would have said if he had been a man and not a child, a well made individual and not a cripple, and if he had been beside her, by night, after a waltz that they had waltzed together, instead of being treacherously lying in ambush behind a window, his mouth gaping and his neck stretched.

The wretched dwarf was suffering to such a point that if his suffering had been suddenly revealed, it might perhaps have caused the two lovers to draw apart and interrupt the kiss that the young man was applying at length to his friend's shoulder...

Elias saw that kiss; he thought he understood it. His eyes were veiled; something broke in his breast; his knees weakened. He fell backwards, his skull hitting the pavement of the balcony, and he lost consciousness.

A domestic who was in the library came running at the sound of the fall. The Baron, transported to his bed, allowed himself to be undressed and laid down without giving any sign of life. The entire house was soon astir. Count de Borg, absent, as usual, would not return until morning. Fortunately, someone had the idea of waking the concierge and sending him to fetch Dr. Delton. Meanwhile the domestic, who thought that his young master was dead, kept vigil by his bed.

Nearly an hour went by before the physician arrived; he had not been found at home, but his mother, with whom he lived, had been able to give precise indications. Dr. Delton ought to be at a ball given to celebrate the engagement of Monsieur Chardin, one of his friends, to Mademoiselle Juliette de Poean. By a favorable chance, the Poean house was very close to the Borg house, and the concierge, on returning, had had the doctor summoned, who had hastened to quit the ball.

Delton went straight to the invalid's bed and took his hand.

"Is he dead?" asked the domestic.

"No, not yet. What has happened?"

Fearing that he might be reprimanded for having allowed the Baron, whose care was confided to him, to remain in the hothouse for too long, the valet said that Elias had gone to bed early, with a fever, and after some delirium, had finally fainted. The doctor seemed astonished that the crisis had not had a more directing determinant cause.

"He'll recover consciousness," he said; and as, by virtue of some presentiment, he wanted to be alone to hear the first, probably delirious, words of the invalid, he made a sign to the domestic to leave, and enjoined him not to come back without being summoned unless Count de Borg returned to the house.

Elias opened his eyes. Delton had positioned himself in such a fashion as not to be perceived immediately. The child put his hands to his forehead and said: "Oh, how hot it is!" Then his arms fell back.

There was a silence then, but very brief, and broken by the exclamation: "Oh! I remember! He kissed her. I saw it. I heard it too. At the window. They didn't know I was there. When was that? Yesterday, I think. No, it was a long time ago, perhaps a week. It was night. Have I been asleep for a week?"

The doctor was stupefied.

Elias continued, with more violence: "No! It was this evening! It was a little while ago! I'm sure of it!"

And it was a horrible spectacle to see the dwarf roll rather than get down from his bed and then, half-naked, delirious, weeping and crying, with hallucinated gestures, crawl toward the door-curtain and, having lifted it, precipitate himself madly toward the glass panel of the hothouse, still ajar.

Delton followed him. He saw him plunge his head into the branches, but, placed behind Elias, he could only see very imperfectly the persons and objects that drew painful exclamations from the child's throat:

"She's still at the window! She's alone. Was I dreaming? No, he's going to come. Ah! He's traversing the courtyard. It's to watch him go that she's put herself there!"

Delton, having hoisted himself up on a stool where there were a few gardening implements that served to prune the trees in the hothouse, was able to see a woman leaning on a window sill; she was leaning forward, speaking to a young man traversing the courtyard, and in a final adieu, she blew him a kiss.

"Again!" cried Elias. "Oh, I don't want to see any more! I don't want to see any more!" And, in turning round, he found himself facing the doctor, who descended from the stool.

"You! You're here! What are you doing here? Get out!"

Like a hunted beast, Elias went to crouch down in a corner.

"Calm down, dear child," said Delton, advancing a few paces.

"Don't come near me!" sad the invalid, in a voice both shrill and hoarse: the voice of a dwarf and a dying man. "You want to cure me, do you? You want me to live, to see them every day, like tonight? What have I to do with living, since she loves that man? Oh, there are women who are worth more than angels? There are women who have pity? You said that. You lied. You're a liar. Don't come near me; I detest you."

The child was breathless. Delton dared not advance any further, fearing to push him to the end.

Suddenly, Elias shivered from head to toe.

"I understand! You love her too! That's why you come here! You come to see her, like me, through the window. You want to take her from me, you too. Oh, coward! Oh, liar! I'm going to kill you."

Furious, with the cry of a jackal, Elias threw himself upon the doctor, seized his hands and bit them. Delton tried in vain to imprison the child in his arms, in order to carry him to his bed, where he would have been able to master him easily. Elias howled, scratched, and tore. He was mad.

"I've got you!" he cried. "You love her! You want to take her from me! You want to cure me! I'm going to kill you!"

Then, suddenly, with an unexpected movement, he escaped from the physician, leapt toward the stool, picked up a sharp billhook, and launched himself with a single bound at Delton's breast.

"Here! Here!" he said. "Are you dead?"

Placed in the necessity of defending his life, the doctor scarcely had time to seize Elias's arms. While he compressed them in his right hand—all his strength was scarcely sufficient—he grabbed one of the child's deformed knees with the other, and finally succeeded in carrying that horrible burden, weeping, moaning, coughing and gasping, to the bed in the next room.

But that last fit had exhausted the energy of the delirium; once lying down, Elias became motionless, his eyes open but not seeing anything, his mouth agape but speechless.

Delton rang. The valet, who had fallen asleep in the antechamber, was slow to arrive.

"Stay with the Baron. It's necessary that he doesn't go into the hothouse. Prevent him from getting up, at all costs. If you can't dispense with it, tie him down. I'll be back shortly."

"Is Monsieur the Baron very ill?" the domestic hazarded, perhaps repenting of having dissimulated the Baron's adventure.

"Yes, he's dying," the doctor replied; and he left, not without having darted a long compassionate glance at the poor recumbent child, who resembled a cadaver whose eyes had not been closed yet.

Elias's delirium was no longer revealed externally, but in the invalid's soul it was still as violent. What thoughts traverse a moribund's mind! Everything surges forth and mingles, is destroyed and recreated. In vague mirages, Elias saw his melancholy childhood on the castle in Dormsoë, his vagabondage among the great trees, and the ancient room where his mother had sat before the painted windows of a high casement. He also saw the unknown woman of the window responding with a smile to her friend's salute, and the kiss, and the doctor, all that in a cloud, without any precise distinction of time or place.

And he was suffering mortally. His lungs lacked air. He was thirsty. He would have liked to drink snow. He thought that someone had put a knee on his throat. He heard gasping, but he thought that the sound came from a long way away, that it was the sound of a sea retreating, a sea from which he might have been able to drink. He was inundated by a cold sweat. He could not see himself there.

He said to himself: "Now I'm dying."

Gradually, however, it seemed to him that something sweet and strange was happening around him. He perceived a faint light, like the early morning clarity that penetrates into the bedroom of a sleeper. There was a delicate rustle near his bed; the light emanated from that rustle; he imagined that someone opened the curtains of a window through which the sunlight entered. His respiration was less painful; a delightful breath refreshed his lungs, and he was like a man on the point of asphyxiation to whom air, daylight and life have suddenly been rendered

When he had recovered his senses completely, Elias found himself lying in his bedroom near a muted lamp, facing a delightfully beautiful young woman clad in a dress of white gauze, who had violets in her hair.

"Her!" he said. "Her!"

He did not know whether he was dreaming or awake; he thought that he was dead and already in the paradise about which his mother had spoken to him.

Juliette de Poean was seventeen years old; the purest azure of the skies would have seemed somber by comparison with the tender blue of her eyes; beneath the gold of her hair the candor of her skin was as white as lilies, but less cold; and her smile was that of a saint.

Next to the soon-to-be-mortuary bed she had the appearance of a angel charged with collecting and taking away the soul of the moribund child.

"Her," Elias repeated; and, with an instinctive movement, he hid his head under the covers.

Mademoiselle de Poean, troubled by the exceptional situation that had been made for her, strove to vanquish a last repugnance and approach the sick child.

"Monsieur," she said, hesitantly, "Monsieur le Baron, are you feeling better?"

The question was banal, but the voice was full of so much compassion! At the sound of that unexpected voice, Elias shuddered; the faculty of rapid and profound perception that people possess who only have a short time to live, permitted him to experience simultaneously an infinite number of adorable emotions, He was suffocated by joy; but he believed himself to be mad.

"How are you here? You! It's you! How do you come to be here?"

"Doctor Delton told me that you wanted to see me; I've come. I'll go away if I'm inconveniencing you."

"He was right, then! There are women who are better than angels!"

Elias took his forehead in his hands and wept abundantly.

"What's the matter, my child?" Juliette asked.

He sat up abruptly.

"Don't call me child! I'm not a child!"

There was so much anger in his voice that Mademoiselle de Poean recoiled, frightened.

"Oh, forgive me! Forgive me! Don't be angry with me. It's because I'm mad. Haven't you been told, then, that I'm mad? Have pity. Don't go away. Since I've seen you, I've be so unhappy. This is the first time I've wept with joy. Don't go away. I've never loved anyone except my mother and you, you more than my mother, and before, for I sense now, clearly, that in her, it was you that I loved already. There were domestics at Dormsoë who beat me. That was when I was little. If I asked them why they were beating me they said: 'It's to teach you to walk straight.' Was it my fault if I was lame? At other times, they beat me because I was hunchbacked—for it's necessary to tell you that I'm hunchbacked, Mademoiselle, and lame too. You can't perceive it because I'm lying down, but if you want to turn away for a moment I'll get dressed and I'll walk in front of you; you'll see that I'm lame and I have a hump. No, no, I'm too ugly. Don't move. Look at me. My mother told me that I have beautiful hair. When people maltreated me, I didn't tell her, in order that it wouldn't cause her chagrin. She was already so ill, my mother; she died of a disease of the lungs. It appears that it's a hereditary malady, and it's necessary that I'll die soon of the same disease. I'm telling you these things in order for you to have a great deal of pity. My father is a bad man. He made us very unhappy, Mama and me. It's high time that someone is interested in me. There's Doctor Delton, but he's a man. Men aren't like my mother. You're like her, but more beautiful. I say that for the sake of laughter. It's no concern of mine that you're beautiful, because I'm a child, a child with much to lament. So, you'll stay with me because you're good. Isn't it quite simple to watch over a poor little creature who is dying? Then, you might be my sister. There, you're my sister. You can see that I'm not as mad as Doctor Delton says. You can stay here without fear, I won't say anything bad to you. You won't be scolded. You've never been beaten, have you, Mademoiselle? If my father comes, it's necessary not to let him in. You can see that I don't have ridiculous ideas. I'm a child and I talk like a child. Don't go away. I'll be very good."

While speaking, in faint voice full of tenderness, Elias contemplated with delight the adorable vision of his last night.

"I won't leave you," said the young woman intimately touched; and she leaned her elbows on the bed, gently.

The child was radiant. One might have thought that an instant of happiness had returned his age to him. He smiled; he talked about a thousand things. He would have liked to ride a horse if he had not been deformed. He asked her what her name was. "My name's Elias," he told her. He asked her what age she was, and when she had replied "seventeen," he added, gaily: "How old you are!"

Mademoiselle de Poean was able to believe that Doctor Delton had exaggerated the horror of the situation; she simply understood that she was giving pleasure to the child, and estimated herself fortunate in being good. Sometimes, Elias burst out laughing, but his laughter, too violent, degenerated into a gasp followed by a coughing fit; then he was horrible to behold; his eyes appeared to want to emerge from their orbits; he was about to die; he died.

At those moments, Mademoiselle de Poean, alarmed, wanted to call out, fearing some terrible eventuality; but soon, by virtue of an effort of will stronger than his suffering, the invalid calmed down; he stopped coughing; he smiled; he spoke; he said: "Don't call for help; I'm better; I'm cured." And the young woman, deceived by that apparent return to life, sat down again, saying to herself: *He won't die.*

Suddenly, after a silence in which he appeared to be trying to reassemble his ideas, Elias cried: "Have you come alone?"

"No, my mother is here, in the drawing room, with the doctor, who is our friend. Would you like me to call my mother? She'll come, gladly. We can both care for you."

"And your brother?" Elis asked, looking at Mademoiselle de Poean with a singular intensity. "Has your brother not come with you?"

"I have no brother," Juliette replied, surprised.

"You have no brother? He isn't your brother, the young man who comes to see you every day? He's your fiancé, then, your husband or your lover? I'm not a child. I love you. I'm jealous. I lied to you. I'm eleven years old, yes, but each of my years has contained centuries of anguish and fear. I've grown old suddenly, without anyone perceiving it, like the legendary hunters of my homeland, dragged away by evil spirits in an eternal black hunt. There hasn't been any time for me. I was born a man as I was born a hunchback. Just as my deformities, immediately definitive, haven't grown, my mind hasn't had any development; it has always been what it is now, the mind of a man, and I love you. Yes, me, I love you like a man. I'm not a child, I'm a dwarf, and I'm jealous. This evening, I tried to kill the doctor. You don't know, the man who loves you, I wanted to kill him too. I hate him. You too, I hate you! What have you come to do here? To see me die, isn't it, in order to be quite sure that I can't kill him? Go away. You're doing me harm. I don't want to see you anymore. Go away..."

Frightened, Juliette stood up. At the sound of Elias's violent speech, a door had opened slightly, allowing the sight of the attentive head of Doctor Delton. The child understood that the young woman really was about to withdraw, that she was going to be taken away, that it would all be over. He could not bear that idea.

He calmed down and said: "Forgive me, Mademoiselle, I implore you! I'm malicious. But when one is suffering, it's easy to be malicious. Don't hold what I said to you against me. I was very stupid. There's no harm in not having a brother. I won't shout again. I'm no longer angry, Stay with me; I'm very tranquil. It was the fever."

Elias saw the door close again. Juliette drew nearer to him again, and said to him, softly: "Poor friend!" The excellent young soul deliberately did not say "child," fearing to renew the moribund's torment.

"I'm malicious because I love you and you can't love me," Elias went on, in a less bitter tone. "How happy he must be, the man you love! Never talk to me about him; that would make me die right away. I love you too, more than him, I'll wager. For a year, I've only had one thought: you! There's a hothouse, there; through a window, one can see your window; it's in that hothouse that I've lived. I see you every day, but you never look in my direction. You couldn't discover me, in any case, I'm too well hidden. When you turn your head, by chance, I retreat right away. It's horrible and charming. Sometimes, I have dreams. I'm twenty years old, I'm handsome, I have myself introduced to your mother at a ball, I dance with you. In the hothouse there are white flowers that I love because they resemble you. When you come to your window I recognize you immediately, in spite of the distance. The first time I saw you, it was a Tuesday. I have a very good memory. You were wearing a white dress. There were forget-me-nots in your hair. I wasn't able to tell whether they were natural flowers; that worried me a great deal. Yesterday you put on a gray silk dress; I'm sure that it was silk because the sun was mirrored in the pleats of the skirt.

"Isn't it true that I adore you? I'm very unhappy. At night, there's only you in my dreams, and they aren't dreams, because I'm not asleep. Doctor Delton can tell you that I don't sleep at all. Only I think, and I see you. You're beside me. But it isn't next to the bed where I'm going to die, as you are now; it's in a great forest, near an old castle, near the castle where my mother lived, in the forest where my mother is buried; it's spring and it's morning. In Norway, there are flowers in the woods, all small, all perfumed: I haven't seen similar ones here, in the Bois de Boulogne. We're walking, alone; I'm a handsome young man; I have a big sword, as in romances; if a tiger comes, I'll kill it, because I have a great deal of courage, although I'm small; in any case, I'm very tall in my dream. We stop sometimes, in order to listen more carefully to the birds; when they fall silent, I'm very happy, because you talk then; soon we arrive at my mother's tomb and we sit down there; you say me: 'Elias, it's necessary to go back.' I reply: 'We have to wait for my mother,' and, in fact, my mother comes; she comes out from beneath the stone; she's no longer dead; she kisses you on the forehead, saying you: 'My daughter!' and all three of us return to the castle, her grave and happy, you laughing, with your head on my shoulder, while I can hear the profound sound in the distance of axes attacking the heart of larches, mingled with the soft and sonorous singing of the woodcutters of the forest."

At those last words, the voice of Elias seemed very distant itself: a voice that was emerging from a vast and unknown place, and which, after having traversed great solitudes, was finally arriving, extenuated.

"That's how I loved you. But now, I love you even more, because you're beautiful and so good—oh, so good, to have come! Then, you don't know, it's because of you that I'm dying. The doctor told me that. Without you, I wouldn't be dead. Thank you. You're an angel. I'm going to die. If I had had to live, I'd never have spoken to you. How good you are to have made me die!"

Mademoiselle de Poean recalled that, indeed, according to Doctor Delton, Elias's malady had been singularly aggravated by the anguish of an impossible amour. Already violently moved by the invalid's speech, she could not bear the thought that she was the cause of that frightful death, and slowly, two tears fell from her eyes.

"Oh, don't weep, Mademoiselle! Am I worth the trouble of anyone weeping for me? You've wept! I thank you. I love you. I'm happy."

Elias took Juliette's hand and kissed it delightedly. Stupefied, the young woman cried out, and the door opened, delivering passage to Doctor Delton and Madame de Poean, who ran toward the bed where Elias, either because the joy of that single kiss had been too strong for his dying sensibility or because he had been rendered desperate by Juliette's gesture of fear, was prey to the ultimate convulsions.

"What's happening?" cried Madame de Poean, taking her daughter in her arms.

"Oh, mother, I believe he's dying."

"Yes," said Dr. Delton, "It's over."

"Oh, Doctor, what have you done?" said Madame de Poean, showing the physician her daughter, almost fainted; and, seizing Juliette by the arms, she cried: "Come, my child, come way!"

At those words, the moribund sat up, extended his arms toward the young woman, and said, in a grave voice: "Stay, Juliette!"

The sum of will contained in those two words was so great that Mademoiselle de Poean, as if vanquished by a magnetic influence, returned to the bed and responded, in a very humble tone: "I'll stay, my friend."

In the brief instants of respite that the death-throes leaves him, when the Christian glimpses the sacred splendors of the paradise of his faith, there is no smile more ecstatic than the smile of Elias was at that response from Juliette. He let himself fall back gently on to the pillow, and extended his fleshless hands to Mademoiselle de Poean, into which the young woman, exalted by the gravity and solemnity of the situation, did not hesitate to put her own.

"Listen to me, Juliette," said the child, in a voice so low that the doctor and Madame de Poean, although they were only a few paces away, could not hear anything of that last conversation, "listen to me: you can see that I'm dying; because of whom? Because of you. At the point where I am, there's no more deformity; in an hour I'll be where neither age nor form exists any longer. What remains of my life, my soul, is so nearly disengaged from the vile envelope that it is already nothing but itself, and that soul, Juliette, has the right to say to you: 'It's because of you that I'm exiling myself before time. Do you want me to depart desperate and blaspheming, and damned for all eternity?'"

Elias was right. The solemn horror of death was upon him; equality was commencing; and, dying, he was a man. Without surprise, Mademoiselle de Poean replied: "What do you want me to do, my friend?"

"I adore you, Juliette, and I'm jealous. Swear to me never to belong to any man."

The young woman recoiled violently; she believed that Elias was delirious; she tried to disengage her hands; but the child held on to them gently, and said, in an almost extinct voice: "Don't refuse me that oath, Juliette! Shall I not have one single joy in dying, me, to whom all joys were unknown while alive? Make me that promise, Mademoiselle. Terrible as the sacrifice will be, accomplish it. God will give you credit for that charity."

Elias's voice was becoming weaker and weaker. Soon, it ceased to express itself by means of intelligible sounds. The death-rattle cut off the words. But while the death-throes took hold of the child, not to abandon him again, all the power of volition of which he still disposed, al his vitality, in a fugitive instant, had taken refuge in his eyes and his hands.

His eyes and his hands spoke clearly to Juliette. The hands said: "Consent; we're only awaiting a word from you to distend and fall dead." The eyes said: "Swear! We'll close on a gaze of ecstasy!"

Between the moribund and the young woman there was a bond so tight that both of them understood ne another without speaking. There was both a fusion and a struggle. But in that struggle, the living woman felt herself weakening. In vain she strove to react against the will of Elias; in vain she recalled her fiancé, their love, their hopes and dreams; she foresaw that it would be necessary to yield to the dying boy's desire; she did not have the leisure to appeal for help to the doctor or her mother; Elias's gaze and hands possessed her entirely, and it was a fatal moment.

Suddenly, the suffering of the invalid appeared to increase; his death-rattle became more profound, his hair stood on end; and his mouth opened, ready to utter the supreme cry. Meanwhile the pressure of his hands became increasingly violent, his gaze had acquired a superhuman force, and Juliette saw Elias raise himself up one last time, in order to fall back forever; and then, subjugated by the hands and vanquished by the gaze, she cried, before the voice of the dying child closed in the last sigh: "Elias! Elias! I swear to you!"

The expression of an immense happiness invaded Elias's face, and he lay down, dead.

At that moment the door opened noisily; Count de Borg appeared, in evening dress.

"How is my son?" he asked, in a conventionally emotional tone.

Without responding to the Count de Borg, the three people who had witnessed the death of Elias withdrew gravely.

"Oh, Doctor," said Juliette, in a low voice, when she had quit the lugubrious room, "if you knew what I have sworn!"

"Mademoiselle," replied the physician, "you are an angel but..."

"But...?" she asked.

"But you are a child."

The Bouquet of Forget-Me-Nots

Very young, scarcely seventeen, and so pretty, albeit paltry and pale, with her unkempt blonde hair and her blue eyes moist with tears, like two little damp skies, the madwoman was sitting on a stone bench in the large courtyard of the asylum.

Around her, the winter sun was blanching the high walls, putting its sheet of silvery snow over the paving-stones and the sand where a few rare trees, black and desiccated, stretched out and spread out the reflection of the skeletons. A keen wind was blowing, fresh rather than icy, brisk and clear, joyful; here and there, sparrows were chirping. If there had been a few leaves on the branches one might have thought that April had returned. January has these one-hour springtimes.

But the poor young madwoman did not pay any heed to that furtive renewal. Hunched up, making herself small in the envelopment of a tight Scottish tartan, with the fearful air of someone about to be beaten, she was sitting on the very edge of the bench, pressing a bouquet of forget-me-nots to her lips, on which her tears were falling, one by one.

The intern who had guided me into the abode of madness and desolation made me a sign that I could approach the child and talk to her. In fact, she could not be malevolent, so sad and so weak. At the sound of my footsteps she raised her head swiftly and looked me in the face, suddenly content, with her soft eyes in which joy dried up the tears as the sun drinks the dew.

"You've come to find me?" he said putting her hands together. "You're going to take me away, take me away immediately? Oh, how glad I am. I have to get out of here, you see, today, before dusk, to console him; he must be so distressed, suffering al alone."

"Who do you want to go and see?" I asked.

"Him."

"Him?"

"Robert Daniel."

"Your lover, perhaps your fiancé?"

"Oh no—Jane's fiancé."

"Jane's fiancé?" I repeated, slightly surprised.

"Yes."

"He's waiting for you?"

"Every day, for six months."

"And where is he waiting for you?"

"Well, where he is. In the cemetery. In his tomb. You don't know his tomb? It's pretty, in white marble, which is sometimes slightly pink in the sunlight. The name Robert Daniel is engraved on the stone, and above it, between the dangling branches, there's a small alabaster urn that the water of heaven fills, where the birds come to drink."

I looked at her, astonished and compassionate.

"Oh yes," she said, "you don't understand, you neither. You think that everything is finished when life is finished, that one no longer thinks, that one no longer moves, when one is buried, that the dead are dead. That isn't true, Monsieur. You don't know how things are. That's because you've never put your ear to a crack in a sepulcher to listen to what's happening inside. I too, before that happened to me, didn't know, like you, that the dead are alive. I don't hold it against you; you can't know what I know."

She interrupted herself momentarily, kissed the little bunch of blue flowers, and went on, very slowly: "Once, I went to Père Lachaise cemetery, on my own, to take a wreath to a friend I had had in the convent, and whom I didn't have any longer. I had put the offering at the grille and I was coming back. There was a lot of brightness in the air, under the azure, and a little shadow in places. Between the tombs, abrupt sunbeams were coming and going, escaping and coming back, like children playing and running after one another. The weather was so mild, so pure so beautiful that I felt happy in that place of sadness—happy and very cheerful.

"Then, as I was passing a tomb where a great many flowers were growing, I had a desire to pick one. It wasn't a sacrilege, was it? I reached out my arm, and stopped, frightened, trembling all over. There, under the stone, someone had spoken, in a very soft voice. Oh, I wasn't mistaken, I really had heard it. The vice had said, in a plaintive and hopeful tone: 'Jane, is that you, at last?'

"I leaned over in order to listen. It murmured again, the voice: 'Jane, is that you, at last? Answer me.' At first, I had been very frightened; now, that was finished. There was no fear; only a great pity and a great tenderness. I raised my eyes. I read the names *Robert Daniel* on the stone, and I saw that he had died at the age of twenty. I understood everything.

"The man that was believed to be asleep in that tomb, and who wasn't asleep, had had a fiancée name Jane, who had promised him to come and see him in the cemetery, and who hadn't come. He was still waiting for her, and every time a sound of footsteps reached him through the earth, he thought that she was finally keeping her promise, and he asked: 'Is that you?' But no one answered him.

"I answered him. He must have been feeling so much anguish, there, in the dark, in the cold, in the rigid narrowness of the coffin. Was I wrong to want to console him a little? I spoke to him and I lied. 'Yes,' I said to him, putting my mouth as close as I could to the stone, 'it's me, it's me, your Jane.'

"Oh, I was very anxious; because of my voice, perhaps he would recognize the deceit, and wouldn't believe that it was Jane who was there. But undoubtedly, through the thickness of the marble, the sound only reached him very faintly, indistinctly, changed, for I heard a slow and profound sigh of contentment. He believed! He believed!

"And we started to chat, softly, tenderly, the two of us. As you can imagine, at the start of the conversation, I only said rather vague things, which could relate to almost any amour, almost any engagement. Most of all, I let him talk, reflecting on the slightest words, noting the details, in order to recompose the history, and to be able to talk in my turn, at greater length, like someone fully informed. It would have been such a great chagrin for him if he'd discovered my fraud!

"Finally, after an hour, I knew everything that it was necessary to know, and I could have been Jane herself and I wouldn't have been able to reply more appropriately. And I stayed there until the time when the cemetery gates were closed. And I went back the next day.

"For three months, every day, we said the dearest and sweetest things to one another. We recalled the day in spring when we met for the first time, the first smile, holding hands surreptitiously while his mother and mine walked ahead of us, chatting together, and not seeing anything. How many times, in the evening, he had come to the door of the little garden. We talked through the wood as we were doing now through the stone. And often, he passed pieces of paper through the keyhole on which there were verses he had written

"Then, our parents wanted us to be happy. But death didn't want that. He fell ill. We told one another about our anxieties and vain hopes during the long illness. But even those bitter memories were sweet for us, and because of the long conversations we were as content as if we had been married.

"Alas, one day when I was about to go out to return to the cemetery, to take Robert a bouquet of forget-me-nots that he had asked me for—they were the flowers he preferred, since he'd died—my mother came into my room with two men I didn't know. They took hold of me, and they took me away. They brought me here. It's much sadder than the cemetery; and although it's as if I'm dead too, we can't talk any more, Robert and I, because our tombs are too far apart."

She fell silent, with a sob. When she raised her head again, she doubtless saw that I had a sad expression, and she understood that I hadn't come to take her away.

"At least," she said, "would you be willing to take a commission for Robert? He's in Père Lachaise, as I told you. The place isn't difficult to find. It's to the left of the main pathway, on the hill. Knock twice on the stone, because he's sometimes asleep. That's the signal agreed between us. Tell him that Jane—Jane, you understand?—has gone away on a voyage with her mother, but that she'll come back, in a week or two, soon, anyway, that he mustn't be sad, or impatient; that she still loves him. Also say that she's asked you to bring him the bouquet, and place it on the marble slab, in the middle. That will please him."

I took the bouquet and went away. And the story is finished.

However, one thing remains for me to say, at the risk of appearing slightly ridiculous, which is that I carried out the commission.

The Unexpected

Are you of the same opinion as Hamlet? Do you believe that there are more things in heaven and earth than all of philosophy has been able to dream? Is it true for you that, in a London tavern, Éliphas Lévi invoked Apollonius of Tyana, the mild prophetic mage, and that the illustrious scientist William Crookes took tea several times a week, for months, with the materialized spirit of a young woman clad in a linen chemise and coiffed with a feathery turban?

Don't laugh. A specter, even in a turban, would chill the marrow of your bones with fear, and the comical aspect might add to the horror.

For myself, I didn't laugh, yesterday evening, on reading in the New York *Herald*—the issue dated 19 March—the report of a criminal trial that will doubtless conclude with the accused being sentenced to death. It's a sinister adventure: as I translate the history of it, reconstructed from the evidence of the hotel bellboy who listened through the keyhole to the conversation of two accomplices and in accordance with the unanimous testimony of forty people absolutely worthy of faith who witnessed the final scene of the drama, I feel a frisson running through my flesh, as if an icicle were melting between my shoulder blades. What would have become of me if I had seen, myself, the beautiful young dead woman, bleeding from the heart, dipping her fingers into the blood in order to bless the forehead of the guilty party with a baptism of red droplets?

On 25 February, at about three o'clock in the afternoon, a famous medium, Professor Benjamin Havenport—the name means "port of salvation"—and Miss Ida Soutchotte, a very pale and thin young woman who had already been lending herself to the professor's experiments for several years, were finishing lunch in their room on the second floor of the Devonshire Hotel in New York.

Benjamin Havenport was, indeed, famous, but it is said that he owed his notoriety to scarcely admissible means. Serious spiritualists refrained from having the confidence in him that they testified loudly to William Crookes or Daniel Dunglas Home. "The harshest assaults that our cause has had to suffer," says the author of *The History of American Spiritualism*, "come from rapacious and unprincipled mediums who, when manifestations are not produced as vividly as circumstances demand, have recourse to imposture to get them out of difficulty." Professor Benjamin was one of those mediums.

In addition, strange stories were running round on his account of armed robberies on the roads of South America, cheating at cards in the gambling dens of San Francisco, and revolvers too rapidly discharged at inoffensive dupes. It was said, almost in a loud voice, that the professor's wife, betrayed, ruined and beaten, had died of chagrin.

In spite of those nasty rumors, and thanks to the skill of his trickery, Benjamin Havenport exercised a considerable influence over simple souls easy to deceive. One would have had difficulty persuading a large number of honest people of the two worlds that they had not seen, heard, and even touched, thanks to him, the corporealized spirits of their brothers, their mothers or their sisters. He was, moreover, well served by a fatal face with a dark complexion, profound eyes full of wild glints, a large hooked nose and a mouth forever twisted in a demonic rictus, and the almost prophetic emphasis of his speech: Satan as a charlatan.

When the hotel bellboy had gone—he did not go far—taking away the dessert plates, the medium said to Miss Ida: "By the way, there's a séance this evening at the home of Miss Joanna Hardinge; many people, important individuals, two or three millionaires. You'll hide under your skirt the gauze cloth with which apparitions veil themselves and the woman's wig, the blonde one."

"As you wish, Benjamin," replied Ida Soutchotte, in a resigned voice.

The bellboy heard coming and going in the room. After a silence, she asked: "Who are you going to evoke, then, Benjamin?"

There was a great burst of laughter, coarse and noisy; a chair grated under the agitation of the hilarity. "Guess!"

"How can I guess?" she said

"I want to evoke...my wife!"

And there was another burst of laughter, even noisier and more brutal, with anger and menace in the gaiety.

But Ida had uttered a scream! By a muted friction of fabric, the listener at the door understood that she was dragging herself over the carpet on her knees.

"Benjamin, Benjamin! Don't do that!" she said, sobbing.

"Why not? It's claimed that I made Mrs. Havenport unhappy. It's a legend that harms me. It will be destroyed when people have heard my wife's spirit speaking to me tenderly. For you'll address very tender words to me from the other world, won't you, Miss Soutchotte?"

"No, no you won't do that! You can't think of doing that! Listen to me, I implore you. In the four years that you've taken me with you, I've always obeyed you; everything that you've wanted, I've done; everything you've imposed on me, I've endured. I've deceived and lied, like you; I've learned to simulate the sleep of somnambulists, the crises, the ecstasies, to bear the weight of men sitting on my back, and pins in the flesh of my arms, and I've never shivered, never uttered a plaint.

"More than that: behind the curtain, imitating distant voices, I've made mothers and wives believe that their sons and husbands came from the other world to speak to them, and in drawing rooms, between the furniture, under lowered lamps, clad in a shroud or a veil with the appearance of a mist, I've dared to be the vague form in which eyes blinded by tears recognize cherished beings. Oh, those sacrileges! If you knew how frightened I was!

"You parody the eternal mysteries fearlessly, because you don't believe in them; me, I'm full of doubts and terrors. God! What if, one day, at the very moment when I pass myself off as him, a dead man were to loom up before me, terrifying, raising his arms, casting maledictions? It's to those terrors that I owe the malady of the heart from which I'm suffering, and from which I shall die. It's because of them that I'm languishing and trailing, feverish, fleshless, exhausted. Well, no matter, I'm yours, entirely. Dispose of me; you can, I want it. Have I ever complained?

"But today, Benjamin, what you're asking is too much. Because of my obedience, because of my suffering, have pity on me, finally. Don't force me to play the role of the poor woman who was so beautiful and so gentle. Oh, how can you even have the idea? Spare me, Benjamin, I beg you!"

He was no longer laughing. As there was, in the pell-mell of overturned furniture, the sound of a skull hitting a wall, it is probable that Professor Havenport had repelled Miss Ida violently, with a punch or a kick. But the bellboy did not go in, because the travelers had not rung.

On the evening of that day, shortly before midnight, in Miss Joanna Hardinge's drawing room, forty people were sitting, facing the curtain that would soon be moved aside by the apparition of the spirit. A single lamp, in a corner of the room, cast a very faint light —the kind of light that makes darkness visible rather than illuminating it—over everything, vague and troubled, while, in the great silence, anxious breaths were exhaled, and the flames in the fireplace emitted furtive gleams, like errant spirits.

Professor Benjamin Havenport had never been as extraordinary as he had that evening. The world of spirits obeyed him, without resistance, as its legitimate sovereign; he really was the omnipotent prince of souls. Hands without arms had been seen picking flowers from the window-boxes; an accordion, put in motion by an unperceived being, had played exquisite melodies; raps struck on all the items of furniture had responded with the most remarkable propriety to the most unexpected questions. The professor, having entered into a somnambulistic ecstasy, had even risen up above the parquet to a height of some three feet—according to the measurement made by Miss Joanna Hardinge—and, with his two hands full of red-hot embers, he had walked in mid-air, smiling, for a full quarter of an hour.

But the most interesting, and most decisive experiment promised at the beginning of the séance, would be the apparition of Mrs. Arabella Havenport.

"The time has come," said the medium.

While all hearts beat with an apprehensive impatience, and all eyed widened in the fearful hope of the imminent vision, Benjamin Havenport stood next to the curtain, very tall in the gloom, unkempt, with infernal gleams beneath his eyelids, as if possessed by a demon, or a demon himself; he was truly terrible, and handsome.

"Come, Arabella!" he said, in a commanding voice, with the gesture of the Nazarene before the tomb of Lazarus.

Everyone waited...

A scream behind the curtain! The shrill, heart-rending scream of supreme terror! A scream in which a soul was fleeing!

The members of the audience shuddered; Miss Joanna nearly fainted; even the medium seemed astonished.

He pulled himself together on seeing the curtain stir, which lifted slowly, giving passage to the spirit.

It was a young woman with long blonde hair, very beautiful, very pale, semi-naked in white garments, whose unveiled torso had a bloody wound under the left breast, in which a dagger was quivering.

Everyone recoiled, coming to their feet, pushing chairs toward the wall. Those who had the thought of looking at the medium saw that he was shivering, frightfully pale, and he too recoiled.

But the young woman. Arabella—the true Arabella, whom he recognized clearly; she had come, since she had been summoned—marched straight toward Benjamin Havenport, who, stupefied and livid, put his hands over his eyes in order to evade the terrible spectacle, and fled, stumbling over the furniture. She dipped the fingers of her slender hand into the wound and she dripped blood, on to the forehead of the medium, on his knees in a bewildered terror, drop by drop, saying, in a slow and distant voice, like the echo of a plaint:

"It's you who killed me!"

Then, as he rolled on the parquet with agonized gasps, the lamps were lit again. The spirit had disappeared. In the next room, behind the curtain, the cadaver of Ida Soutchotte was found, her face convulsed. A ruptured aneurism, said a physician who was present. That is why Professor Benjamin Havenport appeared alone before the New York jury, charged with having murdered his wife four years before, in San Francisco.

Wedding Night

A livid pallor of dawn slid through the curtains. I was not asleep, gazing at that sad light. A bell rang, violently, redoubled, echoing in the apartment, and a few moments later, Sylvain Brunel opened the door of my bedroom, followed by my domestic, dressed in haste, who picked up the lamp.

"You!" I cried.

My surprise was all the more natural because they day before, Sylvain Brunel had married a beautiful young woman with whom he had evidently been passionately smitten. What was he doing in my house at an hour when he ought still to be ecstatic in the delectable triumph of the wedding night?

My astonishment increased, and became a dolorous anxiety, when I had remarked the pale face of the visitor, his eyes injected with red bile and his lips trembling like those of a fever-victim.

As soon as we were alone, he put a hand on my shoulder and spoke very rapidly, stammering, with teeth that were chattering.

"Do you believe in the impossible? Do you believe in the prodigious chimera of the dead who live, like us, who love, hate, suffer and weep like us? In the miracle of the dead who accompany us in the street, take our arm, sit down at our table, lie down in our bed? If those things aren't true, well then, lock me up—I'm mad!"

While I considered him with an increasing stupor, he let himself fall into an armchair next to my bed.

"Listen," he went on, lowering his voice, his speech slowing, "you know how I love Gilberte, my wife! You can divine with what hectic desire, yesterday evening, I waited for the moment when the two of us would finally be alone? That moment came, so hopefully awaited. Heart melted in delight, I was outside the door of the nuptial chamber; my hand touched the key; I was about to go in...

"A frisson ran through me, from head to for, with the zigzag of an icy lightning bolt over all my flesh. What as the matter with me? At first, I didn't understand. The effect had preceded the cause. I had the symptom of terror before the terror itself. But the fear arrived very quickly, sharp and intense. Yes, I was afraid. Why? Because I thought, for no reason, about Madame de Mortales, the poor dead woman who had loved me so much, so close to the dear living one I loved so much! It was like encountering a tomb on the threshold of paradise.

"With the gaze of the spirit, which contemplates past things, I saw her, Laurencia, pale and motionless, in the big bed from which she was not to rise again, having no more life except in the depths of her eyes, where a wild and jealous amour burned; and I heard her repeating to me, with the harshness of her Aragonese accent the words that she had already said to me so frequently:

"'You will never love another woman, will you? No, never? Whether I live or die, you'll be faithful to me, forever? Oh, if you deceive me, Sylvèrte, beware! I'll avenge myself, treason for treason. Resolutely, coldly, if you prefer another woman, I'll deliver myself to another man. Even dead, for I believe that I shall wake from the eternal sleep to accomplish my vengeance.'

"I heard those mad and sinister words yesterday evening, my hand on the key of the nuptial chamber. I heard them confusedly, as if a specter were whispering in my ear. But finally, with a surge of will power, I drove away the chimeras and became master of myself; smiling at my folly, I opened the blessed door. Pale and trembling, in the lace of her peignoir, Gilberte was waiting for me, and became very pink when she saw me. I knelt down before her, like a pilgrim at the feet of a statue of the Virgin and I adored her, full of grace.

"Let those who boast of the vain joys of culpable amours say what they will; perfect intoxication, the supreme delight, is to contemplate the blush of a virgin soon to be a wife, who is frightened, but who wants it dearly. Gently, slowly, as one might touch the wings of Psyche, I had taken her in my arms, and on her lips, scarcely turned away...

"Extraordinary thing! To our kiss, it seemed to me that another kiss responded, also tender, distant, like a faithful echo. I looked at her; she smiled, more roseate; she had not heard anything. I was losing my mind, in truth. I hugged her more tightly in the crumpled malines; I felt through the lace the warm and smooth reaction of her delicate body...

"God! Who, then, outside that room, simultaneously so far away and so close at hand, had crumpled a peignoir as I had? I looked at her more intently: still smiling; this time, again, she hadn't heard anything; and that open garment allowed the sight of the frail pallor, scarcely blue-tinted by a pale vein, of her adolescent cleavage. The folly of being fortunate carried me away, redoubled by a strange rage—that of being prey, me, a man of sense and firm mind, to stupid reveries. I embraced her, I lifted Gilberte up, astonished by my rudeness, and in the alcove, I said ardent things to her, I bit her with frantic kisses, I enveloped her with insatiable caresses.

"Oh horror, horror! I tell you that those words, another voice pronounced them, down below, almost the same, heard by me alone, that those kisses, other mouths gave them, far away, and yet close by, that another body—where, then? where?—was enveloped by those caresses. There was around us an abominable parody of our amour.

"Have you, by some sad hazard, possessed your mistress one night in one of those dismal hotels near railway stations, where the neighboring rooms, only separated from yours by a thin partition, have welcomed other couples? Add to the annoyance full of shame of a dirty proximity, the irresistible conviction that the noises—the noises that were driving me mad!—were not coming from a bed that as too close at hand, but from some unknown, mysterious, terrible couch, a Sabbat camp-bed in which the damned ferment blood and blasphemy, and you will scarcely understand what I experienced!

"I struggled against the terror, always hoping to vanquish it, to drown it in amour, triumphantly to make the frisson of fear into a frisson of pleasure. In vain! In vain! I laughed with ecstasy, I gasped in horror. At one moment, while the words still repeated my words, the kisses my kisses and the caresses my caresses, I even thought, for an instant, that I saw, next to the recumbent Gilberte, so young and so beautiful, tenderly resistant—yes, next to her, in a narrow shadow—another woman, pale and cold, as Laurencia, embalmed in her tomb, must be at this moment, but loving, resisting poorly, like Gilberte!

"And when, from the vanquished modesty of the young girl-woman, I had extracted, in a redoubling of desire, the supreme confession of the sigh, a different voice, equally tender—alas, where did it come from?—died in the same sigh! Then I leapt from the bed, intoxicated by fear, seating in large droplets, and I grabbed my clothes, and I fled, and I ran through the streets, and here I am, finally. I'm mad, am I not?"

I think that there is no need to spell out the arguments by means of which I succeeded in calming the morbid excitation. I did not succeed in that without difficulty. However, after a long conversation, he consented to recognize that he had been, if not mad, at least hallucinated; that only the memory of Madame de Mortales, perhaps mingled with some remorse, had given rise to that singular aberration; and he left my house almost calm almost serene.

It is probable that I would not have thought about that adventure again, and that I would never have narrated the story, if I not read in a newspaper, two days later, a very horrible article. A warden at Père-Lachaise cemetery—a monstrous brute—had been surprised two nights before as he was violating a sepulcher abominably; and that tomb, said the newspaper was that of a young Spanish woman, recently deceased, Madame Laurencia de Mortales.

As for the abject wretch, he was tried by the Court of Assizes of the Seine, but he was acquitted, the reports of the alienist physicians having established that the monster was demented. What contributed above all to conciliating the clemency of the jury was the absurd but evident good faith with which he sustained during the trial that if he had lifted the marble slab it was because, as he was making his round, not drunk, shortly before midnight, he had been invited to do so by a soft feminine voice, which had appealed to him, sliding between the stones of the tomb, through the verdure of the yews.

The Guest

It was a magnificent speech. Never yet had Monsieur Morgan-Level, then minister of commerce, raised himself to such an elevation of views. Rid of arid technical details, developed in a very noble language to which the beauty of the orator—and ancestral beauty, with a broad high forehead and a white beard—added to the solemnity, the question having appeared to be, in fact, vast, general and fraternal, interesting all of the human family. From various parts of the Chamber, continually, applause rose up, with murmurs of admiration, and everyone agreed in recognizing that no finer triumph had ever been achieved at the French tribune. But the end of the speech was marked by a singular incident, which, I believe has remained in many memories.

"Yes, Messieurs, in France as in America, on the old continent as in the New World..."

Monsieur Morgan-Level interrupted himself with the air of a man experiencing a hitch, doubtless slight, but nevertheless sufficient to trouble him.

He made a sign to the usher, who mounted the steps of the tribune rapidly, and, in the great silence, he pronounced these words, very simply:

"You see that skeleton sitting in the third row, between Monsieur Lockroy and Monsieur Madier de Montjau? Go and tell him to withdraw. You can add that I will gladly receive him at my home, and that I do not want to wound him in any way; but he will understand that his presence, in this arena, is somewhat out of place. Go, my friend."

The usher stepped back, stupefied.

"But no, don't disturb yourself," said the minister. "He's getting up and withdrawing of his own accord. That's very good. Thank you."

Then turning to the assembly, he continued: "Yes, Messieurs, in France as in America, on the old continent as in the New World..."

On the evening of that day, Doctor Delton entered without having himself announced into the private apartment of the minister of commerce—an old familiarity authorized that lack of ceremony—and extended his hand to the old man, who was working placidly, his beard whiter under the shade of the lamp, in a large, somber, austere drawing room hung with ancient tapestries, almost devoid of furniture.

"All my compliments, first of all. Everyone says that you were superb. You know, people are talking about you very seriously for the Presidency of the Republic. But damn it, what fantasy took hold of you? I wasn't there; I've been told about it. What's this story of a skeleton? A skeleton in the Chamber? You've made a farce, which isn't in your character, and I don't understand it at all."

"A farce?" repeated the minister slowly, with the melancholy smile of an old man who knows many things. No, it wasn't a farce. I really saw the skeleton, between Monsieur Madier de Montjau and Monsieur Lockroy.[14] He was wearing a black jacket, and in his fleshless hand he was supporting his opera hat on his left femur. What time is it, my dear Delton?"

"About nine o'clock."

"If you have nothing better to do, stay with me. We'll take tea, and I'll introduce my skeleton to you, who will be here before long. Generally, to distract ourselves—for he doesn't speak—we play chess or a game of écarté. This evening, we can play with a 'dead hand,' since there are three of us," added Monsieur Morgan-Level, with a little laugh.

The doctor, having fallen into an armchair, listened, his arms dangling. The old man went on, in a slow and serious voice:

---

[14] Édouard Lockroy and Noël Madier de Montjau were both radical députés in the late 1870s and early 1880s.

"You think I'm mad? I'm not. I have all my reason. In spite of my great age, my faculties are intact, thanks to the hygiene of measured, daily work, too neglected by the men of today. In any case, occupied with numbers and speculations, I've never been inclined to chimerical reveries. The opposite of a hallucinate, that's me. No superstition. I'm even an atheist. However, it's true; I have for a companion, for a guest, for an everyday friend, a skeleton: a skeleton who walks, sits down, extends his hand to me, asks after my health by means of gestures, and thanks me for my bonjour by nodding his head.

"Don't ask me whether I can explain that extraordinary presence. I observe it, that's all. I'm confronted by an impossible fact to which I've become habituated at length. At first, I revolted; I denied my sight, my sense of touch. I was wrong. The being exists, visible and tangible. What do you want me to do? That's the way it is. Nothing fantastic. A reality, which I no longer contest. For me, what would be astonishing now would be no longer seeing the skeleton. Perhaps I'd be afraid if he didn't appear. He's part of my existence. He's like a relative that one has the habit of greeting without paying any great attention to him, like an item of furniture of which ne makes use without noticing its form, by virtue of continual usage.

"Until now I haven't mentioned him to anyone, because my guest, for his part, maintains a certain discretion in his insistence in haunting me, visiting me in the solitary hours, hesitant to hurry things, like a modest mistress who doesn't seek publicity. But since he's manifested himself before everyone today, it seems to me that I too am disengaged from my reserve. I'll admit to him, since he's shown himself; and I see no inconvenience in telling you, in a few words, the history of this strange haunting.

"I was sixteen years old when he revealed himself for the first time. Ingenuous, I was in love, and one morning of spring freshness I was walking with the child of my first amour in a flowery wood. 'I want that rose!' she said. Before I had approached my hand to the branch, a hand had picked the flower and presented it to me—a bony hand, yellow and desiccated—and the skeleton smiled at me amicably, a toothless smile. I fled, mad with fear, and for two months, between life and death, I always saw him, the skeleton, behind my mother, behind my father, behind the physician who shook his head, anxiously. Cured, I still saw him, always at the same hours, reading with me, going out with me, coming back with me, living with me.

"After having known intolerable terrors. I arrived at not being disturbed when he brushed me, when he spoke to me—yes, without a voice—and when he looked at me, without eyes! From then on, through the hazards of work, throughout life he hasn't ceased to follow me. As a soldier, I had him as a companion in arms, as a student, for a study companion. I haven't married, for fear that he might lie next to me in the nuptial bed. And, as I say, he no longer frightens me. He's there, I admit it, I consent to it, I want it; I have the skeleton in my life as another man might have a pet dog.

At that moment, the door opened.

"Monsieur le Ministre," said Baptiste, "Monsieur le Ministre's skeleton is here."

"Have him come in," said Monsieur Morgan-Level, calmly.

Through the open door, what came in was the shadow of the antechamber, and nothing else: nothing at all.

But the old man had stood up, and indicated a seat to the invisible visitor.

The doctor withdrew, and in the antechamber, he said to the valet: "You're wrong. Why do you lend yourself to your master's mania? He's ill. A contradiction might perhaps cure him."

"But Monsieur," protested the domestic, "You haven't seen the skeleton, then? I assure you that he entered the drawing room as soon as the door was open. I know that very well; I introduce him every evening."

"The next day," Doctor Delton—to whom I owe this story—told me, "I tried to see Monsieur Morgan-Level again. The kind of malady by which he was afflicted was curable. I wanted to talk to him, to convince him of his chimera. The door was closed! Every time I presented myself at the house or the ministry, I was sent away, like a solicitor. Perhaps the invalid, after having allowed himself to make confidences, had regretted them? Doubtless he did not want to blush at his weakness before the man to whom he had made the confession.

"I reconciled myself to that new singularity, but I admired from a distance the man that it was impossible for me to encounter. His firm attitude in the midst of the incessant variations of politics, his speeches of an incomparable value and his frequently published books, too, in which a elevated and clear mentality was manifest, recommended him to my faithful admiration. I came to believe, so much did the serenity of his political conduct and his conceptions distance any suspicion of intellectual derangement, that he had mastered himself once again, after a temporary instability and escaped from funeral hauntings and hallucinations.

"That was my assumption, three years later, when I received a telegram signed by Baptiste, asking me to come to see Monsieur Morgan-Level, who was dying. When I went into the moribund's bedroom, the priest stood aside to let me pass. It was all over; in a matter of hours, my friend would be no more. I approached the bed, where the former minister, his eyes red and his lips pale, was convulsing in his death-throes.

"He cried: 'He's there! Still there! Always! I was wrong to receive him, to welcome him, for he has told the others, and they've all arrived, innumerable: the skeletons of children, the skeletons of women; all the exiles of all the cemeteries.' He was gasping as he spoke. 'Look at them, sniggering, sitting on the chairs, between the curtains of the windows, between the curtains of the bed. Help! Help! They're taking my hands, they're taking my pulse. One of them is offering me a cup of tisane, another parodying my oratorical gestures at the tribune.

Oh, I'm dying! There are too many of them. One, I didn't mind; all of them, they're killing me. Leave me alone! I tell you to leave me alone!'

"And he gasped horribly, his eyes wide, biting the sheets, wrapping himself in them like a shroud, spasmodically."

"A madman?" I asked.

"A madman?" said Doctor Delton, suddenly going pale. "I don't know—for while he was speaking, I didn't see, no, I didn't see the horrible assembly of skeletons, but everywhere in the room, between the curtains and under the furniture, I heard the frightful rattling of a heap of invisible bones colliding with one another."

Possessed

Still young, almost rich, the husband of a lovely woman who always has a smile of contentment on her lips, the father of a boy nine years old and a girl of six, who fill the house with a jolly tumult of laughter—having, as they say, everything that is necessary to be happy—Pierre Féraud appears the most miserable of men, so much is his forehead, under gray hair that is already sparse, hollowed out by profound wrinkles, while his staring eyes, which one might think dilated by fear, reveal an intimate and tenacious despair and his mouth is contorted by evil laughter or abandoned to an expression of definitive enunciation.

What, then, is his torment? Some dolorous memory? His life, simple and open, known to all those who frequent him, has had none of the rude shocks that disturb souls permanently. Some remorse, perhaps? A remorse would explain that bleak attitude, that appearance of continuous anguish; but how can one believe that he has committed a crime or a cowardly action? Honest and good, loving, devoted to everyone, ready for sacrifice—in a word, irreproachable—he surely merits the esteem that surrounds him. And it is, indeed, a strange spectacle, that if the infinite desolation on the face of that fortunate and honest man.

I would not have interrogated Pierre Féraud if curiosity alone had pushed me to emerge from doubt, but an amity already old authorized me to ask him for the confession of his mysterious chagrin; perhaps my consolations would ameliorate its bitterness.

At my first words my friend went very pale—even paler than I was accustomed to seeing him—and had a movement of recoil toward the door, as if with an intention to flee. But he stopped, stiffening his entire being.

"No, no, don't interrogate me! Let me be, go away!"

Then, abruptly, as if an invisible hand on his shoulder had constrained him to yield, he let himself fall into an armchair and started to weep, his head between his hands and his breast shaken by sobs.

"Do you believe the old stories of Possession? Do you believe that a man or a woman can be haunted by tempting spirits, to have for a perpetual companion a demon giving bad advice, who whispers in their ear and maddens their conscience? No, isn't that so? Nurses' tales, evil legends, absurd chimeras? So be it; I want that; I grant it. But when, what can explain what is happening in me, what has been happening within me, perpetually, for so many long years? If Satan doesn't exist, how it is that I am damned?

"You're looking at me with amazement; you don't understand; you think I'm mad. Listen.

"Once—I was twelve years old at the time, and it as the beginning of the vacation some friends and I were shooting at a target with an air-pistol. We were cheerful and rapturous under the sun, in the liberty of our pleasure, and I was more cheerful than the others, feeling those surges of joy that one doesn't experience later rising from my heart to my throat. When it was my turn to take aim I took the weapon and loaded it very rapidly. I was entirely given to the glorious thought of showing myself very skillful.

"'You'll see!' I cried to René, my best friend, almost my brother, but as, in the confident hope of the triumph, I prepared to press the trigger—oh, horror! a horror new then, but so familiar since!—the abominable and delectable desire came to me, without any reason, to fire, not at the target, but at my comrade. Yes, I wanted to kill him; I wanted it madly. And at the same time as that idea, there came to my mind, with a lightning suddenness, the entire vision of what would happen when I had killed him: the terror of the other children around the cadaver, my family running in response to the screams, and me, without a word, without any apparent disturbance, ecstatic in my crime!

"I uttered a cry, I threw the pistol into the branches, and I fell, weeping, into the arms of the stupefied René. 'Forgive me! Forgive me!' I said, clasping him to my breast; and I fled, and went to shut myself up in my room.

"An hour later, with the faculty of forgetfulness that fortunate childhood possesses, I was almost no longer thinking about it. I had had a moment of madness, perhaps because of the bright midday sun, and it was finished; I had chased the Evil Thought away forever.

"Finished! Yes, how complete it is, at the first bite of the iron, the first burn of the sulfur, the eternal torture of a damned soul!

"Under all forms, on all occasions, almost at every hour, the imperious covetousness of evil has not ceased to haunt me since that fatal day. Who, then, is within me, or so close to me? Who speaks to me? Who tempts me? I don't know; I sense that it will always be impossible for me to know. But what I can no longer ignore, alas, is that I am subject to the sinister advice, that I try in vain to escape it. And it is a monstrous torture. To be good and to want to do harm; to feel oneself ready to weep with pity for a beaten child, for a maltreated animal, and to want to beat that child oneself, to want to maltreat that animal oneself; to be unable to give a caress that does not want to be a strangulation; to think about theft while giving alms; to take advantage of the various circumstances of life in order to dream, being honest, about treason, being chaste, about debauchery, being full of tenderness, about the delights of murder; to be a worthy man who is simultaneously Judas, the Marquis de Sade and Lacenaire; and always to fear, in the midst of the anguish of an incessantly-renewed struggle, that the conscience will eventually weaken, will cede to the execrable pressure—that, that is the prodigious torment that has turned my hair white and curbed my spine, which has made of me, for whom life is so beautiful, of me, loving, beloved, fortunate, the most deplorable of living men.

"Listen, listen, alas!

"Do you remember my father's illness, last year? You know that, for more than two months, without sleep or repose, almost without nourishment, I did not quit the old man's bedside? You haven't forgotten my cry of joy when, after so much mortal anxiety, the physician declared that the disease was vanquished? Well—this is frightful to say—while he was suffering, the dear man, while each of his plaints was tearing my heart, I thought, and I couldn't prevent myself from thinking, that if he died, I'd be richer, that I'd inherit his house in Paris, his farm in Normandy; I thought about that in spite of myself, perpetually, me, who, in order to spare him a suffering, would have given my last sou, all my fortune, me, who would gladly have sacrificed my life for him; and it was impossible for me not to look at the dangerous potion, of which a few drops too many poured into his tisane would have put my father to sleep permanently.

"Listen again! My love for my wife is as devout as an adoration; I know that Providence has given me, in her, the most chaste of human angels; and I'm not unaware, in truth, of the importance, for her, of my respect and my tenderness. Wretch that I am! That gentle creature, august in the strength of purity, who has all of holy ignorance, I cannot approach, at the hour when her head is about to fall asleep on the conjugal pillow, without the filthy fury of a libertine lust making my temples throb as if to burst, exasperating me, maddening me; and perhaps, one night, finally lacking the strength to rest the Evil Thought, I might make my dishonored marriage bed into an abominable place, like the alcove of a prostitute.

"Oh, how ashamed I am of myself! How I nourish, incessantly, remorse for the frightful desires that are unrealized, but which harass me relentlessly. Such is my fear of myself that I dare not walk alone on the bank of a river or cross a bridge—no, I dare not!—with my son and my daughter, for the thought would certainly come to me—supreme abomination…what am I saying?...it comes to me, I sense it, it possesses me…to seize them, to squeeze their throat, to see, while bursting into laughter, their lifeless bodies, their adored bodies, fall into the water under the stone of the arches, with a splash.

"And it will never abandon me, pure and honest as I am, that inexorable desire for evil. You know that I have conserved intact the pious faith of early childhood, that I believe firmly in the God that proves me. Well, I'm sure of it, on the day when death comes, at the supreme moment when the priest, frightened by my general confession, puts forgiveness and salvation on my lips, then, in my religious ecstasy, the infernal need will torture me to insult my God and damn myself with a blasphemy!"

The Arsonist

The wretch, rescued from the flames, told me his story, while the last fragments of the walls of the burning house collapsed, like enormous blocks of embers.

"Yes, it's me who set fire to it. Listen.

"Scarcely had I attained the age of reason—why did I not die before that detested moment?—than I became singularly surly, saying very little, pretending to read in corners, going to the door as soon as anyone came in, drawing away as one escapes, slipping furtively along the corridors. At school or at home, in the city as in the country, I experienced that need for solitude, for reclusiveness, for flight. I did not know the expansions of first friendships, and when I approached my father or my mother and extended my forehead for the evening kiss, it was with the desire to receive it very quickly and no longer to be there.

"Everyone around me was in accord in believing that I was a timid child, that it would pass with age. I wasn't timid, at least in the fashion that they understood it; I wasn't afraid of others, I was afraid of myself. If I hadn't lost, in long suffering vainly shaken off, the habit of revolt, I wouldn't fail, here and now, to be carried away by furious recriminations against the unknown will that had made me as I am—which is to say, frightful. But I'm no longer irritated, not for a long time now, and I haven't relearned the anger that I experienced in a circumstance of which I shall shortly tell the story. I limit myself to being astonished, while being resigned.

"Was I the inheritor of some ancient curse? Was there in my veins—poor innocent, scarcely born, as frail and gently as the birds and the flowers—a little of the blood of some ancient ancestor who committed unforgivable crimes? I've often interrogated my father regarding the past of our family: a long sequence of honest bourgeois, placid, orderly, home-loving, moderately devout. Had I been spoiled, at the first awakening of intelligence, by the example and advice of some bad companion or culpable books stolen and meditated in secret? I don't remember any; I don't believe so. What is certain is that I bore within me almost irresistible instinctive needs for treason, for theft, for blood under the knife, and also for debauchery, such as my impure precociousness could conceive it; and when I looked at myself in mirrors, I saw that I was very pale.

"I shall never forget with what execrable emulation I sensed myself exalted when I read in the Holy Book the story of the man who betrayed God—and I too, am Judas! It was impossible for me to see gold shining on the arm or the neck of a woman without the impulse to take it, to snatch it and carry it away, clenching my fingers—not that I was avaricious, or attracted, as certain thieving beasts are, by the gleam of the metal; it was the pleasure of theft alone that incited me to steal. I was haunted every day by the thought of stealing the sous from the bowls of blind beggars.

"My sister had a great fondness for two tame turtle-doves that inflated their throats every day on a perch, whining joyfully and preening their feathers: two delicate birds, so pretty, and so weak; I watched them! With the fixity of a cat extended its claws, I watched them! In spite of myself, unable to turn my eyes away, and, holding a compass that I used to draw circles in my geometry book, I had a frisson from the nape of the neck all the way down my spine in thinking that the life might emerge from their throats in a red cooing.

"With regard to my puerile and diabolical libertine perversity, it's better that I don't go on; you'd impose silence on me, incredulous or saturated with disgust, and the story would never end. Anyway, could a few memories of infamous reveries, chosen from a thousand, give any idea of the furious and perpetual covetousness of evil by which I was possessed?

"Fortunately—or unfortunately, for the accomplishment of the worst sins is perhaps the only felicity possible for souls elected by Hell, and who knows whether I might not have found a profound peace in the realization of my chimeras?—

an infinitely sensible and very firm conscience, which would not enter into accommodation, defended me against the temptations. I was criminal and innocent, very abject and very pure. I affirm that I have never committed a veritable blameworthy action, although I was tormented pitilessly by all the appetites of crime. But at the price of what efforts I obtained that victory! And what scorn I felt for myself when, an instant after being mastered by the claw of the archangel, the satans of which I was full surged forth again! And what fears I had of one day being defeated!

"I perceived, in the distance of the future, visions of the penal colony or the merited scaffold. I fled into solitude the possibility of the fall.

"As a young man, I had some respite. Life, with the activity of its first exuberance, with the hazards of facile amours and the cordiality of brief comradeships, interested me and amused me. I was able to believe that I was like other people, that nothing persisted in me, except for a little sadness and savagery, of the wretched predestination of old, and that I was the brother, growing up in good health, of a made child, dead, buried and forgotten.

"One evening, when I was sleeping next to a beautiful girl, I woke up with a start, as if shaken by the shoulder. My mistress, her head amid her scattered hair, her breasts protruding from the batiste, was opening in sleep the smile of her lovely teeth. A soft warmth of white flesh was emanating from her. She gasped, struggling under the strangulation of my two hands, escaped, took refuge, haggard, in a corner of the room, while I fled through the house, and when I slumped against a wall in the corridor, under the clarity of a gas jet, I saw that I had blood under my fingernails.

"Thus, the evil of which I thought myself cured gripped me again, even more terrible. It did not limit itself, now, to troubling me with horrible temptations; it triumphed over my resistance, demanding action and constraining me to it. I was destined to know, not only the remorse of the crime conceived, but the remorse of the crime realized. I had nearly been a murderer; I would be a traitor, a thief; and the sinister debauchee for whom permissible kisses were no longer sufficient, would be me. The demon that held me—yes, truly, I believed in you, Satan!—would not let me go.

"There was only one thing I could do. Living among my peers, I would be a danger for them and for myself; I had to separate myself from men and women, with no going back. A dog sick with rabies is isolated, if one hesitates to kill it; I did not feel the courage to blow my brains out or throw myself from a bridge into the river; I exiled myself from humankind.

"A ship that is setting sail for the polar regions and whose captain anticipates long winter sojourns, is not better provisioned with food supplies of every sort than my house was, devoid of neighbors and servants, beyond the suburbs: a vast and bare house, the doors and windows of which I closed, one autumn evening, not to open them again. Henceforth, I was separated from human joys and dolors; nothing of life could reach me, not even the sounds, for the walls were thick and I took care to pad the windows. The tomb of a living man! The closed door only lacked an epitaph.

"I shall not tell you about the melancholy of the long days, the tedium of solitary meals under the ever-illuminated lamp, the slow walks from one wall to the other in the rooms, the books recommenced a hundred times, which I never finished reading, the awakenings by night with wide eyes, in the eternal silence, and the head falling back, yawning, on the pillow.

"Heartbreaking as my existence was, I sometimes rejoiced in my desolation. For here, at least, I could not yield to the attraction of evil; I had put impossibility between crime and me. I came to know a sort of bleak happiness made of the absence of peril. The redoubtable covetousness no longer frightened me; I even consented to it, without combat and without horror; yes, I permitted my dream to be the coward who, in a civil war, reveals the hiding place of refugees; I permitted it to be the thief who enters a dwelling, hooded lantern in hand, behind the latched doors, the murderer who wipes the blade of his knife on his sleeve, the hideous debauchee, corrupter of adolescent virgins.

"Why not? Why should I perpetuate the torments of a frightful struggle? Did I not know that my desires—hallucinations now—would remain forever unaccomplished? Was my innocence not ensured by my isolation? Did not the impotence in which I had put myself to commit the evil action authorize me to savor the imaginary joy of it? Did I not have the certainty that my crimes would never have any reality?

"Now, one morning, or evening—for a long time I had no longer distinguished one hour from another—I was dreaming, lying back in my armchair, my gaze raised toward the bare wall. I stood up, uttering a cry. There, on the blank wall, as if an invisible hand had blackened it with a abrupt drawing, I saw, and was obliged to recognize that I saw, a man with my face and my clothing, picking up coins from the blood of a murdered woman. Mercy! What did it mean? Who, then, had traced the abominable dream with which, precisely, I had been indulging myself a little while before? What frightful artist had made the portrait of my soul?

"The vision, if it was one, was effaced, as if washed away with a sponge. But from that day on—oh, it was frightful—every time I abandoned myself to one of my familiar reveries, I saw its exact representation, implacably precise, on the wall, or on a door, or the ceiling. Kneeling victims extended their suppliant hands to me. Blood ran from cut throats and white breasts that I had kissed before stabbing them. There were feasts in which naked virgins, served on golden platters, had daggers in the heart, the blades of which were quivering. And to complete the horror, those images were soon no longer effaced. Nothing could efface them. I fled from room to room in vain; everywhere they were offered to me, various, innumerable, similar to my thoughts. If I extinguished the lamp they were paintings, the color of blood and fire, victorious over the darkness; and I lived in a treble museum of my crimes!

"Can you understand now why I set fire to my dwelling, why I threw myself into the conflagration before the eyes of the crowd that came running in tumult? Oh, cursed be those who pulled me from the flames! Now I have returned among people; the rabid beast has been let loose. Cursed, cursed by the imprudent saviors who did not allow my being to be consumed and to vanish on the pyre of my evil thoughts!"

The Flute-Player

Four stadia from Miletus there was a wood of oleanders, and in that wood, as the twilight darkened, a young man was dreaming who was reminiscent of Dionysus, who tamed panthers. A tunic dyed with the blood of Tyrian mollusks[15] enveloped his slender and robust body, and long blond hair hung down over his shoulders in sunlit curls.

When he raised his head the nocturnal Hours were forming choirs on the mountain-tops. He picked up his traveling staff and headed for Miletus.

He had taken a few steps past the western gate of the city when he saw a majestic marble edifice to his right. It was the temple of the Milesian Aphrodite. He went into the temple; his slow steps struck the diamond-shaped floor tiles, and the echoes were stimulated by the sound. A flame that was never extinct was burning at the foot of an alabaster statue that was snowy in the gloom. The head of the statue was covered by a thick veil; that had been the desire, thus far respected, of the sculptor, so no human hand had yet lifted the veil. Undoubtedly the man who had carved the goddess in the lily-white block had been dissatisfied with the ensemble of his work, and had only wanted to show the perfect part—and nothing was more beautiful than the body of the goddess!

A profound and serene joy filled the soul of the visitor. He had seen the Aphrodite of Cnidus, the work of Praxiteles, the victorious Aphrodite of Lacedaemon, and the Artemis of Arcadia, queen of the nymphs. He had seen the temples of

---

[15] The famous dye known as "Tyrian purple" or "imperial purple"—actually crimson rather than the color nowadays called purple—was a secretion produced by sea-snails of a species known at the time as Murex; the extraction of the dye was a difficult but important industry.

Athens, which counted as many goddess of shiny marble on the frontons as suppliant women before the sacrificial altar. But his gaze had never had such enthusiastic caresses for a statue as for that marvelous apparition of alabaster. And he fell to his knees, with the dazzled fervor that the contemplation of the Beautiful inspires in great souls.

"Oh," he said, bewildered, "if a woman was able to serve as the model for that divine work, and that woman still exists, I would possess her! If, for one day, or only one hour, a body of flesh as perfect as that body of marvel could palpitate in my arms, I would be the equal of the gods!"

He remained on his knees for a long time, plunged in the tumultuous joy of hope.

A man who watched over the security of the temple by night came to warn him that the doors were about to be closed and that it was necessary for him to withdraw. The stranger went out. At the door of the monument he encountered women clad in long robes who were passing under the colonnades. Sometimes, the strollers stopped to look at them, and some lingered in order to speak to them in low voices; but the young man, full of his dream, disdained the beautiful courtesans that evening.

One of them approached him.

"I'm Chrysis," she said. "What's your name?"

"Icarion," he replied.

"Icarion of Phrygia? Thanks be rendered to Zeus, for it's said that you're as rich as the King of Pontus."

"That's true."

"Come with me, then, Icarion, and I'll guide you to the joyous young men."

Having said that, she marched toward the center of the city. Icarion followed her, indifferently. On the way, he noticed a low mound on which a mass of odorous logs was fuming, half-consumed.

"What's that?" he asked.

"It's the pyre of Xenila, the daughter of Demophon. Her naked body was exposed in the public square for two hours yesterday."

"What was Xenila's crime?"

"She allowed herself to die of amorous despair."

"I haven't heard it said that it was the custom to punish suicide."

"Perhaps it isn't the custom in Phrygia, but in Miletus it's the rule. There was a time when suicides for the sake of amour were so frequent that it was necessary to pass a law threatening the public exhibition after death of those who rendered themselves culpable of voluntary death. That law, moreover, has had excellent results, since, in the last ten years, only two or three events of that kind have been counted."

"The modesty of the young women of Miletus is such, then," said Icarion, that, not hesitating before death, they recoil before shame?"

"We've arrived," said Chrysis.

Twelve beds surrounded a sumptuous table: twelve ebony beds encrusted with gemstones. Three beautiful blonde women, naked to the waist, were pouring the wine of Chio into sculpted cups; three young boys clad in long linen tunics were slicing meat on golden platters. At the back of the room, players of lutes and citharas were only waiting for a sign from the master to commence the concert; and the guests, crowned with flowers in accordance with the rite observed in festivals, were singing noisily hymns consecrated to the god who holds the thyrsus. Silence suddenly fell, however, when Chrysis came in, followed by Icarion.

"Be welcome," Xantippe said to the Phrygian.

Two slaves brought a bed encrusted with fine stones, in order that the young man could sit down among the guests.

"And you, Phénice," added the host, "take your flute and sing. I want my house to be agreeable to my guest.

Phénice appeared, tall and simply clad. She was the most skillful musician in Miletus, but the young men said that in order to hear her pleasantly it was necessary not to look at her. Alas, she was ugly. Beneath her hair, as stiff and bushy as the mane of a wild boar, the skin of her face was dull and gray-tinted, like the earth in the ardent days of a heat-wave.

She picked up a lotus-wood flute and played. Sometimes she removed the ivory mouthpiece from her lips in order to sing. She narrated the amorous adventures of gods, and that the immortals sometimes deigned to share the couches of humans; she recounted the scandals of Olympus and the quarrels of the celestial households. But suddenly she changed her design; she had just perceived the handsome Icarion at the moment when he moistened his lips with the perfumed wine, and, allowing the desires of her heart to speak, this is what the flute-player sang:

"Young man, O handsome young man, more beautiful than Lyaios,[16] it is not in wine that it is necessary to step your lips!

"The mouth of a beloved is the cup in which your desire ought to be slaked. Are you not thirsty for flavorsome kisses?

"Young man, O handsome young man, more beautiful than Lyaios, it is not on beds destined for feasting that your supple body ought to lie down!

The breast of a beloved is the pillow that befits your divine head. Are you not weary of not being loved?

"Young man, O handsome young man, more beautiful than Lyaios, do not stop at seeking beauty only in the face!

"In truth, the beauty of the face charms the eyes of young men; but it is not on the forehead that lovers collect the sweetest kisses!

"Hear my prayer, young man, O handsome young man, more beautiful than Lyaios!"

Having sung thus, she took up the flute again, and the docile flute expressed all the furies of amour. The guests stood up to applaud Phénice; but then a great sadness invaded the heart of the musicienne and suddenly she broke the harmoni-

---

[16] Lyaios was an alternative name of Dionysus.

ous flute over her knee; for Icarion had paid no heed to her; his eyes, illuminated by the intoxication of good wine, believed that they could see, at every instant, the body of the Milesian Aphrodite resplendent in a distant glow.

The next day, Icarion was accosted in the street by a deformed and lame old woman. She was leaning on a knotty staff; her desiccated hand, with jaundiced skin, resembled the claw of a bird of prey.

"Icarion," she said, "only yesterday you arrived in Miletus, and already your presence had made numerous supplicant women run to the temple of triumphant Eros. This morning I have seen doors ornamented in your honor with odorous garlands, and the interlacement of flowers showing eyes the letters of your name."

"What does it matter to me?" replied Icarion.

"Icarion," the old woman went on, "cruelty befits women, but it cannot be appropriate in young men. What! When the beautiful Milesiennes forget, in order to please you, the restraint imposed on their sex, you affect a severity incompatible with yours. When they make an effort to go toward you, you make an effort to flee them? May it please the Immortals that it is not so, for the vengeance of the god adored in Thespis is suspended over your head."

"What do you want with me?"

"Among the beauties who love you there is one who is more beautiful, and who loves you more. She has told me her trouble and I have promised to change it into joy. If you would care to follow me, handsome young man, I will take you to her."

"I only love one woman in the world, and that woman I do not know; perhaps I shall never know her."

"Perhaps, Icarion, in the one that is waiting for you, you will find the one you seek?"

At that speech, Icarion conceived a strange hope; he made a sign that he was prepared to follow the woman. She put a blindfold over his eyes, and exclaimed, as she took his hand: "By the pruning-knife of Ithyphallos, one might think that one were seeing Eros himself!"

A short while thereafter, Icarion was alone in shadow and silence; a mild sensation of warmth ran over his limbs; unknown perfumes charmed his sense of smell, and a distant music, as seductive as the appeal of the sirens, resonated softly.

"You may take off the blindfold, Icarion."

He obeyed in haste. A woman, covered in a white linen veil, was reposing on a crimson carpet. Modestly, she was hiding her face in embroidered cushions; but does one need to see a woman's face to know that she is beautiful? Has not beauty, a divine flower, in addition to the splendor that strikes the eyes, revelatory scents?

Thus thought Icarion when he knelt before the unknown woman, saying to her in a low voice: "You hide your face from me in vain. In spite of you, I know all that your eyes have of divine languor; I knew the splendor of your forehead, and your melodious mouth, a lyre with two roseate strings, is not unknown to me. But I do not know whether your hair is dark or blonde; that is all that it remains for me to know. Throw back that thick veil and let me kiss your hair, as somber as the throne of Hades or as bright as the nascent day."

"You shall not see my face," said the veiled woman.

"Well, no matter, I love you. I love everything about you, including the mystery that envelops you, including the veil that covers you, for thus you resemble more the one for whom I am searching. Where I was going, I do not know, but it seems to me that I have arrived. The indecisive goal that my dream is pursuing, I sense that I am at the moment of its discovery. Thanks be rendered to you, O woman who restores peace in me! Veiled sun that illuminates me charming sphinx, whether you remain forever unknown to me, or whether you will deign one day to show yourself to my eyes, whether or not it will be given to me to divine the mysterious enigma, I love you and I will love you incessantly."

"And I too love you, O my Icarion!"

Like a she-wolf pouncing on her prey, the breathless Phénice hurtled herself upon the young man more handsome than Lyaios.

"Phénice!" exclaimed the Phrygian.

And with a scornful gesture, he pushed her away from him. In vain she tried to retain him, in vain she threw off the linen sheet that covered her body, saying: "I'm beautiful, look!" In vain she followed him, murmuring: "You will regret me when I am no more, O handsome young man, more handsome than Lyaios."

He had already fled, unkempt, his hands clenched, his bile stirred; violently, he elbowed the passers-by; even a bronze wall would not have opposed an obstacle to his course, so much haste was he in to arrive at the temple of Aphrodite; and when he was kneeling, quivering, before the alabaster statue, he said:

"Be merciful, O goddess; I implore my pardon! But I do not merit it for, blasphemous madman, for an instant I was able to believe that the beauty of a woman equaled your beauty. O most beautiful of immortals!"

As he was wandering through the city, the following day, a god guided him to the public square. In the midst of the assembled people, on a scaffold covered with a black veil, the cadaver of Phénice the flute-player reposed, naked and white. A few kneeling slaves were shedding tears and proffering lamentations.

"Alas! Alas!" said Chrysis, sincerely moved.

"Thus my daughter died," said Demophon, father of Xenila.

"Poor Phénice, who then did she love?" asked Xantippe.

"She loved Icarion of Phrygia," replied the old Titthé.

"Earth and the gods!" cried Icarion, as soon as he could see the beautiful cadaver, her loins and breasts bare and her face covered with a veil, "it's the Milesian Aphrodite herself!"

"No," said Titthé, "it's Phénice the flute-player. Know however, something that only I know. When the sculptor Xanthias came to Miletus, Phénice deigned to show herself naked three times, and Xanthias made a masterpiece."

Icarion did not say a word. He lowered his head and went away, and while he drew away, his heart filled with a bitter sorrow, it seemed to him that a voice spoke in his ear, saying: "You will regret me when I am no more, O handsome young man, more handsome than Lyaios."

The Tearful Day

At the sound of my footsteps the beautiful young woman raised her head in a movement of dread; she was as pale as the dead; her eyelids were a trifle red; her eyes resembled two forget-me-nots that rain had dampened drop by drop, bordered with pink.

"What, you?" I exclaimed. "You're weeping, Madame?"

"It was a mistake to let you in," she said. "I've closed my door, not wanting to see anyone. When I have my sadnesses, any presence, even that of a friend—and you are my friend, since you have never paid court to me and never will — troubles me almost frightens me. I am gripped by an instinct of recoil, or flight, a need for security and isolation. I'm like the glass lawyer,[17] you know; I experience throughout my being—it's doubtless an effect of nerves—the sensation of a fragility that, at the slightest contact, nothing but the proximity of an approach, or the abruptness of a sound, might break dolorously."

I pretended not to understand the plea to go away contained in her words; I was retained by a curious desire, in which a great deal of sympathy was mingled. I repeated:

"What! Veritably? You're weeping?"

"Oh, yes, that astonishes you! It astonishes me, too, I swear to you. Whatever makes one fortunate—a good name, money, a husband who loves you, youth, the triumph of being pretty—I possess, and if something were lacking in my good fortune, I wouldn't have time to pay any heed to it, frivolous

---

[17] The protagonist of Miguel Cervantes' short story "El licenciado Vidriera" (1613), known in French as "Le Bachelier de verre" and in English as "Doctor Glass-Case," who wakes up from a trance induced by a failed love potion believing that he is made of glass.

as I'm known to be, almost always occupied with a thousand amusing social obligations: excursions to the Bois, discussions with a dressmaker, afternoon teas, dinners, premières and dances, hunting, comedies at the château; all the hours of my life are pleasures, one after another. Now and again, when a lassitude wearies me—one can yawn by virtue of laughing—I repose with a serenity of which people would not believe me capable, in the grave tenderness of the man who has given me his name; and you know how I adore my children. As for furtive, culpable amour, with its remorse and its hypocrisies, of which one is ashamed and which one hides, I have always avoided it, always rejected it; my boldest flirtations go no further than permitting the breath of a mouth on my gloved little finger; and I remain a fortunate woman because I am an honest woman. Oh, certainly, very fortunate! If I were not me, I would want to be." Her head between her hands, she added: "However, my friend, as you see, I'm weeping."

"I gazed at her, increasingly surprised. She continued speaking, with occasional sibs.

"Yes, I'm weeping, and I'm desolate, and I don't know why. It was five years ago, one autumn morning, that this anguish seized me for the first time, without reason. And since then, every year, on the same date—the same date, you hear?—it takes hold of me again, wherever I am, whatever I am doing. Oh, don't smile because these days of desperation are rare; don't tell me that a few hours of bitterness ought to count for very little in a year of joy. They are so frightful, those hours; they contain, in so few moments, so much intense suffering that I would prefer to my long series of joys, frightfully interrupted, a whole melancholy existence!

"As soon as the day after the fatal day, I try to forget the tortures. I tell myself, like someone drawing breath at the summit of a hill painfully climbed, that it's over, that I'm out of trouble; I recommence smiling, loving, living; I'm content. I arrive at believing that the abominable torment will never seize me again. Why should I experience it again, at the accustomed date? Have I been subjected, on that day, in the past, to some disaster, the memory of which is periodically renewed? No, I've searched my most distant memories in vain; the detested day is only the anniversary of itself.

"Come on, this time, it won't lead to any chagrin; it will be a day similar to all the others, amiable and charming, when one goes to visit the couturier, when the children smile, when I shall dance in the evening! I'm full of ease and tranquility. But it arrives, similar to itself, similar to itself alone, with the dolors of the previous year! I can assure you that it's horrible. All those I love are alive, are close to me, and will come in at any moment, smiling—but I sense the lacerated heart of orphans and widows. I have lost nothing, but it is as if I were deprived of everything. No disaster has struck me; but I have in my mind, in my heart, and in my body too, throughout my being, something like the weight of a collapse.

"I want to escape that hell. I come, I go, I dress, I order the harnessing of the carriage; the open air, the sun, the chatter of visits, the pleasure of being thought beautiful, will distract me, will triumph over the baleful influence—vain efforts! In escaping, I take my torture with me; I am caught, like a hand in a vice, which follows it. Truly, no words can describe the terrors to which I succumb. Oh, this impression of absolute destitution, of infinite emptiness!

"And—which is even more atrocious—I don't know why I'm weeping, I don't know what I regret. I know that something more precious than anything else has been stolen from me, but that thing, which I no longer have, I did not possess. I know that a person dearer than any other has left me, but that person who has gone has never been close to me. Inconsolable at having lost them, I cannot form any idea of who they were; and the sadness of not having known them complicates the despair of their irremediable absence."

She fell silent. I took her hands in my amicable hands, striving to calm her down, saying those vain words to her that try to console but do not console: that it was nothing, an overexcitement, a nervous irritation, or a fever; the recurrence of her anguish undoubtedly revealed a rather strange illness, but not serious, over which one might triumph with care and calming medication...

"Oh, I'm not ill!" she said, shrugging her shoulders.

She stood up, marched back and forth in the room with long strides, for a long time. Then, stopping in front of me, her head held high, her eyes staring, she said:

"Do you not believe, yourself, that every human birth corresponds to another birth? That every living being is linked to another by a fatal or providential destiny? I believe that! I believe that no one exists for himself, for himself alone, but that everyone is half of a couple premeditated by a mysterious unknown will; and in spite of himself, without knowing what is impelling him or attracting him, the husband seeks the wife, and the wife the husband, through all the immense terrestrial tumult. When they encounter one another, it is the perfect, incomparable joy, the realization of the divine will in human happiness.

"Oh, how pure, sacred and infinite that happiness must be! And how little, compared to that, is the mundane satisfaction of being the wife of a gallant man to whom you were not promised! But to find one another, among the vast crowd, is not always possible, alas! They are rare, hymens down here that correspond to betrothals on high. Many brides don the nuptial robe before having seen their true fiancé; many a time the man who ought to have been the husband dies unknown to his wife.

"Well, who knows? I often dread that, I often think it: the man who was destined for me by providence, whom I have not encountered, I shall never encounter in this world, because he has ceased to live! And I have wept for him, unconsciously, in my distress without a cause. I have wept for him; I am weeping for him. Who he was, I don't know. His country, his race, and his name are things that it is forbidden for me to learn. But I know the day on which he died!

"Invisible and impalpable as our chains are, they could not be broken without my heart bleeding; it was on the day that he died, the lover, that I suffered for the first time. It is the anniversary of my extinct, buried, vanished true happiness, the anniversary of my betrothal in mourning and my desolate widowhood that I am celebrating with sobs and tears."

The Chaste Town

It happened in a small town, devout and solemn, with streets that resembled long, cramped corridors with gaps overlooking the cemetery; with shutters closed like a meditating ascetic's eyes; with the religious silence of a cathedral in which the offices are recited in low voices. And it is, in fact, a church of sorts, that town: a dismal church devoid of ceremonial pomp, with no singing organ or radiant candles. Once invaded by an emigration of Jansenists, it does not consent to the luxuries, tenderness and smiles that the amiable conciliatory doctrine of the Jesuits accords.

No, as sinister and cold as the nudity of a cadaver, it is enshrouded in peace, isolation and bleak reverie; never does a sound of wheels awaken the idea of an excursion, a departure and a return; never is there a shrieking stampede of children after school; one never sees between the partly-closed blinds the profile of a young woman sewing, embroidering and sometimes darting a furtive hopeful glance at the mirror, on the lookout for the image of a passer-by who will doubtless fall in love with her, perhaps a husband. There is no noisy tavern; no Theater; no festival hall.

The living who inhabit that town go to mass, to vespers, and on coming back, devote themselves to the necessary duties of civilization in a mute mystery of phantoms prowling around a necropolis; they go home in the same way that revenants return to their towns; the doors, as they close on them, echo the sound of a funerary slab falling back.

Inside the houses there are meek maidservants with faces of old ivory and a congregation ribbon around the neck, who make no noise, shod in bedroom slippers, when they dust the furniture in the drawing room. The thin and ugly wives do not offer their foreheads when their husbands return, going from the linen cupboard to the larder, signing themselves when the bells chime; wan daughters with rings round their eyes and thin lips, while reading books of devotion, chew bad teeth as they mumble prayers. Young boys, brought up in the seminary, bring to the family home the already overt, or even hateful, slyness of a life tamed by discipline. Meals are silent there, the evenings devoid of conversation, with black gazes, during the reading of the gospel, toward the cold ashes of the heart.

And in that whole town, there was only a single prostitute.

Who did she serve? Everyone: she alone served everyone.

Not young, tall, fleshless, jaundiced, with a shock of black hair, a mouth like an open wound and eyes like two hooded lanterns, bony hands the bestial fingernails of which were long and clawed, she gave the impression of a gypsy left there by some vagabond band. Her feet were often bare beneath the fringe of a ragged red skirt—flat feet hardened by the scarred wounds of stones and brambles—and her forehead flamboyant beneath a scarlet headscarf.

She lodged outside the edge of town in an old roadmender's hut between the road and the river. She had furnished two rooms there, one in which clients waited, the other where there was a bed: a bed devoid of woodwork made of two mattresses of wrack, with a semi-cover of garnet brushed wool over a single sheet, rarely changed, and two pillows devoid of pillow-cases, rent here and there by the rips of enraged teeth, and yellowed by the dried drool of ancient spasms.

In the evenings, at the window of the room where there was a bed, she lit a lamp with a red shade, a filthy lighthouse of desperate lust in the tempests of nocturnal concupiscence.

In the beginning, when she established herself in the hut, where had she come from? Where did she want to go? Oh, who knows where they depart from, and what path they want to follow, the beings whose presence Necessity demands at a certain moment in a certain place?

In the beginning, she had the custom of strolling impudently in the town. Brushing the doors of austere houses, seminaries and churches with her red skirt, casting at the closed shutters the challenge of her mouth, bloody with the offer of kisses, suddenly interrupting with hoarse laughter the religious silence of the streets like corridors open over the cemetery, she roamed indefatigably, the terror of the meek maidservants, the horror of the ugly wives, the astonishment of the thin-lipped virgins; and the chaste men, warmed in their marrow, could not detach their thoughts from the shameless creature who invited them to sin. More than one took flight, not without turning their heads, frightened by having recognized her at dusk in the shadow of some wall, leaning over, and uttering obscene words, sometimes lifting up her skirt in the twilight to the point of revealing, russet and bushy, the abysm of the sexual Inferno.

But soon, some of them—oh, with what precaution, went along the houses closed by night, doors and windows shut—searching for her, and, far from avoiding her, following her, closely or at a distance; and then, after some of them, almost all of them; and then, after almost all, all of them. The virility of the town was exasperated toward her. Now there was no need for her to wander through the streets; it was sufficient for her to light the lamp in the window of the room where there was a bed made of two mattresses of wrack.

Emerging surreptitiously from the austere dwellings, enveloped in cloaks, coiffed in hoods that came down over their noses, they went, the old, the young, the fathers who has read the gospel in loud voices, the adolescents who would return to the seminary the following day, and those who were magistrates, and those who were priests, toward the hut where the dark-skinned gypsy with the shock of hair traversed by flame was leaning on the window-sill. If they bumped into one another as they walked, converging toward a single point, they pretended not to perceive the collision. They did not look at one another, and did not want to see one another. They marched toward their sun without any other thought, like dogs with their tongues hanging out looking for a pod in order to lap water. And, sitting side by side in the first room, they did not recognize one another, awaiting the hour of evil.

Meanwhile, she, unaware of it but in whom the diabolical intention was ardent, welcomed them, wanted them and tortured them by means of the anticipation of delights a hundred times more than by means of the delights themselves, only delaying with regret the damnation of those of whom the nascent daylight had witnessed the infamous joys. In any case, the next day, they returned to their austerity, no longer remembering the sin to which they consented or which they coveted, and, very gravely, after mass, a little apart from their wives, daughters and maidservants, they talked between themselves, in low voices, about the measures that it was appropriate to take against a creature, an inhabitant of a hut beyond the outskirts of the town, they did not know where, who was scandalizing strangely the honest and peaceful town. Amid the blasts of the organ emerging from the oft-reopened doors of the church, the bells rang religiously.

Now, one morning, passing along the new path between the road and the river, mariners found the body of a dead woman in the mud and he pebbles. She was naked, with clotted blood in wounds in the neck and the breast, with green-tinted entrails spilling from the gashed belly. Her black hair was enflamed by a red headscarf. The mariners ran toward the town, awoke the local police, and spread the news. Two physicians who arrived belatedly could not refuse to testify that the possibility of a suicide was scarcely admissible, that the body was that of a woman lacerated by fingernails and teeth, killed by blows of fists and heels. They were even able to ascertain that, dead, she had been possessed.

In what atrocious brawl, of which she was simultaneously the cause, the victim and the prize, had the dark and stiff creature, coiffed with a kerchief the color of blood, perished?

An investigation was ordered. It had no result. It was impossible to discover the criminals: vagabonds, no doubt, who had quit the area immediately after the murder. Or those mariners…yes, the very ones who, perhaps by virtue of a stratagem, had revealed the crime.

The file was closed. The town returned to its calm: the devout and solemn town with streets that resembled long cramped corridors, with shutters closed like the eyes of a meditating ascetic, with the religious silence of a cathedral in which the offices are recited in low voices.

56 *Rue des Filles-Dieu; Or, The Heautonparateroumene*

After the report of Dr. Elysée Beuriot, so clear, so precise and so conclusive—a report that, as we have seen, concluded that he was not responsible for his actions, the acquittal of the accused was no longer in doubt for anyone. Maître Flor Delestang could have been dispensed with his speech for the defense, but we would have lost a remarkable oratory performance. Although flawed here and there by pedantry—carries away by his classical memories, the defender went so far as to describe his client as a *heautonparateroumene*!)[18] his speech was one of the most beautiful that we have heard

Gazette des Tribunals, January 188*.

"Brunois! Brunois, I beg you! Charles! Don't agitate like that! You're grinding your teeth, you're sweating all over, and the sweat is quite cold. What's the matter with you? Wake up, open your eyes. You're as white as the pillow. Your throat is swollen, as if you were about to choke. It's rising, rising, it's beating! Oh, are you going to die? Wake up, then, Charles, I implore you, wake up!"

Outside the sheets, his night-shirt torn, the gray hairs on his chest bristling, Charles Brunois sat up straight; his earthen face stretched and creviced by tics, like that of an electrified corpse, his chest having as if to burst, his eyelids tightly closed, he stiffened in a tension of his entire being; but after a cry ejected like wine from an unplugged barrel, he collapsed

---

[18] Roughly "he who spies on himself," derived from a comedy by Terence, *Heautontimorumenos* (tr. as *The Self-Tormentor*).

on the bed, his stomach flat, his throat slack and his arms flaccid in the annihilation of the expended crisis.

White with fear, Madame Aurélie Brunois, an old lady with gray hair, tightly curled within the tube of her nightcap, leaning toward the pillow in a camisole, barefoot, without feeling the chill of the parquet on her soles, gazed at her husband in the silence of the bourgeois bedroom—mahogany, rep, framed lithographs—in which the tremor of the flickering night-light was blinking in the nascent light of dawn, cut into thin strips by the parallel slats of the Venetian blind.

"I beg you, speak; speak, since you're calmer. What's the matter with you? Answer me."

He stammered, without raising his eyelids, his lips slack and his voice oozing with the slowness of a viscous liquid: "I…I don't know."

"A nightmare, perhaps?"

"Yes…perhaps. Yes! Yes, a nightmare! I saw…I saw things…things..."

"What things?"

"Things..."

"Well?"

"Frightful things!" His temples were sweating, large droplets running like tears.

"In sum, what?"

"Frightful things," he repeated.

"But what? What were they?"

His forehead creased in an intense effort; then, as if in an abandon of discouragement, the wrinkles relaxed.

"I don't remember..."

"Try, Brunois! Let's see…first of all, at what hour did you come in? I was asleep, and I didn't hear you get into bed. What time did you come in? Tell me."

"I don't know."

With a slight irritation: "You don't know anything!"

"That's true. I don't know anything."

"Oh, think! You dined with Richond."

"Richond?"

"My God, you're mad! Now you no longer know Richond. Your friend Richond, your former associate? He was to leave for Le Havre at eleven forty-five. He came to bid us adieu as we were about to sit down at table. He took you to dinner at the restaurant."

"Yes, Richond. I dined at the restaurant with Richond."

"Ah!"

"Yes..."

"Did you eat something that made you ill, which is weighing on your stomach?"

"I...I don't know."

"Or you got drunk? You don't have the habit of drinking. You got drunk on champagne, or spirits?"

"No...not with champagne...with...with spirits, yes."

"That's it; you made yourself ill?"

"Ill...I made myself ill."

"And after dinner, where did you go?"

"With Richond?"

"Of course."

"No...not with Richond..."

"With whom?"

"I don't know."

"You were dead drunk, wretch!"

"Dead drunk..."

"Anyway, were did you go? What did you do?"

"I did...I did...I did...things..."

He had straightened up. He was livid, shivering as if in a fever of agony, and barked between his chattering teeth: "Frightful things!"

Madame Aurélie, terrified, was going out of her mind. However, an idea occurred to her: "A physician!" But they had no domestic; a housemaid came every morning and left at midday. In order to tell the concierge to go and fetch a doctor, it would be necessary to quit Brunois. She hesitated, her eyes wandering uncertainly; she spotted her husband's clothes, in disorder, on an armchair. An instinct advised her to investigate them, to search for some clue there. She lifted them up and shook them; there were trousers, a waistcoat...but where was the frock-coat? What? Brunois had come home in his shirt-sleeves? Stupefied, she returned to him.

He repeated, his mouth white, his skin the color of lead, his hair standing on end: "Frightful things! Frightful!"

She threw herself on to the bed.

"But you're driving me mad! What does frightful mean? What have you done that's frightful?"

"I've...I've...I've..."

She wailed in anguish

"I've..."

A howl sprang forth, as if from a torn throat, and the man fell back on the disturbed sheets, not another word, not another gesture. Slack, heavy, annihilated, he stagnated, his face white, striped with green daylight; not even a frown. He was asleep, the sleep of a drunkard, or a dead man. The only sign of life was a snore that sharpened to the point of a shrill plaint, like a little dog under torture, or thickened into the bitter and greasy gasp of a wild beast with its throat cut.

Madame Aurelie, her eyes bulging with fear, gazed at him in the livid morning light, where the tiny flicker redness of the night-light sizzled, about to go out.

A few hours of sleep restored him. At midday, he ate lunch with a good appetite, in a good humor, his tongue scarcely heavy. Without remembering what he had done after leaving the restaurant—drunk as a Pole, no doubt—he had some suspicion of it, hypothesis substituting for memory. Well, at forty-five years of age, a man isn't "finished," especially after drinking Chambertin.

This, he knew: Richond and he had drunk Chambertin, very expensive, excellent. The probability of some escapade counseled by the burgundy and conversation over dessert, infatuated him, tickled him, made him wink his eye, not without malice; at the same time he was slightly enraged. If the adventure was funny, as was probable, he would have been pleased to remember it, in all its details. He smiled at the idea of "details." No matter. It was already amusing, and, more than once, he was on the point of laughing aloud at the thought of the "spree" that he had undertaken.

As for Madame Brunois, sullen at the beginning of the meal, she did not take long to cheer up. Older than her husband, by whom she knew that she was tenderly and gravely loved, she had some indulgence for the worthy man who still young, without permitting himself a single day of rest or pleasure, had drudged for twenty-five years in a wholesale ironmongery business in order to amass the seven thousand francs of rent on which they lived in comfort in the entresol of a house in the Rue Legendre in Batignolles. At present, he had the right to divert himself twice a year when the opportunity presented itself.

Jealous? Not at all. Not very pretty, even in her youth, she had always been more of a housekeeper and companion than a wife; it was not at fifty-five years of age that she was going to start hammering her head because Brunois had committed some folly. But she held against him the mortal anxiety that she had experienced last night, and the lost frock-coat. Was it possible that one could drink to the point of getting into such a state? It must be very bad for the temperament.

"No, no," replied Charles Brunois, heartily. And he sang a song by Boileau to a vaudeville tune, the sole memory of three years at the Collège d'Étampes.

If Bourdaloue, a bit severe,
Tells us to treat lust with stealth,
Escobar says to him, 'Father,
We permit it for the sake of health.'

What also tormented Madame Aurélie was that he could not remember anything at all about the employment of his evening. Drunkenness, even excessive, did not explain sufficiently such a complete forgetfulness. Scantly knowledgeable as she was, she was not unaware of the terrible maladies that abolish the intellectual faculties and render a previously robust and healthy individual infirm of body and mind, motionless, speechless and drooling. She had a frisson at the thought her dear, worthy husband as an old man in a wheelchair that she was pushing.

She had thought aloud; he burst out laughing. Oh, there was no danger of him becoming decrepit. It often happens, because one has drunk too much, or following an intense emotion...

"Emotion?" she interrupted. "Have you had an emotion?"

He could not help smiling, a trifle conceitedly.

"Anyway," he said, "for one reason or another, one can have a partial amnesia"—having read scientific articles in newspapers, he employed that mysterious and solemn term in order to impress his wife—"without it being a reason to conceive any anxiety for the future."

And he cited examples. There had been some very curious ones in his own family. His grandfather, as a young man, had embarked at Le Havre for New York: a voyage on business. On the third day of the crossing, there was a terrible storm, "and grandfather was so frightened that when he arrived in America he had completely forgotten everything that had happened between the commencement of the tempest and the disembarkation. That didn't prevent him doing excellent business in New York and living to the age of eighty-two with all his common sense."

Madame Aurélie shook her head. "With all his common sense?"

"Yes indeed."

"It isn't mad, then, to want to fire revolver shots at people who haven't saluted you in the street? This isn't the first time you've talked to me about your grandfather, you know."

Monsieur Brunois smiled. "Yes, on certain days the poor man got angry; that was when someone had irritated him—but it was necessary not to irritate him. Tell me Aurélie, don't you know any people like him, who get annoyed, grumble and sulk because someone has upset them without meaning to? It seems to me that, without going very far..."

She shrugged her shoulders, laughing; fundamentally, she was not anxious, she was not annoyed. She consented, after lunch, to a little glass of Benedictine. That cheered her up. She gazed with an amused complaisance at her husband, who had played the young man.

Drawing his chair closer, he nudged his wife with his elbow and said, a trifle roguishly, his expression almost lewd: "Come on, admit that what's annoying you is that I didn't wake you up when I came in!"

"Bad lot!" she replied. And the lunch ended, chatty and joyful, in the waxed walnut dining room, shiny with light, while two canaries, their cages hanging next to the open window, twittered in the sunlit fresh air rising from the garden. Then when the coffee had been drunk and the little glasses emptied, while his wife, occupied with household chores, cleared the table and hastened the work of the housemaid in the kitchen, Brunois pushed an armchair toward the window, installed himself there after picking up the *Petit Journal* from the marble of the stove, not yet unfolded, took off the rubber band and commenced reading, in the perfect wellbeing of digestion, while the odor of roses drifted in the healthy air, amid the birdsong.

"Aurélie!"
"What?"
"Aurélie! Aurélie!"
"Well, what?"
"Come here!"
"What's the matter? Why are you shouting like a dead man?"

She came back into the dining room wearing a blue cook's apron that came up to the neck, with the front of her skirt tucked up and wrapped around the belt of the apron.

Brunois, in an extreme agitation, was brandishing the newspaper, which trembled, traversed by daylight.

"Another one!" he said.

"One what?"

"A crime."

"You're disturbing me for that? Crimes aren't rare in Paris."

"No, undoubtedly..."

"And you read about them every day."

"This one..."

"What's extraordinary about it?"

"Here, look."

She approached and took the newspaper condescendingly, scarcely interested.

"Where is it?"

"On the third page, at the bottom of the second column."

"Good." She read aloud. Brunois, leaning forward ardently, a palm, of each arm of the chair, looked at her, his eyes staring and his mouth moving, as if he were spelling out the words on his wife's lips.

What Madame Aurélie read was:

"Toward the end of the evening the news spread of a murder in the vicinity of the Rue Poissonnière. One of our reporters immediately went to the neighborhood. He telephoned that, indeed, at about ten o'clock in the evening, the attention of neighbors and rare passers-by was attracted by plaints and screams emerging from a furnished hotel in the Rue des Filles-Dieu that bears the number 56. Then a window opened on the third floor of the hotel and a woman fell, or was thrown, on to the cobblestones of the street. When she was picked up, her face entirely lacerated and bloodied by the stones, she was dead, but the fall was not the cause of death. On the cadaver, transported to a pharmacy in the Rue de Cléry, a physician summoned in all haste observed three deep wounds, one in the neck and two beneath the left breast, seemingly due to a very slender and sharp knife. The strange thing is that there is no agreement regarding the identity of the victim. Although disfigured with cuts and bruises, the people of the quarter believed that they recognized her as a prostitute

named Félicie Bonheur, known as "the Big Jewess," who frequently occupied a room on the third floor of the hotel where the crime was committed. But the manageress of the hotel, who is also the concierge, is sure that Félicie had not appeared at the hotel that evening and did not possess a dress like the one the dead woman was wearing. As for the author, or authors, of the crime, suspicion has not yet fallen upon any individual...

"Well, what of it?" said Madame Aurélie, interrupting herself. "Such filthy atrocities happen too often among the vagabonds of Paris."

Monsieur Brunois, calmer, was sitting back in his armchair. He crossed his legs and said almost indifferently: "In fact, you're right. Nothing very curious about it."

"Nothing! Nothing, I tell you. Have you read the stop press?"

"No."

"There isn't even a mystery any longer. Listen."

She read: "*Latest news. The murderer has been arrested. He is a pimp greatly feared in the quarter, where he is know by the name of Eudoxe le Marin. Having entered a liquor shop in the Rue Sainte-Foy about an hour after the crime he was expelled for disturbing the nocturnal peace and taken to the police commissariat in the Rue d'Aboukir. 'The Big Jewess is my girl!' he said. 'I've settled her account this evening.' It is, therefore, Félicie Bonheur who has been killed, and this affair, which appeared mysterious momentarily, is reduced to a bloody brawl between a prostitute and a pimp; a banal story, in sum. Tomorrow morning, after the usual formalities, Eudoxe le Marin will be sent to the Dépôt.*

"You see!" said Madame Aurélie.

"Oh, my God, yes, a banal story. The newspaper is right. I hadn't read the end, you understand...but since the victim and the murderer are known...and then, in fact, it's all the same to us, people like that. The woman is dead, the man will be guillotined; that will be two scoundrels fewer."

"Exactly, and if all the villains cold destroy one another like that..."

"It would be all the better for honest folk!"

With that, while Madame Aurélie returned to the kitchen, Brunois, very satisfied and blissful, sprawled in the armchair, lifted up the newspaper, and resumed reading. His eyes, disdaining the articles, were attached to the feuilleton.

The retired ironmonger owed to the reveries of leisure a mind that took great pleasure in romantic inventions. For a time he had even devoted himself passionately to reading judiciary romances in which agents of the Sûreté, in whom the subtle soul of Edgar Poe survived, investigated, pursued and finally caught undiscoverable criminals. It was doubtless by virtue of an old habit of interesting himself in stories of that sort that he had pad heed, a little while ago, to a mediocre item of reportage. But the *Petit Journal*'s actual romance soon caused him milder emotions

It was a matter, in that work, of a young woman who, having been stolen on the day of her birth, was taken in later by her own mother without being recognized. That situation gave rise to very touching scenes between the two women, invincibly borne to love one another without knowing that nature had destined them to do so. Brunois had eyes moistened by tender tears now, and gradually, no less soothed by a compassionate sympathy than the amiable lassitude of digestion, he slid into a smiling somnolence while the newspaper fell on the parquet.

With a seemingly automatic, even uninterrupted movement, his eyelids covered and uncovered his porcelain blue eyes, until they were entirely covered. His full lips rounded out into a chicken's backside opening and closings again after laying an egg. Alongside one wide and sniffing nostril, the curly hairs of a large wart put a discordant note into the expansive bonhomie of the face the breeze from the garden and the odor of roses enveloped the honest sleeper with freshness and charm. His continuous snoring, devoid of roughness, doubled the hum of a wasp that came in and went out again through the sunlit window.

It was the custom of Charles Brunois, especially in the summer months, to take a stroll on the exterior boulevards before dinner. He stopped, very interested, at the displays of bric-à-brac merchants, but without ever buying anything.

That day he did not fail to follow his habit.

He paused for a long time before the shop on the corner of the Rue Lepic; he cast an eye over the painted flowers of faiences, weighed up cast-iron andirons red with rust, and tapped copper plates with the tip of his bent middle finger. He became absorbed in the contemplation of a colored lithograph in a small mahogany frame, representing Mazeppa dragged by a furious horse; with great fixity he considered the legend in verse beneath the image, and said to himself, in a soft voice: "But why was he in that liquor store so close to the hotel where he had just murdered Félicie?"

His eyes never quitting the lines of the legend, he added: "That he confessed his crime at the police station is explicable, since he was drunk. So be it; I admit it, although it's absurd; he could admit the crime, he admitted it. The incredible thing is that his first concern, after the murder, wasn't to reach safety by quitting the neighborhood; that, on the contrary, he went to drink in a place where he must have been known. Was he thinking about creating an alibi? No, since the news of the crime must already have spread when he went into the wine merchant's shop."

Brunois had ceased gazing at the image; he was giving the greatest attention to a carriage lantern, dislocated and bent out of shape, which only retained one of its four windows, dusty and cracked. He added, in a slightly louder voice: "In sum, it isn't clear. No, it isn't clear. What evidence do they have against Eudixe le Marin, in sum? His confession—good—and the fact that he had a relationship with Félicie Bonheur. Very good! But what if he was talking at cross-purposes because he was drunk? And what if it wasn't Félicie

Bonheur who was killed? For after all, it's not certain that it was her..."

One by one, as if counting them, Brunois handled the old blackened iron keys on a ring hanging from a nail. He murmured: "They can say what they want, but something tells me that it wasn't Eudoxe le Marin..."

A newsvendor cried: "The *Liberté!* Third edition. The mystery of the Rue des Filles-dieu! Murder of Félicie Bonheur! Eudoxe le Marin released!"

Charles Brunois, his face expanded with pride, leapt forward, called to the newsvendor, bought the paper and started reading with a feverish eye. "What did I say? What did I say!" Then, almost running, he returned home, His neighbors were astonished, never having seen that placid man hastening in such a fashion.

As he went into the dining room Madame Aurélie was putting dinner on the table. Brunois, sweating and out of breath but triumphant, with the air of someone bringing admirable news, said: "Well it wasn't him!"

"What? What's that you say?"

"I said that it wasn't him!"

"Who's him?"

"Eudoxe! It wasn't Eudoxe who struck the blow."

"Eudoxe?"

"Eudoxe le Marin. He's innocent. Look, read this, he's been released. Oh, I have a nose for such things!"

And in an enthusiastic joy, he strode back and forth in the dining room, holding up the unfolded newspaper, which palpitated in the air.

Madame Aurélie, finally understanding what it was about, shrugged her shoulders.

"Truly, you're too stupid, getting yourself in such a state over things that don't concern us. What can it matter to you whether the fellow is innocent or not?"

"What! What can it matter to me…?"

He stopped, astonished.

In fact, why was he taking such an interest in an adventure so foreign to his life, so distant from him?

"When his wife said: "Come on, to table," he sat down, a little ashamed, and ate his soup in silence.

However, he could not distract himself from his preoccupation; he needed to talk about the mysterious affair. In order to excuse himself in his wife's eyes, and also his own, he said: "In sum, one might as well chat about that as about something else. It's the news of the day. People are searching, imagining, trying to divine—it's amusing."

"Oh, if it amuses you!" said Madame Aurélie, ladling more soup. "But I don't share your opinion, you know; of course it's that filthy swine who's the murderer."

"Not at all! Not at all! Eudoxe had nothing to do with the crime. That's proven, absolutely proven."

Monsieur Brunois had recovered his enthusiasm. With the newspaper open on the table, rereading and developing, in abundant words, the reporter's article, he said:

"Follow me, and you'll understand. The examining magistrate interrogated Eudoxe today: 'You admit having murdered your mistress, the prostitute Félicie Bonheur, yesterday evening at about ten o'clock in an ill-famed hotel in the Rue des Files-Dieu?" Then, do you know what he did, Eudoxe? He writhed with laughter. He laughed so much he couldn't respond. The magistrate frowned. 'You're lacking respect for the law.' The other was still writhing. Finally, he explained things. He couldn't have killed Félicie yesterday, in the Rue des Filles-Dieu at about ten o'clock since he had been, almost all evening, from eight o'clock until ten forty-five, in a creamery in the Rue Vieille-du-Temple, from which he hadn't budged, and where twenty people had chatted with him. He only had to ask the owner, the owner's wife, Fifi Romain, fat Adèle, Cadenasse, all those who were there.

"As for Félicie, he had seen her, yesterday evening, in that same creamery; they had dined there together, but she had quit him after coffee because she was working that evening. It's true that she should have come back to met him to go to the Vaux Hall, only she hadn't come. Because of that, not content, and a little dunk, because one gets bored waiting without drinking, he had come back to the Rue Poissonnière quarter at ten forty-five; he thought he would find her in the wine-shop on the Rue Sainte-Foy. No, he hadn't found her, and had been thrown out because he had taken out his anger on the tables and the bottles on the counter. In sum, he couldn't have killed Félicie since, after dinner, he hadn't even seen her, and the magistrate only had to send for the people at the creamery to establish his alibi."

"Well, so what?" said Madame Aurélie. "What does it prove that he said that? He lied, that's all, since he admitted himself, at the police station, that he was the murderer?"

"Very well, yes!" exclaimed Brunois. Delighted to see his wife finally taking an interest in the mysterious rime, and proud to be able to confound her. "A serious objection; the judge said precisely what you've just said. But you'll see. Listen, listen..."

The put his finger on the newspaper at the top of a column. He read:

"'*However, according to your own expression, you settled your account, yesterday evening, with Félicie Bonheur!*'"

"Well, that's what he said," said Madame Aurélie.

"Certainly that's what he said. But that doesn't prove anything at all. Here: '*Yes, Monsieur le juge, I settled the girl's account—which is to say that I gave her a few slaps because, for three days she'd been for a stroll. It's necessary to explain that I love Félicie. I have her in the blood and the bones, and it's not a matter of business. When it doesn't please me that she goes with others, it doesn't please me. So, she got a slap because of her escapade, and I promised her a better one if she didn't come to fetch me to go to the Vaux Hall. But kill her, me? Never in this life. I loved her too much for that, and the fellow who did it only has to hold still; there won't be any need to try him; I'll take care of him in two ticks!*'"

In spite of the reporter emphasizing the tone of sincerity in which Eudoxe le Marin had pronounced those words, Madame Aurélie declared that she was not convinced.

"All criminals try to get themselves out of trouble by inventing stories…"

"But damn it, it's not a matter of invented stories. The examining magistrate summoned witnesses. Seven people, you hear—I haven't invented those seven people, it's in print—came to affirm that Eudoxe hadn't quit the creamery in the Rue Vieille-du-Temple before ten o'clock."

"Fine witnesses, Big Adèle! Cadenasse! Fifi-Romain! Prostitutes and pimps. As if one can believe what people like that say!"

"And policemen, it's not necessary to believe what they say either?"

"Policemen?"

"Yes."

"What policemen?"

"Those in service in the Rue Vieille-du-Temple, who saw Eudoxe come out of the creamery shortly before eleven o'clock—no sooner."

"Who reported what they'd seen?"

"They did."

"Them?"

"Exactly; you can read their deposition."

He put the newspaper before her eyes; then, standing up, his arms folded, superbly, as if from the height of a pedestal, Brunois cried: "Well, what do you say to that?"

"I say…I say…"

She stood up as well—they had finished dinner while chatting—and began clearing the table.

"Yes! What do you say to that!"

"I say that you're irritating me, and that I have other things to do than think about such horrors."

With that, turning her back, she got down on her knees in order to put away the sugar-dish, the carafe, the bottle and the plates that had not been used, in the bottom of the sideboard.

For a moment, Brunois looked at his wife, not without a scornful expression; truly, she had never been very intelligent, and, although she was a good person, she was a stubborn one. Then he began to stride back and forth, anxiously.

The wrinkles on his forehead and the fixity of his stare, between almost-closed eyelids revealed the intense effort of his meditation. He only interrupted his reflection to look at the clock.

Eight o'clock chimed. He picked up his hat.

"Oh! Where are you going?" asked Aurélie.

"I..."

"Yes? Where are you going?"

The truth was that he was going out to buy the latest evening newspapers; they ought to contain further details about the affair of the Rue des Filles-Dieu.

But he lied.

"Where do you expect me to go? I'm going to play a game of dominoes at the Café Guerbois."

"Oh! Good. Don't be too late back."

"No, no..."

He went to the door, seemingly indifferent, without hurrying. But scarcely was he on the landing than he grabbed hold of the banister and went downstairs with long strides.

For several days the investigation, although conducted very assiduously by Maître Legrandin, the examining magistrate, did not uncover anything except for the probability—a detail devoid of any real importance, in any case—that the murderer must have escaped, as soon as the crime was committed, not via the corridor opening on to the street, on which side he would have encountered the crowd that had gathered rapidly, but at the other end of a courtyard, or rather, a narrow open passage, through a door opening on to the Impasse Saint-Spire, always deserted after nightfall.

Every day, a new trail was followed; as soon as the next day, it was abandoned.

Interrogated several times, no longer as a suspect, for there was not a shadow of a doubt as to his innocence, Eudoxe le Marin had not been able to furnish any useful indication. He affirmed that Félicie Bonheur, not accommodating after aperitifs but, in sum, a good creature, had had no enemies, and lived on good terms with the local prostitutes and their lovers.

Was it, then, a crime analogous to those of the likes of Prado and Pranzini? Had some passer-by, taken to her lodgings by Félicie Bonheur, murdered her in order to rob her? What rendered that hypothesis improbable was that the unfortunate woman, drinking everything that Eudoxe le Marin did not extort from her, possessed neither money nor jewelry—which was well known. Not elegant, wearing an old dress, the same one for a year, going out hatless, there was nothing in her attire that could awaken the temptation of a lucrative murder.

The memory of a recent affair, not without resemblance to this one, gave birth to the suspicion of some family drama, enquiries were made as to whether Félicie had relatives. The people of the quarter did not know of any. Only Eudoxe remembered that he had a sister, in the suburbs of Paris or the provinces, who was a domestic or a shop assistant, a sister much younger than her, and very pretty, who was honest, or nearly so, who sometimes came to visit Félicie in the evenings, but he had never seen her, and all he knew about her—very little, next to nothing—he had from his mistress, who might have lied, in order to make herself look better by claiming an honorable relative, or for some other reason.

After a week of uncertainty, however, one point was established by the investigation: the murder really had been that of Félicie Bonheur.

It will be remembered that at first, there was some doubt about that. The testimony of the first people who had seen the victim lost much of its value because the fall on to the cobblestones of the street had almost completely disfigured her, and the concierge-manageress—without being able to explain how anyone else could have introduced themselves into Félicie's room, and without being able to say who had taken the key to that room from the nail in the lodge—had been obstinate in declaring that her tenant had not come to the hotel on the evening of the crime, and she had not recognized the cadaver's clothes.

All hesitations ceased, however, because Félicie Bonheur did not reappear. She would have had no interest in hiding; therefore, she was dead. In addition, the concierge began to show herself less affirmative. Yes, it might be—she thought she remembered now—that she had gone out shortly before ten o'clock, and that, during that absence, Félicie had taken her key and gone upstairs, alone or with someone, to her room.

In brief, the identity of the victim was sufficiently established—all the more so as her linen, chemise, bloomers and handkerchief, bore the initials F.B.—for the judge to give permission of the inhumation, after an autopsy that discovered nothing new, fully confirming the statements of Dr. L.M., according to which the three mortal wounds, one in the neck and two under the left breasts, had been produced by a very slender pointed knife.

Longer than all the other readers of the daily newspapers, Charles Brunois, who followed the strange affair with a increasing ardor, conserved doubts regarding the identity of the victim. To tell the truth, he did not know to what cause to attribute the persistence of his uncertainty. Perhaps he remained struck, unconsciously, by the discord between the names Félicie Bonheur, significant of joy and contentment, with the horror of a bloody end? Yes, perhaps. In the end, though, it was necessary to yield to the evidence, and he had repudiated all doubts in that regard some time before the day he went to visit the dispatch room of *Le Figaro*.

There, the portrait of the victim was displayed, photographed the day after the crime, and the portrait of Félicie Bonheur, also a photograph, taken two months before and supplied to the newspaper by Eudoxe le Marin.

It was not without difficulty—for the crowd in the hall was compact—that Charles Brunois was able to slide toward the wall, but he finally succeeded.

Looking over the shoulders of the curious, his eyes fell first upon the photograph provided by Eudoxe, and before even having read the inscription written below the portrait he had recognized Félicie Bonheur. There was nothing extraordinary about that. The prostitute had been described so frequently in the newspapers—not beautiful, too fat, lips swollen, bare-headed, an old maroon dress, no corset, slack breasts—and then, all these streetwalkers look alike.

He advanced further, using his elbows; he was in haste to see the other portrait, that of the murdered woman.

He shuddered.

In that worthy man, with a mild and feeble soul, and a heart easily moved, such a movement of horror was perfectly natural at the sight of the stiff cadaver, with its cut in the neck—the wounds under the breast were not visible, the bodice being closed—and her face all torn and soiled with blood, so that it seemed masked by wounds. Monsieur Brunois' hands, which he had raised, trembled above the crowd; his lips stirred like those of a frightened ape.

Then, suddenly, he was quite different. He stiffened, his eyes wide and staring, and extending his arm, he said in a declamatory tone: "It's not her!"

Proffered in a loud voice, those words attracted the attention of several people, notably a man with a ferrety face and an unkempt beard, wearing a tilted bowler hat and a dirty frock-coat buttoned up to the top.

But Brunois, without noticing that he was being observed, repeated: "No, It's not her. That isn't Félicie Bonheur, no, no, no!"

Then, abruptly, the man in the dirty frock-coat said: "Why do you say that?"

Brunois kept silent, either because he had not heard or because he had no response to make.

The man said: "I asked you why you say that that isn't Félicie Bonheur."

This time, with the suddenness of a triggered release: "Because…!"

Brunois stopped. He no longer knew what he had wanted to say; he searched for it in vain; there was a sort of vacillation in his head. It was only a very brief disturbance. Then he looked at the people round him, tranquil and smiling. But he was in no hurry to reply. He could not imagine himself why he had cried out, in such an affirmative tone: "It's not her!"

He understood it when he had looked more closely at the photograph of the dead woman.

That correct, modest, dress, very clean wherever the blood and mud had not stained it, the hair in virginal bangs, which even death-throes had not been able to ruffle, the strictly-buttoned bodice and the little white collar—in sum, the entire appearance of the victim—had nothing in common with the costume and appearance of Félicie Bonheur in the neighboring portrait, and, in a general fashion, contradicted the idea of disorder, effrontery and extravagance that the estate of common prostitute implied.

Ingenuously, not without some pride in his sagacity, Charles Brunois gave his reasons to the man who was questioning him. They did not convince anyone. People shrugged their shoulders. The man was talking nonsense. Between the two portraits there was, in fact, a difference of costume, but that did not prove anything. Prostitutes often affected modest exteriors in order to tempt men, and so far as could be judged between the wounds, the two faces were similar: the same form of the nose, the same curve of the eyebrows, the hair planted in the same fashion, and, on the cheek near the left ear, quite visible, a similar birth mark.

Charles Brunois could not deny that resemblance of the features, but, shaking his head, he did not appear to attach any importance to them. Suddenly, with the air of someone who has made a resolution, he went out rapidly, without another word.

For him, there was no doubt. In spite of the general opinion, it was not Félicie Bonheur who had been murdered.

Slightly conceited, he told himself, rubbing his hands, that he would have made a fine prefect of police. A simple civilian, he would fulfill his duty as a citizen by enlightening the law.

The investigation could not have any satisfactory result while it was emanating from a false point of departure. The guilty party had not been found, and would not be found, because it was obstinate in searching for him among people who, in one way or another, had a relationship with Félicie Bonheur. The indispensable thing, to begin with, was to discover who the victim was; when that was done, the murderer would be arrested before long.

So he went into a café and asked for writing materials.

He picked up the pen, but only traced the line: *Monsieur le juge d'instruction...*

He searched for phrases, for words...

To tell the truth, when he came to formulate it, his conviction no longer seemed to him to be based on evidence sufficient to make anyone share it. The reasons he had furnished just now in the dispatch hall had not been very convincing, opposed to so many contrary appearances.

He did not change his mind, He was sure that he was not mistaken. Since he had divined correctly with regard to the innocence of the supposed murderer, why should he be any less wrong in his appreciation with regard to the pretended victim?

But in reality, he did not have enough evidence. No, he did not have enough evidence yet. And, with that thought, he dropped the pen...

Someone whom he did not see, standing on the sidewalk, was watching him through the window of the café: the poorly-dressed man with the ferrety face and the unkempt beard.

The next day, at nine o'clock in the morning, Madame Aurélie uttered an "Ah!" of surprise as she woke up. Her husband, standing in front of a mirror-fronted wardrobe, was finishing buttoning his frock-coat. He already had his hat on—a top hat, although it was summer. In his costume and his attitude there was something grave: ceremonial, one might have said.

"What? You're going out this morning, in formal dress?"

He replied that he was going to the funeral of a friend, a former businessman, one of the domino-players at the Café Guerbois.

"You didn't say anything about it yesterday evening."

No, in fact, he had forgotten to mention it yesterday evening. He had only remembered it this morning. He could not dispense with following the procession, and he was already late. He would be obliged to go directly to the church. He kissed his wife and told her not to worry if he only came back in the afternoon, or a little later. It was possible that there would be a "consolation lunch" after the burial. Then he went out. He marched at a firm pace, with a self-important and thoughtful expression.

Once again, Brunois had lied; the domino-players of the Café Guerbois were in good health; he had made up the pretext in order to avoid the mockery of his wife, to whom, moreover, he had no longer mentioned the mystery of the Rue des Filles-Dieu for several days. The truth was that, not having enough evidence to enlighten the law, he wanted to gather more, entirely persuasive; and, doubtless incited by his memories of detective stories, he was going to carry out his own investigation of the crime, on his own.

He climbed into a cab.

"Rue des Filles-Dieu."

For it was necessary to begin, as the saying has it, at the beginning; which is to say that, before anything else, to inspect the scene of the murder and its surroundings, to make the nearest neighbors talk.

"What number?" asked the coachman.

Charles Brunois knew very well that Félicie Bonheur has longed at number 56. However, he replied: "Stop at number twenty"—a subtlety for which he congratulated himself. He might have attracted attention by getting out of the cab in front of the house where the crime had been committed; one observes better when one is not observed.

During the journey he reminded himself, coldly, of the principal points on which his investigation would bear, and coordinated them in his mind, logically, repudiating all the suppositions published by the newspapers, in order that no preconceived idea would trouble the clarity of the impressions that he might receive, and would not expose the information that he was going to gather to an erroneous interpretation—admitting, on the contrary, his own hypotheses as indisputable verities.

So, a woman *who was not Félicie Bonheur*, had been stabbed three times, and had been picked up, dead and unrecognizable, from the cobblestones.

Such were the facts.

To establish the identity of the victim and to discover the veritable murderer, *who was not Eudoxe le Marin*.

Such was the objective.

When the vehicle, which had quit the grand boulevards a few moments before, had engaged in the labyrinth of cul-de-sacs and back streets that twists and turns, winding back upon itself, between the Rue Poissonnière and the Porte Saint-Denis, Charles Brunois observed without surprise the rather ill-famed quarter that the bourgeois from Batignolles, homebody as he was, he had few opportunities to see. He was scornful, but he did not find it singular or unexpected that, between the few new houses, there were leaning, cracked buildings with dirty, crumbling plaster, and windows decked with red curtains, half-closed by a chain, where the nudity of an arm or a shock of red hair emerged between the open shutters, and sordid narrow shops spilling forth streams of vegetables devoid of baskets, ragged clothing on hooks, and liquor stores with facades painted blood red.

He ought, truly, at least to have experienced some sentiment of novelty in confrontation with those things.

No, he did not experience it.

But he had no difficulty deducing the cause of that absence of astonishment; it was because that vile and obscene corner of Paris appeared to conform in every way with the image he had formed of it, in accordance with reportage, especially after the ignoble murder.

Only one thing surprised him, seemingly abnormal: the brightness of the daylight on so much ugliness and baseness. By night it would have seemed to him to be quite natural and necessary, doubtless because his mind, in his vision of that corner of Paris, so closely in harmony with the crime that made it more sinister, inevitably associated it with the idea of the nocturnal hour when the crime had been committed.

Scarcely had he entered the Rue des Filles-Dieu than he shouted: "Driver! Stop!"

On that order, the vehicle stopped, but outside a door but next to a street-light. Neither the houses to the right nor the left of it bore the number that he had indicated, or that of the hotel that he intended to inspect. By virtue of what whim, therefore, had he told the coachman to halt? He did not know.

It was singular, the instinctive impulse that had obliged him to cry "Stop!"

Behind the street-light, between a façade and an advancing wall, there was a rather profound corner, which, in the evening, must be very dark, in spite of the neighboring gaslamp: one of those recesses in which, in the low quarters, prostitutes lurk, from which their hands spring forth to grab the arms of passers-by, accompanied by filthy promises.

Why had Brunois evoked that image? Because he remembered having seen such corners and such whores…but when? Well, quite often, in the evenings, when going home after playing dominoes at the Café Guerbois.

At any rate, he descended from the cab and paid the driver.

He was in the Rue des Filles-Dieu; he would go on foot to number 56.

But on the sidewalk, he did not budge.

That place interested him, that corner, that recess, which must be very dark in the evening, with the shadow of the wall over the façade.

If the victim was a streetwalker, if the murderer was a prowling drunkard in search of good fortune...a drunkard? yes, the supposition of a drunken murderer had occurred to him suddenly, doubtless because of the many liquor stores that he saw in the quarter...they might have encountered one another in such a place, doubtless in this very one, since it was near the hotel in which the murder had been committed.

Perhaps, after exchanging a few brief words, the prostitute going ahead, the drunkard bumping into shop-fronts already shuttered, they had headed toward the hotel...

Certainly, certainly, things could have, must have happened like that! And Brunois, following his idea—living it, so to speak—went along the walls at an ill-assured pace, as if he wanted to imitate the individual evoked by his imagination.

Abruptly, he stopped in front of a pharmacy.

The thought rose into his mind in a single jet, like a rocket of divination, that a quarrel between the man and the woman had taken place in the street, on this sidewalk, here! Here, in the pink-tinted radiance of that enormous bottle, now extinct, but which, in the evening, was flamboyant...

That hypothesis—he remarked the fact—had nothing, with regard to the place, that was not perfectly normal, the pharmacy being a few paces from the hotel. But what had suggested to him the idea of a quarrel in the street between the two people who had encountered one another?

He asked himself that question, and knew immediately what the answer must be. Nothing was simpler! It happened so frequently...he had seen such altercations himself, many a time, near the door of some dive, between a prostitute and a passer-by, haggling over the price, or for some other reason.

For some other reason.

He was inclined to think that, in the case in question, the quarrel had not been a matter of bargaining.

Perhaps the prostitute had refused to take the drunken man home? No, no, they were not so delicate, these streetwalkers. Perhaps she was one of those who, at certain hours, limit themselves to enticing the passers-by, not going up themselves into the shady houses where the women whose turn it was to welcome visitors were waiting—and the drunkard was annoyed, because he wanted, precisely, the woman who had accosted him in the corner behind the street-light?

By virtue of a strange faith in himself, Brunois now admitted, as established facts, the most gratuitous hypotheses suggested to him by his chimeras, or memories of things seen in the street, or remembrance of things he had read.

He would have sworn that the woman had not gone into the hotel with the drunkard, that they had separated there, in the radiance of the pink bottle.

On the other hand, he was dissatisfied with the idea that she was only a tempter, conducting men as far as the door.

Perhaps she had had a rendezvous with her lover, a pimp, jealous n his fashion...

Brunois could hardly retain a triumphant cry. He remembered Eudoxe le Marin's deposition. On the day of the crime, Eudoxe had ordered Félicie Bonheur to come to join him in the creamery in the Rue Vieille-du-Temple; the hooker of the drunkard, who was none other than Félicie, alias the Big Jewess, had planted him there, fearing that she might be beaten by her lover if she was too late.

Thus, reality adapted marvelously to Brunois' suppositions.

But the Big Jewess had not wanted a good opportunity to be lost to just anyone. She had told the passer-by to go to her room, at such-and-such a door on the third floor of the hotel at number 56; he only had to turn tight, without saying anything to the concierge; and in her room he would find another young woman, much younger than her, much prettier than her, a friend who had come to see her that evening, yes, a friend, a relative...

Brunois lifted his hand violently to his forehead and cried: "Her sister!" and, certain of having divined correctly, he swelled with pride.

But he was soon obliged to admit that, correct or not—he would have wagered that it was correct!—that new hypothesis had nothing of which he had reason to be proud; he had not arrived at it merely by supposing that the Big Jewess had a sister, younger and prettier and her, whom she had mentioned to the drunkard, since Eudoxe, in his deposition, had mentioned that sister, still sage, very pretty, a domestic or a shop assistant in the suburbs of Paris or the provinces, who came to visit Félicie sometimes in the evening. What Brunois had admired as the result of an extraordinary intuition was only a memory.

Slightly disconcerted in his vanity as an observer, he recovered assurance by thinking that, among the facts acquired by his investigation, there were many others whose discovery he owed entirely to his personal sagacity; and he followed the line of his inductions ardently.

So, after a brief quarrel, followed by an agreement, the Big Jewess and the drunkard had parted company outside the pharmacy, she to go and rejoin Eudoxe le Marin and he to go to the designated hotel; and, as that man must have done, as he surely had done, Brunois hastened forward, staggering a little in imitation of the person he was imagining.

Oh, he had no reason to complain, the drunkard! Instead of a streetwalker, not beautiful, getting old, and so banal, he would have a young and pretty woman, almost honest—that was in Eudoxe's deposition—a royal morsel, in a word. Deep down, he had had some remorse...

What! What, then, had led Brunois to think that, at that moment, the drunkard had already felt remorse? Yes, why suppose that, at that moment, had been feeling remorse, already? Because, involuntarily, he was confusing the state of mind that must have followed the crime with the one that had preceded it? That explanation did not satisfy Brunois. He clung to his idea that the future criminal, here, in the street, had experienced disturbances of conscience—strangely, he clung to that idea—but, at the same time, it seemed to him that it must have been for reasons unconnected with the crime itself.

What reasons?

Men who ran after whores were not disconcerted by the idea of an adventure in a furnished hotel, undoubtedly. But where was the proof that the drunken man—he no longer thought *the drunkard*—was a habitual libertine, a recidivist of vulgar orgies? Brunois was astonished that he had admitted that point to begin with, without discussion.

It was not only vile prowlers who, sniffing musk and flesh washed with Lubin,[19] stopped when accosted by a whore in the angle of some wall. Worthy men, habitually very chaste, bourgeois of good morals, might allow themselves to be tempted from time to time by the facile pleasure that was offered to them, and was not very costly. A little escapade, discreet and not dangerous—one took precautions—is not implausible, especially after a meal in a restaurant with friend, who, in order to celebrate the sealing of some deal, or to drink to the success of some enterprise—a voyage for example—have had the best wines brought up from the cellar. Friends…or a single friend. It is not necessary to have many people in order to eat well, to drink well, and to lose one's head, in a word. There is nothing like burgundy to give one ideas; and when one's brain is lit up by good wine, it only requires the odor of a woman on top of that to set everything ablaze.

So, probably, yes, very probably, the man having strayed, on the evening of the crime, into the Poissonnière quarter, was none other than a worthy bourgeois—perhaps some retired businessman—not at all debauched, but a little

---

[19] Pierre-François Lubin became one of the most successful Parisian perfumers when his "eau vivifiante" was adopted by the Empress Josephine. The company he founded is still active and thriving.

crazed by Pommard or Chambertin; and given that, nothing was easier to admit than the remorse by which he had been assailed, and which had obliged him, hesitant and moved, almost fainting, had perhaps obliged him to catch his breath before this door.

At the same time, Brunois, so much was he living his chimera, stopped and leaned his shoulder on a hinged door. For that libertine by virtue of hazard and circumstance, after dessert, had to be married; so that, at present, on the brink if this villainy—kisses bought in a dirty hotel room—he thought about his wife, not very pretty, but such a good and old friend, who was waiting for him, awake, with her head on the pillow and her eyes on the hands of the clock.

And, as one is easily overtaken by emotion when one is drunk, he wept into his hands, shaken by the somersaults of his breast. Fortunately, there were few people in the street, and those who went by did not pay any heed to him. In any case, they do not last long, the chagrins of drunken men; suddenly, the fellow—Brunois drew away from the door, joyfully, and resumed walking—must have burst out laughing, and, his lips moist and his eyes hot, no longer thinking about his wife waiting for him in bed, in the bedroom furnished in mahogany and ornamented with lithographs, had started to run—finally, it was not forbidden for him to amuse himself for once—to run to the point of running out of breath, toward the hotel, very close, a low door with a grating, before which Brunois stopped, out of breath, without even having seen, under the window of the entresol, the number 56 in white, on a background of blue enamel.

Furthermore, there was nothing at all extraordinary in his halting there, before having seen the number, because the shady and sordid hotel, with its little windows lined with red cotton, was opposite an open drinking den in which the enormous distillation apparatus at the end of the counter imitated the winding coils of an enormous copper dragon, the façade of which had tall mirrors here and there, which reflected the cobblestones, the gutter, the sidewalk and the passers-by, and the overhanging first floor and the narrow door to the corridor between walls of dirty plaster, certainly offered the resemblance of a crime scene; the sagacious Brunois could not have made a mistake.

However, he was in no hurry to open the door with the grating; he reflected.

Desirous of inspecting the staircase that the murder had climbed, the room where the murder had been perpetrated, should he present himself to the concierge-manageress simply as a curiosity-seeker—as, indeed, he was—or should he make up some pretext that would permit him, alone and at his leisure, without chatter around him, to examine the inhabitants of the sinister house?

He opted for the latter course. But on what pretext? The most plausible of all. If one occasionally lodges in dives of this sort, it is the custom to hire there, for a few hours, rooms in which one does not sleep, Well, he would adopt the fashions and the appearance of someone who has a rendezvous with a woman here, and, having arrived first, will wait for her. So, putting a little impertinence and conceit into his attitude, he advanced toward the concierge's lodge, cockily, his gaze licentious, with the air that the man in whose footsteps he was following so ingeniously must have had on the evening of the crime.

"Yes, yes, Monsieur," said the concierge-manageress, an obese, sweaty quinquagenarian with a moustache and gray hair, "there's a room free on the entresol, the best in the house!"

Having entered part way into the lodge, he did not linger to observe the woman who was speaking to him. Strangely enough, he hardly glanced at her, and, although she could doubtless have furnished him with interesting details regarding the bloody adventure that preoccupied him, not for a moment did he have the idea of interrogating her.

Was that by virtue of a disdain, permitted to him by his recent discoveries, of usual police procedure, or by virtue of the pride of owing nothing, in his investigation, except to his own clear-sightedness? What is certain is that he was not interested in the landlady. But, flexing his neck, his eyes wide open and his gaze intense, he considered the corridor walls avidly, and the dirty copper banister-knob of a narrow turning staircase, and the steps, one after another...

With the result that he made no response.

Then, abruptly, he extended his hand toward the panel where the lined-up keys, with copper numbers, were hanging from hooks, and he seized one.

"Oh, no, no, Monsieur," said the manageress, "don't take number thirteen. That room wouldn't suit Monsieur. It's not very well-furnished the bed isn't wide enough, and it's on the third floor. And then, well, it's not a cheerful room, since the affair...you know, Monsieur...since the affair that was reported in the newspapers..."

To tell the truth, Brunois experienced a great admiration, not devoid of some amazement, for the instinct that was guiding him in his difficult research. Thus, without any kind of indication, uniquely by chance—which was veritably prodigious—he had put his hand immediately, without hesitation, on the very key to the room in which the sister of the Big Jewess had been murdered. In truth, it would not have taken much for him to admit some supernatural intervention—at one time, he had nearly devoted himself to spiritism—if he had not remembered that men endowed with a superior talent for the accomplishment of some kind of work are often aided in their task by the good will of circumstance. Destiny likes to serve genius, and Brunois, after so many successes, which had permitted further successes, could not forbid himself a little pride.

But it was only a brief surge of conceit.

Fundamentally—he was obliged to recognize it—there was nothing marvelous in the fact that he had extended his arm toward that key, and not another. The number 13 displayed on the little copper oval had naturally attracted his eye and struck his mind by virtue of the concordance of the "fatality" of the number with the horror or the crime; hence the gesture; nothing was more easily explicable.

However, he kept the key.

"Good, good," he said, his hat tilted slightly sideways, rakishly, "it doesn't matter that the bed isn't wide when the girl is pretty, does it, Madame? You'll see, when she arrives, that she's very pretty. I'll take number thirteen. That's my decision."

And he put a ten-franc piece in the hand of the manageress.

"Oh!" she said. "As Monsieur wishes. That's what I say myself…if Monsieur would care to follow me, I'll show him the way…be careful, the stairway is a little narrow, and dark…"

"I know, I know."

"Monsieur knows?"

For what reason had he said *I know*? Well, obviously, because it isn't in houses like this one, with sooty walls, devoid of sunlight or gaslight, that there are spacious steps whose ascension is easy.

"No, Madame, don't disturb yourself," he added. "I'll find the room on my own. On the third?"

"The second door in the little corridor."

"To the left."

"To the left? Exactly. Monsieur has been to the house before, then?"

He shuddered, and was then immobilized, in a tension of his entire being, and, his eyes staring, in a voice that was not talking to anyone, a slow, vague, neutral voice, he repeated: "Been…to the house…before…"

But very quickly, extracted with a start from the brief absence of mind, he said, cheerfully: "Good, good, to the left; thank you, Madame, thank you."

In any case, he did not marvel for long at having thought immediately that the door was to the left. It was a question of room number 13, and was there not in the unevenness of odd numbers, a kind of analogy with the kind of incompleteness, of awkwardness, of "gaucherie" that there is in the sinister side? Yes, that was why he had divined immediately that the door was on that side. And then, thirteen, sinister, the murder: all of that went together.

He took pleasure in that subtle reasoning, observing and analyzing himself. He was interested in his own thinking, as if in a scrupulous study of a mental state in some novel, and it seemed to him that he was reading himself.

Now, while the concierge-manageress went back into her lodge murmuring: "An eccentric, for sure," he went up the first flight of steps to the first floor, in the turning stairwell, where, through a narrow bay, the window of which was half-open, daylight entered at an angle, dirtied by a dusty steel reflector

Abruptly, he felt very vigorous, like a man who has dined well and is going to see a girl.

Ah! After a good meal there is nothing like a pale creature, who has a lot of flesh, flesh on to which one can put one's open hands, in a caress as broad and sonorous as a smack. Thin ones too are amusing! It's even funnier, it excites more. She must have been small and thin, with small breasts, Félicie Bonheur's sister, since she was so young and so sage, in the room up there, in room 13.

What amused Brunois, in his investigation, was the facility with which he was putting himself in the place of the man he wanted to deliver to the law. He felt that he had got into the skin of the character, as they say, so well that he was sure that he was thinking and acting as the other had thought and acted. And that incarnation, which had already aided his research a great deal, would aid him even more powerfully.

He burst out laughing because, at the turning of the stairway, he had nearly fallen flat: the good humor of a drunkard who had almost broken his neck. Then he continued climbing in the glom, slightly illuminated by the light from the first-floor window; and, tottering from the banister to the wall, striving to be exactly as "the other" must have been. If he succeeded in that, he was very cheerful—with returns of melancholy because of the poor wife who was waiting for him at home, her alert eyes on the hands of the clock. But giving oneself a good time isn't forbidden; one isn't made of wood, damn it!

And, still climbing, he had the refrain of a song heard in a café-concert on his lips: "*Oh, there you are, Mathieu, how are you my old chap...*"

On the second floor, "*there you are, Mathieu…,*" he paused to catch his breath, gripped the banister again, "*how are you, my old chap…,*" and, cheered up by the song he recommenced climbing, "*there you are, Mathieu…,*"

For sure, he wouldn't be bored in a little while, "*how are you, my old chap…,*" with the girl, *there you are, Mathieu…,*" and he hastened, taking the steps two by two, and he turned into the corridor, and he saw the door, to the left, and he opened it, and brutally, "*how are you, my old chap…,*" received full in the face the bloody pool of a red curtain!

Scarlet, the curtain of the only window tinted the floor-tiles, the wallpaper, the tablecloth, the chairs, the marble of the wash-stand, the basin and the bed with murder.

Splashed all over by the crime, Brunois uttered a cry. For, in sum, he, a worthy man, a good bourgeois, married and tranquil, suddenly, he was in that frightful room, all red, where nothing was lacking of the murder but the victim bleeding from the neck and the breast, standing near the window...and yet, no, she wasn't lacking, for he thought he could see her, he did see her! It was enough to drive one mad.

In a paroxysm of terror, he turned round and ran down the stairs. He arrived outside the lodge, but did not go toward the street, and, without knowing what instinct was impelling him, he traversed the little courtyard, the narrow uncovered passage, toward the Impasse Saint-Spire ("Monsieur! Monsieur!" shouted the concierge), not hearing, still running ("You're mistaken, Monsieur, it isn't that way!"), reached the wall, pushed the door, and fled.

Then the old woman, very astonished, said: "Well! Well! Can it be, by chance…?" and, emerging into the street, she called to a neighbor, the fruiterer: "Look after my lodge for a minute!"

And then, very quickly, because of a suspicion that had occurred to her, she went to the commissariat in the Rue de Cléry, while Monsieur Brunois fled via the Impasse.

He went on and on, running between the long double row of water-sellers' barrels that shrank the narrow passage even further, and the surprise of wine-merchants' waiters washing bottles in the back rooms, and the sniggers, at half-open windows, of prostitutes in blue or pink peignoirs, who advanced beneath red shocks of hair the horror of make-up seen in broad daylight.

Certainly, he ran like that, frightened and bewildered, until he ran out of breath, or until he encountered some obstacle—wall, carriage, passer-by—with which he collided, so great was his terror of the horrible room that he had glimpsed, so urgent was his need to be far, far away from it, at any cost.

Alas, poor man, so mild, so calm, so quiet, slightly dreamy because of the leisure of the commerce finished, a trifle romantic and subtle because of judiciary romances read with passion in the slow wellbeing of evenings! The crime of the Rue des Filles-Dieu, so much did it remain, in spite of its reality, nonexistent and chimerical, because of its resemblance with the imaginations of Gaboriau or Jules Mary, had interested him without troubling him—had amused him, in a word. It had been, in his monotonous life, a distraction, not devoid of arrogance, to play the role of the man who, at a given moment, would emerge, saying to the policemen and the examining magistrate: "You're all imbeciles! What you haven't been able to discover I've discovered, myself, although not in the profession!" and would then withdraw, worthy and proud, between the hedge of amazements and congratulations; and people would run after him to offer him well-deserved recompenses, positions in which he could exercise, for the public good and his own glory, his almost-miraculous surety of investigation.

In sum, it had been the pastime, which did not harm anyone, of an idle mind, a game, a conundrum, an absorbing puzzle, and, for a salary, something resembling the vainglory of the Oedipus who had obtained first prize in a competition in the "Games and Recreations" section of a weekly supplement.

But he had seen the crime at close range, on seeing the abominable chamber in the red shadow of the curtain! And it was no longer a chapter in a novel, or a puzzle: it was a real murder, with real blood, and abomination close at hand, living and tangible. And he had fled, and he was still fleeing, in a fear comparable to that of a criminal who had been taken to the scene of his crime, and perhaps in a fear that was even more disconcerting, for, after all, someone who had committed murder must have had, in remembering the wounds, a sort of familiarity with the redness on the wall, on the carpet and on the table, whereas, for a weak and ingenuous person like him, so easily moved to pity, and so fearful of any barbarity—he would have died of hunger in a poultry-yard rather than strangle a chicken—that there was something maddening in the sight of such a room, impregnated with the murder.

Oh, how wrong he had been to read the *Petit Journal*! Oh, how well he would have done to follow the advice of his wife!

He was running, he was breathless and sweating, he would fall ill for sure; all that because he had wanted to follow a trail, like an agent of the Sûreté. As if crimes were anything to do with him! Oh, that room, that room! He could not stop thinking about the man going in, the man leaping forward, the man raising the knife, and striking!

He ran, and ran, and kept running, still running, painting and sweating...

At the end of a side-street, wooden beams, stones and rubble were scattered in a muddy building-site, an interrupted construction; a pile of sand in front of an unfinished wall was rounded out and hollowed out by a sort of low crater, in which lime had hardened in a plaster-like sheet.

As he went past that pile of sand, Brunois was tempted to take off his frock-coat and throw it into it.

Eh? What? His frock-coat? Take it off? Throw it...there?

Oh, yes! Since, from so much running, he was so hot...

But Madame Brunois would have uttered loud cries! She had scolded him so much, because of the other frock-coat, lost on the evening of the dinner with Richond, the frock-coat that he had had to replace immediately, at the ready-made garment shop.

Now he was no longer running, because of the numerous, better-dressed passers-by. He had emerged from the back streets and blind alleys, and was in the next quarter, commercial, populous and not proletarian. His gait, however, jerky and brutal, like a condensed, collected surge, was no less fatiguing than the reckless race a little while before. His chest expanded and collapsed like that of an actor n a melodrama, while, with a fixed, haggard stare he could still see the frightful room, and large drops of seat emerged on those temples, his forehead and below his eyes...

A Wallace fountain!

He approached it, held out his open hands, washed them in the falling jet, filled them with water, bathed his face with it, and felt a delectable freshness that cleansed...and calmed...

That was a strange idea he had had! I ask you, is it what a well brought-up man like him does, washing himself in the street? Truly, among all the extraordinary things that had happened to him, there was none as extraordinary as that one. Damn it, one doesn't wash oneself at a public fountain when one is someone respectable, when one has an income of seven thousand francs. That is fine for louts without a domicile, for prowlers who have slept on benches...or for murderers soiled with blood, who hope to cleanse themselves of their crime...

Oh! Had the murderer of the Rue des Filles-Dieu washed himself in this fountain, perhaps? Just as, perhaps, he had thrown his frock-coat on to the pile of sand, amid the stony ruts of the house under construction!

Once again, Brunois could not help admitting the truly amazing sagacity thanks to which he discovered, divined and repeated all the actions of the criminal; and for a moment, his pride urged him to continue an investigation for which he seemed to be so manifestly destined.

But the sight of the room of the crime had impressed him too cruelly for him to persist in an adventure that doubtless reserved even worse terrors for him.

In any case, the cool water had suppressed his fever; he was now walking at a regular pace, not too promptly; he recognized that he was in the Rue d'Aboukir, near the boulevard where he would find a cab-stand.

He breathed deeply, and recovered possession of himself. No, no, no, a hundred times no! He would no longer belabor himself with a hundred blows in order to render himself useful to the law. Whether the guilty party was found or not, it was perfectly indifferent to him. He would return to the nice little routines of his everyday life. Oof! It was over. He put his hair in order, which the running had tousled, buttoned up his frock-coat—his new frock-coat—arrived on the boulevard among people who were strolling, climbed into a cab, gave his address, and remained pensive during the journey, in a somnolence almost devoid of thought—as one is liable to do after a violent shock—and went home.

He was slightly troubled when Madame Aurélie said to him: "There wasn't a consolation lunch, then?" but he remembered the pretext he had used in order to explain his morning excursion and recovered very quickly.

"No, no, after the cemetery, everyone went home." He took off his ceremonial clothes, put on a dressing gown and sat down at the table, where the housemaid had just brought him an omelet. Through the window open to the sunlight, amid the chirping of the canaries, came the air from the garden and the odor of roses. Oh, how pleasant it was to be at home! And he would not go running around again, for affairs that were not his concern.

Like a tracked beast going to ground in its lair, huddling there and never wanting to come out again, Brunois returned to his simple and secure life, in his stay-at-home egotism. No, he would not take it into his head again to spend the morning playing Lecoq. Those antics produced excessively strong emotions. To each his lot, and his was getting up late, having a good lunch, taking a siesta, idling for a hour or an hour and a half on the exterior boulevards to give himself an appetite, playing manille with his wife or dominoes with his friends at the café, and going to bed on the stroke of ten, after a "Sleep well, Aurélie" to the latter, already asleep.

In order to be sure of not being caught up again with his silly obsession, Brunois forbade the housemaid to bring the *Petit Journal*. The result was that, five or six days after his return to his habits, he had lost all interest in the mysterious crime that he preoccupied him so intensely. In truth, he would not have crossed the street to learn the identity of the real murder, and he had soon forgotten completely that a poor girl had been killed in the Rue de Filles-Dieu. In any case, he had never felt better, had never enjoyed a more regular appetite. "Charles, Charles, you're getting fatter by the day!" And for twelve hours—a complete rotation of the hands of the clock—the rhythm of an even snore cradled his slumber without starts or dreams, his mouth open blissfully.

One night, all of a sudden, he sat up in bed. In a corner of the room, as if in a hollow in the wall, the flame of the nightlight was sizzling redly above a somber disk, about to go out with the eye-blink of a dying owl. And, with his elbow on his knee and his fist under his chin, his eyes staring into the void of solitude and shadow, he thought:

The extraordinary, inconceivable thing is that such a crime has been committed by a man of placid mores, mild humor, polite, even timid. What would be quite simple on the part of a brutal prowler accustomed to using a knife becomes incomprehensible when it's a matter of an honest and calm bourgeois. And yet—that is established, and proven—such is the guilty man. What, therefore, can have pushed him to commit an action so contrary to his nature, to his species?

He was drunk? Yes, yes, undoubtedly he was drunk; but having drunk too much can give a worthy man funny ideas,

ideas of "having a ball," but can't giving birth in him to a ferocious needed for cutting throats and bloody murder. I admit that in room 13 there was some quarrel between the sister of the Big Jewess and the visitor. That isn't sufficient to motivate him to hurl himself upon her, stab her in the neck, and stab her in the breast twice. What, then, was the matter with him? What was it that connected with a latent rage in him, ready to burst forth? That's what it's necessary to know. Surely someone in the evening, had crossed him, exasperated him. Yes, undoubtedly. But where, and who?

Brunois shrugged his shoulders.

I've got it! I've got it! Really, it was too stupid not to have thought of that right way, He had dined at a restaurant with friends, or a friend—that's also established, and proven—on the occasion of a completed deal, or a journey. Well, at dessert, there was an argument. He wasn't malevolent, and only wanted to laugh, but by means of bad jokes, nagging, aggravating remarks, the other put him beside himself. One can be the best man in the world, but one loses patience if the teasing goes on to long, one can no longer restrain oneself. They're not rare, very mild people who wouldn't hurt a fly, but whom it's necessary not to excite. Grandfather was one of those people! Good, good, everything is explained; the argument became a dispute: harsh words, insults, perhaps punches exchanged over the crockery and glasses. Who can tell whether the man, beside himself, the man who had been driven into a fury, might not have lunged, mad with rage, and grabbed a bottle from the table, or a carafe...or a knife...

Monsieur Brunois started.

A knife! A knife! Yes, one of those small, light, slender knives, sharply pointed, that there are in restaurants...exactly the kind of knife with which he had wounded and killed, later, the sister of the Big Jewess. The physician said that the wounds appeared to be due to a very slender, sharply pointed knife. How would the murderer—a placid man, who would surely not have gone out armed—had such a murderous instrument on him, if he hadn't taken it from the table in the restaurant, and taken it away with him, doubtless by mistake, when he quit his friend at a run, for fear that, if he stayed any longer, he might do something bad?

Sweating, Brunois felt his chest heaving violently, so vivid was his emotion in reconstituting so plausibly the preliminaries of the crime, and so much was his pride in his perspicacity stimulated.

He contained himself, and succeeded in not budging anymore; it was necessary not to wake Madame Aurélie, sleeping alongside him. He continued talking—or, rather thinking, his mouth moving but mute.

And afterwards? After he had left the restaurant? What did he do? Oh, that isn't very difficult to divine. Calmed by the open air, but the gaiety of the shops, still illuminated—it must not have been later than nine o'clock or nine-thirty, since the crime was committed at ten—content, moreover, with not having done his friend any harm , he started strolling along the streets, looking in the shop windows, amusing himself making signs to the shop-girls. Certainly, he was still angry, nasty rages don't go away so quickly, but the gaiety mingled with his ill humor, teasing him, tickling him, wanting to make him laugh. That diabolical burgundy!

And soon, stirred up by the wine and the pretty faces of the girls behind the widows, he quit the bright, spacious, busy streets. He plunged into an obscure quarter, where, in the solitude and the mystery, there were possible encounters, pleasant encounters, and in corner, he found Félicie Bonheur, and she didn't want to go upstairs with him because Eudoxe was waiting for her, but she showed him the hotel and told him the number of a room where he could find another woman, much younger, much prettier, and he went to the hotel, and went past the lodge, where there was no one in, and he went upstairs, and he saw number 13 on the door, n the corridor, and with a song in his mouth, he went into the room, into the room... "into the room..."

Those last words, Brunois had not only thought but had pronounced, almost shouted.

"Eh? What? What's the matter?"

It was Madame Aurélie who spoke, half-awake, lifting herself up toward him.

"Nothing. I turned over in bed. I woke you up. Go on, go to sleep, my good friend."

She put her head back on the pillow, snoring very softly.

Through clenched teeth, he muttered: "Yes, he went in. He went in singing, with the knife in his pocket…with the knife…and then…"

He did not finish.

Then…then…

He had lost the track. He felt impotent to divine for what reason, once he had entered the room, the man had murdered the girl who was there. One is drunk, one is cheerful; one sees a pretty young woman beside a bed. One doesn't have any desire to kill her, damn it! On the contrary! You speak to her, smiling, you take her in your arms, or you make her sit down beside you, or on your knees, you caress her hair, her neck, and you start to kiss her, and as she doesn't forbid it, as she is also laughing, as she lets you do anything you want…

"But no! But no!" uttered Brunois, in a contained exclamation. *She didn't let it go—exactly! She wasn't a streetwalker, like the Big Jewess. A domestic or a shop assistant, very young, almost honest…yes honest. That's certain. Eudoxe said that to the magistrate, and Félicie Bonheur said it to the man outside the pharmacy. If that child, very slim and pretty, simply dressed, with modest airs (aha! that's what I said before the second portrait in the dispatch hall!) if that poor kid was in the hotel that evening it's because she had come to see her sister, quite simply…her sister, the Big Jewess, who must have been enraged, and humiliated, to see that girl remaining sage, not going with men, and who must have thought it funny to send her someone.*

Yes, she had sent her someone, the first comer, for a joke, for a laugh—in order that the poor kid would finally be a whore, like the others.

Yes, yes, yes! Brunois continued, with the enthusiasm of a miser gradually unearthing a treasure. *But Félicie Bonheur's sister didn't want to lend herself to the joke. She refused herself, she got annoyed, she didn't want anyone to touch her. Then, lit up by the little girl who escaped from his arms and ran round the room, shouting for help, he no longer knew himself, he went mad. With the wine, the exasperated desire, and his bile, not entirely appeased since his dispute in the restaurant, rising into his throat, into his mouth, into his eyes, like hot alcohol, he grabbed the girl again and she escaped again. He caught up with her near the window.*

"You don't want to?"

"No!"

"You don't want to?"

"No. no! Leave me alone! Help! I'm not what you think. My sister lied to you. Leave me alone. Help! Help!"

And she bit him and stuck her fingernails in his eyes. Then he took the knife from his pocked and he struck Françoise...

Monsieur Brunois stiffened, stupefied.

Françoise?

Why had he said Françoise? Where had the idea sprung from that the victim was named Françoise?

That the murderer knew that name was possible, the Big Jewess might have told him, or the poor child herself. But he, Brunois, how could he suppose it. How did he know that name, which Eudoxe le Marin, in his deposition, had not pronounced?

For a long time, a long time, fearfully, he finally thought about the intuitions that had leapt to mind continually throughout his investigation; and this time, it was a matter of a name, a precise reality, which could not have been concluded from another fact...

But he smiled. We, no, he was not a sorcerer, nor lucid in the fashion of somnambulists. An intelligent, perspicacious man skillful in drawing conclusions from the faintest indications, that was what he was, and nothing more. If he had supposed that name, Françoise, it was because he had read in the newspapers that the underwear of the dead woman was marked with the initials F.B. That dead woman—Bonheur but not Félicie—had to be called Flora, Francine or Françoise. Most likely Françoise, since, not going on the spree, she was in a shop or in service in a bourgeois household.

And he followed, his temples clasped between his fists, his eyes open on the blackness—for the night-light had just gone out—the now-torrential course of his divinations...

The drunken man struck Françoise in the neck and in the breast, with the little pointed knife, which came out again all red. Not yet dead, she advanced toward the window, screamed, howled, broke the glass with her fist, howled, howled, opened the casement and threw herself out, while the murderer, mad, haggard and terrible, ready to kill again if he encountered anyone in his path, ran down the stairs—precisely as Brunois had done the other day—did not go into the street, escaped through the narrow uncovered passage, threw himself into the alley, ran, ran, between the water-sellers' barrels, breathless, sweating, unable to do any more, stopped, out of breath, saw, in a ray of moonlight, blood on his sleeves and his buttons, saw at the same time, at the end of a street, wooden beams, rubble and stones in muddy excavations, a building-site, where a pile of sand in front of an unfinished wall rounded out and hollowed out a kind of crater, where lime was still fuming; took off, or rather tore off his bloody frock-coat, his denunciatory frock-coat, and threw it into the fuming lime, which would burn it, which would suppress it, and plunged it into the lime with rage, with thrusts of his heels...

Brunois was neither a fool nor a madman, and, in sum, he was not overly given to deceiving himself. He understood perfectly that if the suspicion had come to him, at that peaceful hour, lying in his bed, beside his wife, that the murderer, bewildered by his crime, had gone past the building site, had stopped at the pile of sand, and had hidden his bloody coat there, it was because he, Brunois, the other day, had halted in the same place, had been tempted, because of the hat, to take of his coat. Yes, undoubtedly, naturally, it was because of the one that he had imagined the other.

But just because that imagination was the consequence of an event completely independent of the crime itself, it did not imply that it lacked all probability with regard to the crime itself. Quite the contrary.

Why had Brunois fled, after the horror of the glimpsed room, toward the alleyway and not toward the street? In order not to go past the lodge, where the concierge was doubtless on watch. Well, the murderer, not without reasons even more pressing, could have—must have—obeyed the same apprehension.

Why had Brunois, after having run between the water-sellers' barrels, halted in front of the building-site? Because he could do no more, having run out of breath. Well, the murderer too had run out of breath while running, and—respiratory endurance being equal, or every nearly, in all men—he had had to recover his breath in the same place.

Why had Brunois, then, been tempted to take of his garment? Because he was hot, because he was sweating. Well, the murderer too, at that moment, could have been—must have been—hot, and in order to tear off and throw away his frock-coat he had had an additional, frightful reason: the red sleeve and the bloody buttons.

With the consequence that the things that Brunois had experienced and done confirmed the logic of his hypotheses with regard to the emotions, and with regard to the actions, of the murderer! And again, again, still (his temples throbbing between his fists, his eyes aimed into the blackness of the night, already green-tinted by a little morning light), he followed the man, the murderer.

He saw him, in shirt-sleeves, a flying white shadow, drawing away, further away, disappear, reappear, still drawing away, running toward the Wallace fountain, washing his hands there (well, doubtless, since he was on the road, the criminal too had noticed the fountain) and then, calmer, with a hope of salvation, reach the populous quarters, the boulevards, where there were cab-stands, where one could lose oneself, melt into the crowds, be unobserved, not be seen, not be discovered!

But at that point, Brunois' investigative vision stopped. He strove in vain to see more: just a hint of white sleeves, in the distance, in the darkness, in the silence, in the streets, vanishing. Then, the absolute disappearance of everything, the perfect effacement of all beings, all things...he had arrived on the sheer brink of the void.

He retraced his steps.

He clung on to the previously established realities. One, above all, attracted, retained and absorbed him, hypnotizing his mind: the frock-coat.

Yes, the murderer's frock-coat, the frock-coat thrown on the pile of sand, plunged into the fuming lime.

It was so extraordinary (in spite of the aid that he found in the concordance of his own adventure with that of the criminal) and so marvelous that he had divined the murderer tearing off and burying his bloody coat, at the very moment of his escape, that the excess of his merited admiration sometimes made him hesitate to judge himself worthy of it, and he dared not believe, entirely, in such a prodigious clairvoyance.

Oh, anything that one might have wanted, he would have given, in order to be certain that Françoise's murderer had, in fact, thrown his coat there, there, out there...for that certainty, apart from the fact that it would fill him with a legitimate and incomparable pride, would be the confirmation of all the other hypotheses that he had hazarded in the course of his investigation.

Well, why should he not test it?

Undoubtedly, the quicklime—now cold—must have corroded, burned, and swallowed, so to speak, the cloth of the frock-coat...but not entirely; the ashes of the fabric must remain, perhaps shreds, with gray moss, and those remnants even if he had to break his fingernails and wear away his flesh on the hardened lime, he would find...if they existed!

But in the day, people passed by. He would be seen near the pile of sand, advancing his hands, digging his fingers into the cracks. People would be astonished.

The lividity of the morning was trembling in strips—the Venetian blinds were stirring in the wind—over the face of the clock. Four o'clock...

Madame Aurélie was a heavy sleeper; she would not wake up before broad daylight. He had time to go as far as the building site neat the Impasse Saint-Spire.

Without making a sound, very slowly, he extended a leg out of the sheets, stood up, his feet on the bedside rug, groped for his clothes, found them, and began to get dressed, silently, holding his breath.

Wet with rain and livid with the distress of the pre-dawn light, the abandoned building-site, with its scattered, whitening stones, its soil excavated her and there, where shadows lurked, resembled, in the silence and the solitude, a ruined necropolis. The incompleteness of a few standing walls imitated the rigid silhouette of ancient phantoms escaped from graves that remained there, gorgonized by their own horror; the beams, all along their horizontal length, put bridges over the emptiness of sepulchers; the flight of a cat, gliding and disappearing, awoke the fear of some cowardly hyena, a licker of bones after chewed flesh. And between the black clusters of the surrounding houses, the site was like a clearing of desolation and pale mourning

There was a sound of rolling stones under his feet. Bent over, with one hand over his eyes, a dense form, totally black in the pale shadow, Brunois drew nearer. Sometimes, he turned his head, fearful of being followed. What would he have responded to someone surging forth, a night-watchman or a policeman, who had suddenly asked: "What are you doing here?"

But no, on all sides, under the finishing night, there was the desert of a cemetery. The nocturnal prowler kept walking, getting his bearings, knowing where he was going. He saw the pile of sand hollowed out into a sort of low crater. The lime, a dull white in color, displayed a plaster-like crust, cracked in places.

After another backward glance—no one, no, no one had followed him, or was on the lookout for him—Brunois knelt down (the soft and fleeting and came up to his thighs) and, head forward, his fingers in the cracks in the hardened lime, he began searching for the relics of the coat. But the cracks, irregular and bristling with sharp ridges that scratched his skin, were so narrow that he could not insert his whole hand into them. By means of a key that he took out of his pocket, he had to crumble the edges, enlarging the hollows. He finally succeeded in detaching a thin white strip, and beneath it, his fingernails scraped more friable chalk.

But he found nothing: no remnants, no residue of cloth; nothing.

A great sadness took possession of him. What! He had been mistaken in supposing that the murderer had buried his bloody jacket here? But in that case, all his other hypotheses, so patiently and so logically founded on the indications observed with so much subtle zeal, were perhaps also false?

At that thought, an anguish squeezed his heart. It would be horrible if, throughout his scrupulous research and his ingenious deductions, he had followed a false path. What humiliation! What a disappointment! No, it was impossible that he could have been mistaken.

And seized by rage, he broke the mass of chalk, here, there and everywhere, sometimes with his fists and sometimes with the key.

Something soft, light and fluid passed between his fingers. He dug down further with a whole hand, and pulled it out full of a kind of gray scum, almost pulverized. That was the remains of cloth! Yes, yes! It was the remains of the frock-coat buried several days before!

And, having leaned over the widened crack again, he saw, not in the chalky pallor but a little further away to the left, in the sand itself, a black shred, with a button, a piece of the murderer's coat! Then, having taken it in his hand, he stood up on the pile of sand, triumphant and superb, and at the risk of raising the alarm, of making people come to the surrounding windows, he uttered a cry of victory, raising his arms toward the sky.

Brunois' first thought, on waking up, at about nine o'clock in the morning, in the bed to which he had returned, while his wife was still asleep, before broad daylight, was to go immediately to the court, to make the law party to the truly miraculous results of his investigation. Oh, he had proof now! That fragment of cloth, which he had put under his pillow, which he could feel with his hand, was not a chimera; it confirmed all his hypotheses, to the extent of perfect evidence.

He was swollen with pleasure and pride, thinking about the surprise of the examining magistrate, and the praise with which he would be recompensed. And his wife, who had made fun of him in the beginning? It would also be necessary for her to admire him, that she be convinced of his intellectual superiority, of which he had given proof! He had a good mind to tell her right away...

But no.

He would not speak to his wife yet, nor to the examining magistrate.

Certainly, his work, worthy of the highest praise, was almost complete. He had reconstituted all the preliminaries of the crime; he knew the slightest details of the crime, and he even knew the name of the victim...but he did not as yet know that of the murderer.

Although he knew what kind of man he was, he still did not know who he was, or where he was.

In order to merit admiration fully, it was necessary for him to learn that. He would learn it!

Scarcely had he got up that he shut himself in the drawing room, to the great astonishment of his wife, who said to herself: *But after all, what's the matter with him? For a few days he was tranquil, now, his anxieties have got hold of him again. What can be wrong with him?*

She looked through the keyhole, and saw that he was writing.

In fact, he was drafting a report, in which he related scrupulously all the circumstances of his investigation. That labor took him no less than two hours. When the last line was written he put the sheets of paper in his pocket, asked for lunch, ate very rapidly, without speaking to Madame Aurélie—who, astonished and also intimidated, dared not breathe a word, and gazed at him open-mouthed—and then he went out, without saying where he was going.

He went to the Rue des Filles-Dieu.

He was not unaware of the imprudent but urgent instinct that impels criminals to haunt the scene of their crime or its surrounding area. Thus, he would install himself in a café or liquor shop near to number 56 and observe the passers-by, and certainly—so clear an idea did he have of the man who must be the murderer, he would not fail to recognize him if he chanced to roam in that direction.

He remembered, in fact, that there was a red-painted drinking den, at a street corner facing the hotel, with a large counter where the distillation apparatus resembled the spilled entrails of a copper dragon, and that the scarlet façade had mirrors in which the sidewalk, the roadway and the passers-by were reflected.

Brunois took his placed before a small round table inside the shop, near the door, asked for a glass of Madeira, and waited, his eyes fixed on the hotel on the other side of the street.

The first afternoon passed without incident. The owner of the drinking den, after being astonished by his obstinate presence, no longer took any account of it, doubtless supposing that he was some agent of morality keeping watch on the local prostitutes, and thus of no importance.

For one moment, Brunois' attention was attracted by a rather poorly-dressed man with a ferrety face and an unkempt beard, a bowler hat and a dirty coat, who went past number 56 two or three times, not without darting sly glances toward the drinking den. That person with the sly and mean face was not unknown to Brunois, but he surely could not be the murderer. No, no, the murderer was quite different: a worthy bourgeois, slightly plump and well-to-do.

Six o'clock chimed. The day had not been good, and the observer withdrew, rather sullen.

But the next day he came back, and did so every day for a week, without result.

No one went past in the street resembling the image that Brunois had formed of the murderer.

Toward the end of the eighth afternoon, and idea occurred to him that he should have thought of sooner. If the guilty party were prowling the surrounding area, he must have had a desire, in order to see the sordid house that he had bloodied, to go into the drinking den, but the presence of a stranger placed near the door and on watch was bound to make him anxious and drive him away. Brunois realized that his observation post was worthless, and resolved to find another, more distant and more mysterious, and isolated.

He paid his bill, got up, opened the door, crossed the road diagonally and turned round because of the sound of rapid footsteps, the footsteps of someone running...and in one of the large mirrors in the red façade the profile, the fleeting reflection of a man...a man, yes, who was, yes, yes indeed, the murderer!

Oh, Brunois was certain that he was not mistaken. That man, who had appeared in the mirror and disappeared, was the murder himself, and he ran toward the liquor store into which the man, after having passed the mirrors, must have gone.

No, the drinking den was empty. Well, yes, doubtless the man, on the contrary, had turned the corner and gone into the side street. Brunois launched himself in that direction, but the side street was empty. What! The guilty man had escaped? Full of anger, Brunois stamped his foot and bit his fingers, alone, all alone...

But at least he had seen the murderer, and although his reflection had vanished quickly, the observer had remarked all his features, his whole appearance, down to the slightest details—yes, down to the slightest details—and he went home rapidly in order to add to his report, already so scrupulous and so convincing, the description of the criminal.

On Monday 15 September 188 , at eleven o'clock in the morning, Monsieur Brunois went into the courtyard of the Palais de Justice, asked for directions from the guard standing near the gate, turned left, and went up a broad stairway that turned at a right angle. Dignified, even a little arrogant, Brunois appeared perfectly content. Evidently, he strove to maintain a grave expression and a moderate demeanor, as is befitting when one is carrying out a serious mission, but his intimate joy was betrayed by the gleam in his eyes and the smug opening of his mouth. He went up, looking straight ahead; he did not perceive that a man with a mean face, an unkempt beard and a dirty coat was following him, with an astonished expression.

He arrived in the wide corridor where witnesses were sitting on wooden benches between the doors of the examining magistrates. He approached a uniformed employee standing behind a kind of pulpit.

"Monsieur Legrandin, examining magistrate?" he asked.

"Do you have a citation?"

"No. Here's my card." He handed over his card and added: "You can say that I've come about the affair of the Rue des Filles-Dieu."

There was almost majesty in Brunois' gesture and tone.

"Very good, Monsieur," said the employee. He traversed the corridor, disappeared, and came back almost immediately.

At that moment, Brunois was so convinced of his importance that he was not astonished to be received right away, even though he was not expected. All doors ought to open without delay before a man who had come to aid the law to punish a crime.

He went in.

He bowed with a slightly condescending politeness to the magistrate, who had stood up, and the clerk, who did not budge. He did not notice that Monsieur Legrandin's face revealed the most profound astonishment; nor did he notice that he was not invited to sit down.

"Monsieur," said the magistrate, "you have come...you..."

"I have come," said Brunois, "to bring you the most complete and decisive information regarding the crime of the Rue des Filles-Dieu."

Slowly, he took the papers from his pocket, unfolded them, and in a loud and clear, magisterial voice, he commenced reading his report while Monsieur Legrandin and the clerk exchanged amazed glances.

The report related, with many details: the dinner of the future assassin at the restaurant with a friend; the drunkenness, the argument, the dispute, the knife taken away; the promenade past the still-illuminated shops; the encounter with Félicie Bonheur in the Rue des Filles-Dieu in an obscure corner; he advice given by her to go to the hotel at number 56, room 13, where he would find a young woman, her own sister, named Francoise Bonheur; the departure of Félicie—if she had not reappeared since the crime it was doubtless because, having been the cause of it, she feared being held responsible[20]—the arrival of the murderer at the hotel, the climbing of

---

[20] This tentative and unsatisfactory explanation leaves several questions unanswered. If Félicie left the murderer in order to go and meet Eudoxe, why did she not do so? Surely she cannot have found out about the murder until after the time when she would have found him—which, according to his statement she did not do; and even if she had heard about the murder so quickly, how could she simply disappear, untraceably? Surely Eudoxe must have lying when he said that she had not found him, and perhaps the reason he laughed so uproariously when the police accused him of murdering Félicie at ten o'clock in

the stairway with a song on his lips; the entry to the room; the resistance of Françoise Bonheur; the violent altercation; the three wounds, one in the neck and two in the breast; the dying woman opening the window and throwing herself into the street; the flight of the murderer via the Impasse Saint-Spire; the bloody frock-coat hidden in the quicklime…

At that point, Brunois ceased reading; he took from his fob pocket a small piece of black cloth on which there was a button, and said: "A frock-coat of which this was the sole fragment that I was able to recover."

And he looked triumphantly at the magistrate and the clerk: the law, served and vanquished by him.

After a moment of silence, employed in looking at the man who had spoken, Monsieur Legrandin said: "Yes, yes, indeed, the majority of the facts that you relate are confirmed by the investigation…"

Brunois made a grimace. He had not read the newspapers for many days; after having erred for a long time, the police had found the right track, then? That was annoying.

But the magistrate added: "And several facts, unknown until today, which you have revealed to us, are entirely plausible."

Brunois relaxed. So the value of his information was recognized. That was less than he had hoped for, but it was something.

And he smiled.

"But," said the judge, "do you have precise information regarding the murderer himself? Do you know his name?"

Brunois was still smiling.

"His name? I confess that I don't know his name. But I have his description, as complete and as exact as possible."

"His description?"

"Yes, Monsieur le juge."

---

the Rue des Filles-Dieu was because he had actually murdered her at half past ten, in a much more discreet location, where he could dispose of the body undetectably….

And, his face expansive with victory, Brunois, without having any need to read it, because he knew his whole report by heart, said:

"The murderer is a man of about forty-four or forty-five years of age; he is rather stout without being obese; he is dressed without extreme elegance, but very correctly, in a black frock-coat; his coiffure is a top hat. He is gray-haired, with prominent, very large blue-eyes, and thick lips; his entire manner respires mildness and benevolence, the calm of a settled and honest life. One identifying mark: near the left nostril he has a birthmark, or rather a wart, with rather thick hairs…"

Then abruptly, the magistrate said:

"But, wretch, that description is your own."

"Mine?"

"And the murderer is you."

"Me!"

Brunois would have fallen on the floor if, tottering, he had not bumped into a chair, on which he sat down, his arms limp.

And he stayed there, his face stupid, his eyes mad.

He understood. He understood.

A room endowed with life, absolutely black, which was suddenly illuminated with an intense light, and revealing itself, entire, with everything there was within it: that was what Brunois' soul resembled after the magistrate's words, frightfully revelatory.

Everything, everything: he understood everything. It was him who had committed the crime! Yes, he had committed it, drunk, after the dinner with Richond; then he had forgotten it, forgotten it totally. No, not totally, since, without knowing why, he had interested himself in the Rue des Filles-Dieu affair. And during his investigation, what he had taken for discoveries of his subtlety were only unconscious reminiscences of the details of his crime, the details of his flight, and, finally, it was from his own image, glimpsed in the mirror of the drinking den, that he had traced the description of the murderer!

Then, suddenly—while, the magistrate having rung, a municipal guardsman came in followed by the badly-dressed agent with the unkempt beard—Brunois dissolved in tears, desperately.

Poor fellow, so mild, so good, full of horror of himself, he thought about his wife and the Court of Assizes, and the judgment, and the scaffold; and he wept, and wept, with great sobs, not daring to hope that the indulgence of the jury would spare him death or convict prison…an indulgence from which he benefited however, thanks to the report of the expert physician—who concluded that the murderer was not responsible for his actions, less because of his state of drunkenness on the evening of the crime, but because of the state of mind that later obliged him to be his own spy and delator—and thanks to the speech for the defense of Maître Flor Delestang: an admirable speech, a trifle marred by pedantry, since the orator, several times, labeled his client "the Heautonparateroumene."

A Village, Near the Road...

I have already tried to write this story—and by "story" I do not mean "work of fiction"—twenty times over, and twenty times the unexpected jealous emergence of another idea, or the interruption of work by some visit, or some other cause, prevented me from completing my design. Added to certain circumstances not without analogy to them, which I shall mention in due course, the frequency of these contretemps has not failed to induce me to suppose, at times, that a mysterious will, under the probability of various pretexts, is opposed to these matters being known.

An absurd hypothesis, evidently. What will? It could only be superhuman, since it disposes of hazard, and what means is there of believing, without being mad, that a being or beings superior in essence to humankind has some interest in maintaining, if not secret, at least only known to a small number, a fact—yes, a fact, unless, for a duration of an hour, eight supposedly sane people were possessed by a common and identical dementia—in which there is no great strangeness or solemnity to be found, and of which an extraordinary implausibility does not suffice to heighten the mediocrity or the puerile fertility?

But then, why were none of those who, one evening, saw and touched the fact, able, or daring enough, to establish its reality or its chimerical nature by means of a second proof? Why did they all avoid talking to one another about it, the next day or later—much later—during the twenty-three years that have elapsed since that evening? Why am I certain that I am going to disquiet them and darken the depths of the soul by reminding them of an adventure that caused them so much hilarity at first and made them faint with irresistible laughter? Why, if I invoke their testimony, do they try to avoid the issue, stammering, with a smile that does not say yes or no, as when someone mentions something that, although doubtless veritable and of no great importance, is better left unmentioned? And why have I never been able to put this anecdote—for it is nothing more than that—on paper? And why, even today, having already traced fifty lines, can I not swear that I will go on until the end?

I shall write quickly, without literary artifice, without getting up from the table for a cigar or to glace at my favorite trinket, and without rereading my work, like a traveler hastening because the route is not sure.

It was in Munich, before the war. It was about nine o'clock in the evening, perhaps a little later, certainly not yet ten o'clock. We were coming out of a theater where Richard Wagner's *Die Walküre* had just been performed for the first time.[21] As I have said, we formed a group of eight: a French composer, already illustrious; a magistrate recently initiated

---

[21] The first performance of *Die Walküre*, at the Königliches Hof- und National Theater in Munich, was on 26 June 1870 (less than a month before the outbreak of the Franco-Prussian War), at the insistence of Wagner's patron, Ludwig II of Bavaria; the composer would have preferred to wait until he had completed the entire Ring cycle, which was first presented in full in 1876. Wagner had worked on the opera extensively in 1868, while he was resident in Lucerne, where Mendès and Villiers de l'Isle Adam were both staying at the time. Mendès, who was 28 when the Munich première took place, was present, as was his then-wife Judith (Théophile Gautier's daughter), although the two had already separated, and she is unlikely to be the "musicienne" featured in the story; the latter might be Augusta Holmes, with whom Mendès had a child—the first of five—in 1871. As well as Villiers de l'Isle Adam, the French party at the première included the composers Camille Saint-Saëns and Henri Duparc, and the writer Edouard Schuré, later to become a significant figure in the French Occult Revival.

into musical drama, of which he had become an enthusiastic apostle; an admirable musicienne, one of the purest and highest glories of the French school; a Hungarian choirmaster who was to become illustrious directing the *meistersingers* at Bayreuth; an Austrian dilettante, a friend of Wagner who had soon become ours; the great and subtle Villiers de l'Isle Adam; another French poet of lesser importance; and, of even less, me.

Take note that we had dined before going to the theater—which is to say, four hours previously—so it is necessary to set aside the idea that a few glasses of Rhenish or Hungarian wine predisposed us easily to admitting the marvelous. Our only overexcitement originated from the sublime drama that we had just heard; it was fortunate, healthy, serene and lucid. In order to talk about the Wagnerian masterpiece far from the noise we decided not to go into the Opera Café near the theater yet, where we were accustomed to have supper, and we followed the broad and long Maximilienstrasse, where silence had already fallen between the luminous tumult of taverns.

At the extremity of the street a broad bridge crossed, with great arches, the almost dry river, where rare pools of mud scarcely streamed between islets of sand. Under the first arch, a dike retained the water, making a channel whose current hastened and gleamed. We went on to the bridge, chatting loquaciously, enthusiastically and joyously, going toward the monument on the other bank, then incomplete, made of pink granite if my memory serves me right, which gave the impression of a smiling ruin traversed by moonlight.

Now, something happened n that bridge: something comical and extraordinary. It was what might be called a farcical miracle. And why, in fact, should the supernatural not be comical sometimes? Why should the impossible not like to laugh? And why, because it is droll, should a marvel be any less marvelous and less frightening? But humans are borne to believe that prodigy never loses its seriousness, and what is amusing is scarcely frightening.

However, a frisson ran down my spine because of what happened on the bridge; I believed that I remarked, under the street-lamp, that more than one of my companions had an anxious smile on their lips...

A gust of wind had blown away the hat—a top hat—of the French composer, who was then walking beside me, very cheerful and very loquacious. In those days the great artiste, nowadays sober, was still subject to youthful exuberances, like the sudden joys of a schoolboy escaping from class. He laughed heartily at his headgear, flying into the air, doubtless to fall far away, and while we were diverting ourselves similarly by virtue of the petty incident, he said: "Wait! Wait!"

He had spotted, in an opening in the parapet, a narrow stone stairway that descended toward the almost dry bed of the river.

"I'm going to look for my hat!"

He disappeared. We waited for him, still laughing, the conversation already resuming.

A man who had doubtless climbed another stairway on the other sidewalk of the bridge approached us and offered us something round and black, which we could not quite make out at first in the semi-darkness.

"Messieurs," he said to us, in French, "here is the hat."

Good. It was a lock-keeper, or a bridge guard who, happening to be there, had seen our friend's hat fly away in the wind and had hastened to go in search of it, in the hope of a small tip. No: he went away without asking for anything, after bowing to us very politely.

It was to me that he had handed the top hat. I shouted to the composer, who ought to have been paddling in the mud: "Come back! Come back up! We have your..."

I did not have time to finish. Our friend had just reappeared. Seven cries of amazement greeted him, for he had his hat on his head. Yes, his hat was on his head, found, he told us, near a pile of the arch, stained with mud, but, in sum, his hat.

And as I raised my arms, full of amazement, another gust of wind carried away the other hat—we never knew where—

that I had in my hand, which the vanished passer-by had brought us.

Certainly, it could be—chance coincidences are innumerable—that two top hats might have been on the river bed at the same time, that an obliging stranger had picked one up and given it to us while our friend was picking up the other. Nevertheless, it is necessary to agree that in that coincidence there was something resembling a prodigy, and that, if what was grotesque in the incident—perhaps less than an instinctive desire not to get to the bottom of things, for every soul carries within it a fear of mystery—had not induced a fit of mad laughter in us, I think that even the most skeptical among us would have been unable to help bring singularly disturbed.

Personally, I have always thought that that small miracle—explicable, but surprising all the same—had been offered to us by fate, or something akin to it, in order to prepare our souls for the far more extraordinary adventure that was reserved for that evening, in order to put us in a state to endure the thing, the other thing, also comical, stupid and puerile, but incontestably marvelous, which, for twenty-three years, we have not been able to remember without shivering, of which none of us has been able, or has dared, to establish the reality or chimerical nature—the thing that it has never before been possible for me to write.

I want to; I shall write it, and I affirm that I shall tell the truth, the whole truth, and nothing but the truth; and the people who were there, who saw it, and touched it, as I did, will not belie me...

Still laughing, slightly nervously, we had reached the other end of the bridge. We turned left. We went along the bank of the almost-waterless river, whose rare muddy puddles gleamed in the moonlight. Having almost forgotten the adventure of the two hats, we were praising in ardent terms, with surges of enthusiasm and amour, the incomparable masterpiece that we had just heard, and with which we were still vibrant.

The beautiful musicienne whom we had the honor of accompanying sang in the starlight the ferocious and strident appeal of the Valkyries riding the crimson and gold of the clouds. But suddenly, one of us, the French composer...

Someone has rung! Who has rung? Oh, yes, seven o'clock already; it's the comrades arriving who are dining with me this evening. I have to receive them, to stop working. Once again, it's impossible for me to write this story! Why? Oh, why? However, yes, it's necessary; I want to; I shall write it tomorrow, or the day after, if I can...

I said that I would write the end of this story and I shall. Not without difficulty. The impending storm is weighing on my skull. Behind the skin of my temples, where the veins are swollen, the little blacksmiths of a migraine are hammering, hammering, hammering the anvil with the ponderousness of cyclopes and the briskness of flies moving their feet. It seems to me that my head is about to fall on the table, fall, turn over, roll, go toward the window, bounce on to the pavement of the street. How nice it would be to lie down, the nape of my neck on the pillow, my eyes half-closed against the light, mouth open to a few fresh perfumes, or, at least, to relate, without thinking about it, almost with an amiable nonchalance, some futile tale, not wearisome for me or for you. But I promised to accomplish my design. I shall say what happened near the roads along the waterless river...

Oh, I don't want to believe that this heaviness in my forehead, and the fever of my hand, in which the pen is trembling, and this fearful anxiety before the blank page, going on, going on, are produced by a mysterious will, by a will that is opposing the divulgation of the fact that we saw, that evening, that we touched, that evening...

I've already affirmed that I don't believe in the existence of that will, and I affirm it again.

I ask you, what can it matter to superhuman powers whether an anecdote, so futile and devoid of real interest, is related or not? However, at this time of day I am usually very well, with my mind clear and my hand firm. It's singular that today, and precisely at the moment when I'm recommencing the promised story, such a languor should invade me, and that the blacksmiths of the migraine are beating the anvil behind the skin of my temples, and that I'm so desirous of not working, of not thinking, of going to sleep...

I shall write. And I've taken every precaution not to be interrupted. The two doors of my room are double-locked. My domestic has received the order not to open the door of anyone rings. There are enough cigars in the drawer of the Japanese box for the desire to smoke not to furnish me with the pretext for a derangement. Matches? Yes, within arm's reach, next to the inkwell. I shall write. I want to. I shall write.

I'm writing.

Where was I? I no longer remember. Ordinarily, however, my memory, of which I'm justly proud, is very reliable, very prompt. It happens that I'm able, the day after quitting a piece of work unexpectedly, to finish a sentence without rereading the beginning. But today, I don't remember.

Ah! Last week's article is on the piano.[22] I've kept it; I put it on the piano, beside the table. I thought I might have need of it. I only have to reach out my arm. I don't reach out. See how one let's oneself go, sometimes, to childishness! A gesture would suffice; I don't make that gesture. Why? Because I'm afraid that that *Écho de Paris*, there, close at hand, might not be the one I need. I might be, yes, it might be that it's the *Écho de Paris* of another day.

What would that prove? Nothing, assuredly, or very little: that I'm mistaken, that I've misread the date of the issue, that my eyes thought that I saw the title of my article in a place where it wasn't. One commits these errors every day, even when one is very attentive, even when one takes, as I

---

[22] As literary editor of the *Écho de Paris* Mendès was responsible for the newspaper's weekly literary supplement, in which the present story appeared in three sections, this passage being the beginning of the second.

have, all precautions not to make a mistake. And it wouldn't prove that, for the newspaper in which I began this story, another had been substituted by some ever-alert malice. No, certainly, it wouldn't prove that...and I'm going to reach out, take that paper, and reread...

There's no need. I remember now.

We had crossed the bridge, where we had been so amused by the adventure of the two hats. Pure coincidence, anyway, that adventure. A coincidence, wasn't it, and nothing more? These things happen every day, which surprise us at first and make us say: "All the same, that's truly extraordinary!" But afterwards, when one reflects, one finds the thing that had seemed very strange at first quite natural. And I'm almost ashamed to have recounted such a silly thing. Anyway, believe that we didn't attach any more importance to it than it merited. In reality, it simply appeared comical to us, and it's necessary to admit that it was, in fact. Think about it: two top hats on the bed of a waterless river at the same time! Even for a vaudeville, it would be too implausible. But it was only a funny coincidence. We were already thinking about something else.

For my part, I can assure you that I was thinking about something else, or at least I was trying hard to think about something else. The admirable voice of the musicienne that we had the honor of accompanying was launching the vibrant appeal of the Valkyries to the echoes! And over the long road, over the river where the black puddles were gleaming, over the city, over the plain in the bare and pale distance, hung a nocturnal peace, like the outspread wings of an immense transparent blue bird, through which the stars were visible.

For a few moments, the French composer—it's because of him, most of all, that I've hesitated so long to write this story; I know how his great dreamer's soul shivers at the breath of mystery![23]—had been walking a little ahead of our group; for an instant, we lost sight of him in the semi-darkness, and, searching for him with my eyes, I was tempted to think that he had turned back toward the city, when a burst of laughter, and another burst of laughter, and another, and another—we recognized the voice—rang out furiously in the silence.

Where was our friend? What was he laughing at in that fashion, and laughing again, and still laughing? We hurried on. Finally, we saw him. His hands on a parapet of unpainted wood, not on the side of the river but on the side of the plain that extended at a lower level than the road, rather profoundly, he was agitating, leaping, writhing, laughing, laughing, laughing...and his laughter, sometimes dull, sometimes shrill, sometimes prolonged and sustained, sometimes broken up into roulades and trills, resembled the never-ending climactic note of a Paganini gripped by madness.

"Well? Well? What? What is it? What is, it, then? What are you looking at down there? Why are you laughing?"

One of us—it was Villiers de l'Isle Adam, I think—asked...perhaps he was wrong to ask it; I don't know why I thought he was wrong, but I thought immediately that he was wrong, all the more so as his voice seemed unnatural, not as light-hearted or as indifferent as it ought to have been: "Is there a third hat?"

The more I think about it, there more I think that there was to need to say that, at that moment...

But we had joined the musician, and already, like him, we were writhing with laughter. That was also because, truly, it was impossible to see anything more astonishing, more comical, or crazier.

Imagine!

---

[23] In 1870 Saint-Saëns had yet to write his famous *Danse macabre* (1874) but he was already working on the music for the Faustian lyric drama *Le Timbre d'argent* [The Silver Bell], although it was not produced until 1877.

Below the road, four or five meters from the wooden parapet, under the sky full of stars, in the pale solitary plain, little houses were spaced out, almost as far as the eye could see, little houses no bigger than dog kennels, little gardens no bigger than a napkin, little churches three feet high—on the bell-tower of one, which my cane would have surpassed, I noticed a cock no bigger than a tiny sparrow—little stables, little sheds, little farms, little cottages, little barns, a deserted village, absolutely deserted, a Lilliputian village, miraculous and real.

It was so prodigiously funny, all those little buildings as far as the eye could see, in the perfect solitude, that we held our sides, that we uttered cries, that we leapt, that we danced, out of breath, until we could do no more, by virtue of laughing.

But it was quite something else a moment later.

The composer had discovered a narrow stairway of sticks, more ladder than staircase, that descended toward the plain. He set forth on it, we followed him, tumultuously, still laughing, and through that little village we went, like a crazy band of schoolchildren. We stepped over garden walls, we leapt over gates with our feet together, and we sat down, as if on a low bench, on the thatch or slate of roofs. The windows didn't come up to our knees. I nearly twisted my ankle when I stumbled over the porch of a chapel.

"Here! Here! Come on! Come on, then! Come and see!"

We were all calling to one another, each wanting to show the others some new marvel of infinite smallness. The magistrate had discovered a Stadthaus whose portal wouldn't have been sufficient for the appearance of a cuckoo. The Austrian dilettante was astounded by pig-sties into which mice would have had difficulty sticking their noses. Small as her feet were, the beautiful musicienne could only put one at a time in the driveway of a park only spacious enough for the blooming of a single dwarf rose-bush. Around little flower-beds there were little circuits of box-hedges. On his knees before a church, the Hungarian choirmaster nearly broke the rose-window of the façade with the amulets on his watch-chain. I knocked with the toe of my boot, without lifting it very high, on the door of an elegant villa. The composer, bending down as far as he could, went "Ooh! Ooh!" into the chimney of a small building that came up to his hip. That building was the village monument! And all eight of us, leaping, gamboling, running, shouting, here, there and everywhere, our joyous stupefaction, exasperated to the point of making us feel ill, confused the desert silence of the night with our bursts of laughter.

We stopped laughing. At a casement—a casement, to tell the truth, a little higher than most of the other windows—a light had appeared, the light of a candle or a lamp, behind a curtain, and a white form that seemed to be moving…

But the laughter took hold of us again, more impetuous, more imperious, more furious, and so intense, so urgent, so uncontrollable, and also so legitimate, was our gaiety that now, here at my table, writing, peacefully, the mere memory of it obliges me to laugh, to laugh, to laugh again, to writhe with laugher!

Truly, I can't continue this article. The pen is crushed by the shaking of my hand. I'm going to walk around the room, in order to recover. I'll finish it later.

I've pulled myself together. However, today, once again, I can't finish the story. I'm no longer laughing. I'm calm. But the spasms have redoubled by migraine. How they're beating the anvil, behind the skin of my temples, the blacksmiths of the migraine! That's why I've stopped writing, and for that reason alone. Don't think that I'm afraid of continuing this comical, ludicrous, puerile story. Why would I be afraid of continuing?

And if I'm stopping, it's not because of what happened while I was going back and forth in the room. For something happened. Oh, nothing very astonishing. Another coincidence, a simple coincidence. You can judge for yourselves: nothing but a coincidence.

One of those who was with us that evening has departed from life, as you're not unaware. His present abode is the unknown region where one knows everything, and the reason for things. I loved him; I admired him. There is therefore nothing extraordinary in the fact that one of his books, open, happened to be on the corner of the mantelpiece. To tell the truth, I don't remember having taken that book from my bookcase recently. I would gladly have bet that I hadn't touched it for two or three months. It was up there on the third shelf of the bookshelf, between Edgar Poe and Jean-Paul Richter. But I would have lost my bet, since it was there, open. And certainly, it was me who had put it there, for, if not me, who could have done it?

In sum, there is nothing extraordinary in a book being on a corner of a mantelpiece; it is quite natural, too, that my eyes, while I was walking back and forth in the room in order not to laugh any longer, should have fallen on the offered page, and that they read a few words. Undoubtedly, I might have been astonished at first, before having reflected, that the words in question, a fragment of dialogue in I know not what tale,[24] were these:

"Dear, dear, leave, leave that alone..."

But that has nothing to do with the fact that I've stopped wiring today. I didn't see that line as the advice of a friend departed for the country where one knows things. I've interrupted myself because I'm tired, because the migraine is laboring me horribly. That's all. And I'll finish my story soon. The day after tomorrow. Not the day after tomorrow. The day after tomorrow I'm writing poetry. But soon, next week. Yes, I'll finish my story next week, certainly.

---

[24] The fragment, as cited here, is not traceable in Villiers' *Contes cruels* (1883), although that is presumably the volume to which reference is intended. Villiers died in 1889, four years before the appearance of the present story in the *Écho de Paris*.

This time, I'll finish my story. Yes, whatever happens, I'll finish it. To tell the truth, just now, I was hesitating, I was on the point of telling you another amusing tale, slightly foolish, at which you would have smiled. And how can it interest you that there was a Lilliputian village in the plain, in the moonlight, that evening? But the scruple that the fear of boring you with this little story, which is even sillier than odd, might only be a pretext, a ruse of my cowardly obedience to not continuing it, obliges me to follow my design. I'll finish...

Anyway, there isn't much left for me to tell. I could do it in a few lines. And I won't think about it anymore. I don't know why I sense that I'll be very content, as content as after a perilous task, when I've finished, when I won't think about it any more...

I've said that in the midst of the little buildings, the laughter had taken hold of us again, more impetuous, more imperious, more furious, and, even more wildly, we were running and gamboling between the houses, over the walls, over the roofs. But that the casement a little higher than the other windows, a light reappeared, the light of a candle or a lamp, behind a curtain, and for the second time, a white form seemed to pass: the very slow passage of a being.

Mouth open, eyes staring, feet nailed to the ground, in the immobility of a man suddenly petrified, I gazed at that light, that form. As I no longer heard and laughter or any sound nearby, it's probable that my companions, no less stupefied, no less immobile, were also gazing at it.

And the being (what being? Something resembling a nightcap surrounding the pallor of a vague face) disappeared, came back, disappeared again, came back again; doubtless it was moving back and forth, holding up a lamp, from one wall to the other, inside the house. But when it reappeared the third time, it stood still, as if it had perceived us, as if it too were observing us intently.

Then I heard noises close by, but not laughter: the sound of labored, hoarse breathing, torn, one might have thought, from the lungs, almost gasps, sometimes the shrill rise of a plaint, as when one is afraid, as when one of horrible afraid, as when one is dying of fear. Aha! They were afraid too, then, my companions, to whom I dared not address a word, toward whom I dared not turn my head? They too, rigid and cold, mutated into statues of ice, were subject to the unshakable horror of a fear never experienced before.

The living thing, the being that was standing behind the blanched curtain of the casement, remained still for a long time; then, with a slow gesture, a gesture that advanced the lamp, it opened the window, and an arm, clutching the light, an arm from which a pale piece of cloth hung down, extended toward us, in a circular movement, as if with an order to go away...

How did it happen that, all launching ourselves simultaneously toward the stairway of sticks, more ladder than staircase, jostling one another, shoving one another, we managed to get back to the road on the river bank so rapidly? In less than a few seconds we reached the parapet of unpainted wood; and all eight of us, at a rapid pace, marched toward the city. We didn't speak to one another. We didn't look at one another.

What thoughts haunted my friends? Were they still afraid? If they were hastening in that fashion, without wasting time in an unnecessary glance or a vain word, was it because it was a matter for them, above all, of getting as far away as possible from the plain where the little village was laid out, where a pale gesture had opened a window? For myself, a cold sweat on my temples, a cold sweat on my back, sometimes shaken from head to foot by a convulsive frisson, without thinking, without daring to think, I drank in avidly with my eyes, with my entire being, the city, the city with its large houses, luminous, inhabited, the city devoid of chimeras, the habitual abode of the possible.

Having crossed the bridge—the bridge where we had been so amused by the coincidence of the two hats—we went along the Maximilienstrasse. Veritably, I began to pull myself together. I began to march less rapidly. I breathed more easily. The gaiety of the noisy, song-filled taverns, the flamboyance of a few shops that were still open, brought me back from the extraordinary, the phantasmal, into the ordinary and simple life. My fear, which persisted for a long time, was succeeded by the curiosity to discover the natural cause.

You can imagine that, calm and serene again, I was far from believing that there was anything truly miraculous in the real existence or the illusory vision of the little village on the edge of the road, inhabited by a single being. Surely, the mystery that had excited us must have, like so many things that seem singular at first, some natural explanation, which we would discover without difficulty, or with which anyone could furnish us.

My companions evidently had the same thought as me. Their pace had slowed at the same time as mine; they were looking at one another; they were smiling; they would not take long to speak, I divined, about the thing that had frightened us so much, after having made us laugh excessively; and it was without visible embarrassment, even with the tone of irony, scarcely affected, by means of which one commences to take revenge, so to speak, on the extraordinary, on the humiliation, that the Austrian dilettante hazarded: "Yes, yes, it's funny, very funny. But you see, we were all overexcited by the music, and it might be..."

To tell the truth, the opinion that eight people, at the same moment, could have been dupes of the same hallucination, did not get much support. Generally, there was agreement on the point that we really had seen, seen and touched, the little houses, the little churches and the littler farms. That astonishing village existed! And it existed naturally. The magistrate, a precise intellect, emitted the opinion that perhaps a breeder of animals...

"Of very tiny animals, then?" objected Villiers de l'Isle Adam.

...had, by some caprice, prepared for the animals lodgings resembling miniature human habitations. There was some plausibility in that hypothesis, which satisfied, for want of anything better, or seemed to satisfy, two or three of us.

But the French composer shook his head. "You haven't got it," he said, "and I've divined the enigma. That singular hamlet, quite simply, must be the result of one of the hundred fantasies of Ludwig of Bavaria. A little extravagant, in spite of his very reasonable and very admirable passion for musical drama, he's had a miniature Lilliputian town built, as he might have given the order to construct, in order to marvel the eyes, a colossal Brobdingnagian village!"

A sigh of satisfaction escaped our breasts.

Good! That explained things neatly. There was nothing fantastic in our adventure. And the being that appeared at the window a little higher and a little larger than the others was some guardian of the village who, disturbed by our laughter and our antics, had made us a sign to go away. In truth, it was absurd that we had not found such a simple and plausible explanation immediately.

We no longer conserved any doubt...no, none...even though it was rather surprising that, having stayed for more than a month in Munich, we had never heard mention of such an extraordinary fantasy on the part of the king...

No matter, there was no doubt; and when we went into the Opera Café, where we were accustomed to have supper, we were convinced that anyone we encountered, as soon as they were interrogated, would respond in such a fashion as to confirm the French composer's hypothesis fully.

We were as disappointed as one can be.

As soon as we had commenced questioning, a Bavarian musician who knew us slightly and was sitting at the table next to ours, looked at us with an expression that was alternately bewildered and annoyed, as if he had imagined, successively, that we were mad, or that we were making fun of him. I persisted; I described, as best I could, the things we had seen; I recounted our laughter, I confessed our fear...

The musician got up and gave the order to have his glass taken to another table, at the back of the café.

"He didn't understand you," said the choirmaster, "because you speak German poorly and he doesn't understand French."

At that moment, Ottilia, a beautiful waitress in the restaurant, accustomed to foreigners, brought the plates and napkins for our supper. Ordinarily, she understood us, and obligingly spoke our language as best she could. I asked her if she knew about the little village near the road that the king had probably had built. She burst out laughing, laughed again, and all that we could obtain from her was: "My God! My God! How funny these Frenchmen are!"

Other attempts to obtain information had analogous results. No one knew that the king had had the fantasy of a Lilliputian village; no one appeared to know about that village so close to the city. Only one old man, the first alto at the Royal Theater, very mild, with soft, benevolent eyes, who was generally held to be an arrant drunkard, accorded us a slightly sustained attention. For a moment we thought he was about to inform us, but, his eyes becoming softer and his head nodding, he said "Oh, my children, my children!" and he left the room very rapidly, as if we had frightened him.

Then we ceased to seek information, and, with our eyes lowered toward our plates, isolated, anxious and nervous, in the tumult of the restaurant—it seemed to us that people were looking at us strangely—we finished our supper in silence...

Well, wasn't it necessary, the next day, as soon as it was daylight, to return to the road, to find the little houses again, or not to find them, to establish their existence, or our illusion; and if they did exist, in fact, to interrogate passers-by in order to clarify everything, to address ourselves to the "being" who had ordered us to leave from the window?

Yes, it was necessary to do that.

But we didn't do it

None of us—not one you hear—accomplished the simple, the facile action of crossing the bridge and following the road. Why not? I don't know. I assure you that I don't know.

Were my companions prevented by more pressing concerns, or were they haunted by some apprehension of what had been so strange by night, simultaneously so comical and so terrible, might be in the lucid light? At any rate, they all quit Munich without retracing the route that we had taken together after the first performance of *Die Walküre*.

As for myself, it wasn't dread; no, certainly, it wasn't dread—what dread could I have had, I ask you?—that turned me away from such an easy stroll. But the next day, I had to write an account of the Wagnerian work; that labor absorbed all my time. In the following days, my time was taken up by visits, and suddenly, a telegram obliged me to return to France.

It is true that, ten years ago, when I returned to Munich, I could have gone to the plain where we had seen the Lilliputian village; I will even say that the desire finally to inform myself regarding that extraordinary reality or chimera was one of the motives for my further sojourn in the capital of Bavaria; but I did not have the leisure to satisfy my curiosity; no, I did not have the time.

For what reason? I've forgotten; I'm not even sure of having known what it was ten years ago. One is so disorientated, when traveling, by the suddenness of arrivals and the abruptness of departures.

What is certain is that I have never learned, and that I will always remain ignorant—yes, always, I believe—of what that little village near the road was.

The Exigent Shadow

It was in the condemned cell at La Roquette.

"Thank you, Messieurs. You have brought me paper, envelopes, a pen and an inkwell"—he arranged the objects on the little table as he spoke—"and I thank you very much. I also thank the governor of the prison, since he has authorized me to keep the light for part of the night. No, you're too kind! I won't play cards this evening; I have a letter to write. It won't take me long. I think, yes, I think"—he uttered a little laugh, almost malicious—"that I don't have many hours before me. So goodnight Messieurs, sleep well, while I write. I fear that you'll be woken up early tomorrow morning. So, goodnight, goodnight."

One of the guards left the cell; the heavy bolt grated as it plunged into the wall. The other guard lay down on the mattress of a camp bed extended in front of the door; he did not take long to start snoring placidly, with no concern regarding the condemned man.

The latter was a small man, already old and sickly, his fingers always stirred by a sight tremor, softly-spoken, seemingly very gentle in spite of the atrocity of the crime that he had committed. There had never been any need to put him in a straitjacket. Surely he would allow himself to be led to the guillotine as meekly as a sheep—a sheep who knew, but was obliging anyway. In the white and brown cell, where the candlelight did not flicker, the little man's nose almost touching the page, only the regular scratching of the pen was audible in the intervals of the snoring.

In accordance with the habit of certain methodical individuals, he had first put the address on the envelope: *To the Almoner, La Roquette Prison*. He added to that the underlined instruction: *Not to be opened until after my death*.

Good; now for the letter. And he traced the characters, carefully, without haste or disturbance—the sight tremor in his hands was habitual—like a conscientious employee copying a report calmly. His handwriting was very neat.

Monsieur Almoner, I beg your pardon for having delayed for so long, in spite of your charitable entreaties, in revealing to you why I rendered myself culpable of that abominable murder. It was necessary that the cause of my crime not be known until its author was beyond the reach of any absolution, and mercy; for my salvation would be a disobedience. But today—this afternoon, and again this evening—I have recognized by certain signs that the definitive moment is near; even in the moments when, given the placement and height of the two narrow windows, its emergence seemed to defy all the laws that given the figuration of bodies on walls, and just now, in the penumbra of the cell, while I was talking to my guards, placed not behind but in front of the candle, it has notified me, by such a clear and sharply outlined absence of what I still have, of the imminent necessity of not having it any longer, and has intimated the order of a perfect resemblance. At dawn, the prison governor will enter here with other persons and announce to me that I must resolve to die. I have, therefore, just time to write this explanatory letter.

Yes, it is quite extraordinary that a man like me, not wicked, not fanatical, quite simple, born of honest folk, who has been well brought-up, who exercised a tranquil profession—I was, as you know, a hat-maker in Remy-sur-Oise—should have rendered himself culpable, without hatred, as if for pleasure, of such a frightful and refined murder. I understand the amazement of the jurors, the Court and the physicians commissioned to examine my mental health (I refrained from telling them the truth; they would have thought that I was mad, and acquitted me, and I would not have been able to satisfy destiny); I also understand the astonishment that you have been kind enough to testify to me, Monsieur Almoner, for you do not know the thing, any more than the others.

Personally, I know it.

What is surprising, even for me, is that I did not perceive it immediately—I mean, as soon as I had reached the age of reason. Was it because, still a child, with frivolous eyes and mind, I did not pay any heed to the strangeness of my case, or, perhaps, that I considered it common to all living beings? No, instinct alone should have been sufficient to warn me of the anomaly to which I was subject. Is it necessary to suppose, then, that the disposition of the places in which I was accustomed to work and play—the large schoolroom, the little kitchen garden behind my parents' house—did not permit me the observation of the anomaly? No, again. The light played through the casements of the school as freely as through other casements; as for the garden wall, it far surpassed the height of my shoulders.

After having reflected on the matter for a long time, gravely, I have come to think that during my childhood and early adolescence I was, in regard to conformity with the laws of natural phenomena, and particularly the one whose deregulation obliged me to commit murder, with a view to expiation, similar in every respect to other boys. The thing that was to decide my life was only produced later, with the expansion of active virility. And, in fact, is it not normal, and logical, even in the most inconceivable violation of eternal rules, that an irregularity implying for an individual, as in my case, some fatal exigency, some ineluctable duty, would only manifest itself from the hour when that person finds himself in a state to obey that exigency and fulfill that duty?

I will tell you in a few words. Monsieur Almoner, in what circumstances the necessity appeared to me for the first time that I have obeyed with horror, but with resignation, and perhaps also with pride—for does a man not have the right to be proud who has, even by means of a crime, undoubtedly saved humankind and nature from incomparable disorder and disaster?

As my father was dissatisfied with the education I received at the school of Saint-Remy-sur-Oise—the teacher, a very pale young man of strange appearance, occupied himself very little with teaching his pupils holy history or the four rules, but more often read aloud in class works dealing with matters of death and eternity, of which I understood very little but which frightened me nevertheless—and as, in addition, it is unnecessary to be very knowledgeable to be a good hatmaker, my father, who planned to leave his business to me, made the resolution when I was fourteen years old to keep me with him perpetually. I no longer saw the schoolmaster, who, if I remember rightly, was obliged to hand in his resignation because he was judged to be slightly mad.

I was a very docile apprentice, and quite content. I grew up, not very tall, but in good health in spite of my paltry appearance. I no longer gave any thought to all the obscure and troubling nonsense that the young teacher proffered with his wild eyes and unkempt hair. My parents were very good. They let me play in the garden or the street between the hours of labor. I ate well and slept well. I already savored, with pleasure, the tranquility of the life that would be mine henceforth.

Even when I was fifteen years old, I scarcely experienced the troubles of imminent virility. My mother rejoiced in seeing me so placid. However, I have to confess to you, Monsieur Almoner, that once my sixteenth year was accomplished, I did not take long to gaze a little more frequently than was appropriate at the female apprentice, very young, still almost a child, who came to the house every day and occupied herself, in the room behind the shop, in sewing round hats and the peaks of caps. That put many little black dots in her fingertips. But she had such pretty eyes, so lively and shiny, beneath bushy hair that was almost red, and, between patches of redness, her skin was very white.

She was the daughter of the druggist, our neighbor. She was a trifle thin, with long arms with which she did not know what to do, which dangled awkwardly as soon as she was no longer working. It charmed me that she was like that. When I looked at her, sitting on the other side of the table, she laughed, or else she cried; when she cried, she was prettier.

You will forgive me, Monsieur Almoner, for telling you about these follies, in which there might have been some sin. My excuse is that I hoped to marry her, when I was established.

We met up, on spring mornings, in the willow grove beside the water. There we held hands, not too close to one another, and we did not say a word, or look at one another. But I heard her breath, and mine, very forceful and precipitate, as if we were out of breath. Then it was summer; I was seventeen; now, when we walked, I no longer kept so far from her. I dared not speak to her yet, but I drew her toward me, as if I wanted to whisper words in her ear. She turned her head toward the trees, or lowered them toward the sand of the path. Once, abruptly—there were flames in the air and we were walking in a hum of bees and golden flies, which were like fire flying everywhere—I clasped her against me and, without knowing what I was doing, I put my lips on her mouth. We stopped, astonished, delighted and bewildered, and I kept kissing her, kissing her beautiful little warm mouth, which couldn't close again.

How did it happen that at that very moment when my child's heart blossomed into a man's heart, my gaze—without my kiss entirely quitting hers—moved away from her slightly and considered our two shadows, our two thin, long shadows, clearly designed on the pallor of the narrow path?

I saw, scarcely blackened, her body next to mine; I saw our arms mingled; I saw, a little higher than her shoulder, my inclined shoulder; I saw, a little higher still. her forehead, and the pretty shock of her hair...but white I inhaled her breath, I no longer saw...no, no, I did not see on the pallor of the path, my own face; I did not see my forehead, I did not see my hair. My true lips brushed her lips, but above the neck, my shadow had no mouth, nor forehead, nor hair.

My shadow had no head.

It would be difficult for me, Monsieur Almoner, to express the extent to which I was troubled by the discovery that my shadow had no head. I ran toward the place of the road where my shadow had been interrupted a little while before, supposing that that there was some abrupt crevice there into which the head had disappeared, cut off by the edge. No, there was no hollow: a smooth and continuous terrain. And further on, in front of me, my decapitated shadow extended.

With an instinctive fear, I put my hand to my cheeks, to my temples; I touched, I could still touch, my skin, fleshy, hairy and alive, but I saw, on the road the blackness of my palms palpating the absent contours of nothing.

I contracted a malady in consequence, Monsieur Almoner, that kept me in bed for fifty days. Having entered into convalescence, I opened wide, wandering eyes, and I remained obstinately taciturn; people were obliged to wonder whether, because of the disease—it was a typhoid fever that I had had—I might have gone mad or become an imbecile. Neither one nor the other: I possessed all my reason; but I could not help thinking about my incomplete image. I thought about it with fear, with rage, and with vertigo. I had, at the same time, a quivering terror and an enraged desire to know whether, after my illness, the thing was in the same state as before. Perhaps my shadow now had a head? Oh, how I would have liked it to have one, and how I dreaded that it might not.

Curiosity finally triumphed over apprehension. One morning, when I was alone in my room, seated in a great armchair like a valetudinarian, I stood up slowly between the casement and the wall. I turned round slowly. Above the back of the chair, there were the shoulders, the neck, and nothing else. I fell back, unconscious.

For many days, many weeks, many months, I was very morose, my eyes staring—which made my mother anxious. Truly, one can have no idea, unless one has experienced it oneself, of the anxiety proximal to anguish, of the embarrassment prolonged into torture, than can be caused, especially in the early days, in a somewhat sensitive individual, by the conviction—corroborated continually by experience—that his shadow has no head. I do not know whether one can accommodate it any more gladly than not having one oneself. For in that case, in order to keep the mind at rest, it would only be necessary not to want to touch the face or the cranium, and carefully to avoid mirrors. Perhaps one would end up forgetting that one is acephalous. But what means is there of avoiding, unless one always lives in total darkness, the apparition of one's body on the wall, the floor or the sidewalk?

For myself, I suffered all the more because I dared not reveal the singularity of my case to anyone. Confessed to my parents, or to friends, my torment would doubtless have been less cruel; but an instinct—I have understood since how right it was, that instinct—advised me to remain silent, warning me that I ought to keep the secret of the derogation of natural law produced in my person, or at least the seeming incompleteness of my person.

What proved that I ought to do that is that, by virtue of an antinomy in which a superior and mysterious will was affirmed, I remained alone in perceiving it. Never has any other living being appeared surprised in seeing beside his shadow one that has no head. It is therefore the case that, by virtue of a necessary illusion, he sees one, and that the thing was an affair between me and…someone.

In any case, thanks to the habitude that one finally owes to time and the frequent return of the same facts, my anxiety became gradually less painful. The astonishment slackened first, and then the fear, of the neck that did not bear anything.

My father died in the year following the decease of my mother; after the distraction caused by my double grief, I was obliged to occupy myself with putting order into our commercial affairs, which were somewhat troubled. In order to conserve the clientele I was obliged make visits, and publish announcements in the Saint-Remy-sur-Oise *Indépendant*. Then I got married, to the little apprentice, the daughter of our neighbor the druggist, who had become a beautiful young woman. I had children, two boys and a girl. All of that diverted me from troubling thoughts. I only retained a hesitation in speech and a restriction in gesture, which were in conformity with the timid amiability of my character.

I reached the point of almost no longer paying any heed to the anomaly from which I had suffered so much, or rather, I considered it without disturbance. I even arrived at treating it with familiarity and good humor. Once—I'll always remember it, it was so funny—I was trying silk top hats on the proprietor of the Three Emperors Hotel; not knowing where to put down one of the hats, too small for my client, between the table and the cluttered chairs, I put it on my own, and then writhed with laugher—literally writhed! And why? Because I could see the shadow of the hat on the wall, so narrow that the head of a child could only have fitted into it with difficulty, touching with its vacillating brim the shadow of my shoulders! I can assure you, Monsieur Almoner, that it was very comical; you would not have been able to help clutching your sides, in spite of the gravity of your holy character.

And to the "infirmity" of my image, I also owed a joy. That was when, on Sundays in summer, when the shop was closed, I went for walks in the country with my daughter and my two sons. As they were already growing tall, and I am rather small, our shadows were almost the same height, because of the missing head—and that gave me pleasure.

In consequence, I might have been able to continue and complete peacefully a very happy life—unless I too had been the victim of the perhaps-universal disaster from which I have, thank God, saved humankind and the worlds—if last winter had not presented anomalous and very disturbing characteristics that gave all persons endowed with a sound intelligence much food for thought. As soon as the fifteenth of January, Monsieur—I'm certain, Monsieur Almoner, that you have retained the memory of it—a sun that one is not accustomed to see so ardent in July, a sun that might have been able to excite a brain less well-founded than mine—dried up the fields and the roads, drank the rivers, forced the trees to become green and roses to bloom. Long sandbanks, like the backs of yellow beasts, emerged from the thin sheet of the water, and one day, I saw the apple tree in the courtyard all white and decked with a thousand flowers. Never, certainly, in Saint-Remy-sur-Oise or in any country in the world, had such an astonishing inversion of the seasons been observed. I had to agree with my wife on the morning when, gazing through the window at the cloudless sky, from which not a drop of water had fallen for a month, she felt obliged to say: "Something in the world must surely be out of order."

That observation did not astonish me, but it moved me strangely. And as, at that very moment, my headless shadow loomed up along the wall, I repeated, almost voicelessly, between my tremulous lips: "Yes, something is out of order. There's something out of order in the world."

I would be lying, Monsieur Almoner, if I told you that, from that moment on the perception was established in me entirely and clearly of the connection there might be, that there really was—as I recognized later—between the prodigy of the estival winter to which we were subjected and that of my incomplete image. No, that connection didn't appear to me at first in its evidence, and even less the relationship of cause and effect between the two anomalies. But, as one sees threads of spider-silk extended from one side of the road to the other in a dusk that makes them increasingly luminous, connections, it seemed to me, as light, as tenuous and as vague, divined rather than observed, linked the two phenomena.

Yes, I sensed that I was no stranger to the strangeness that was being produced, and that the transgression in me of a natural law might correspond mysteriously to the transgression of another law in nature...

However, Monsieur Almoner, the preoccupation—albeit very vague, uncertain, scarcely presented—that the acephaly of my shadow was not without a relationship with the irregularity of the winter that was so ardently estival, did not take long to dissipate, as the season, vanquished by the eternal law, reverted to its normal temperature; and I think that nothing similar would ever have haunted my mind again if, quite a long time after the complete disappearance of the idea, in the early days of the month of April, the newspapers had not reported, with many details, the unexpected and frightful cataclysm that had overwhelmed the island of Java and almost completely destroyed it.[25]

It was, according to the rare survivors of the long disaster, more than a week of unparalleled horror. Amid a rightful and incessant din of thunder, in a darkness in which the sun no longer rose and only lightning provided illumination, mountains sank in the suddenly-split earth, and accumulations of rock and metal in fusion surged forth from lakes of plains: instant mountains soon swallowed up in reopened abysses, while an immense and thin torrential sheet, not of water but of lava, passed over the entire island like an immeasurable scythe, and, cutting through everything—hills, forests, houses—left behind sheaves of ruins.

A formidable inversion of all the rules that regulate matter! Enormous rocks were seen flying, carried by a wind that did not come from the sky; flocks of doves and swans were seen to collapse, made heavier by an unknown weight. The contrary was triumphant in the chaos of the end of a world: a restricted world—less than a continent—but a world nevertheless. And the inhabitants of our entire earth—without conceiving, however, that a sign had been given to them—were astonished by that upheaval, and shivered.

For myself, I understood that sign, that warning. I understood that the Destroyer—the one who was, in the beginning, the Creator—was testing by means of the narrow ruination an universal ruination; that the partial collapse of an island was a sketch of the total catastrophe of the universe.

But why had that sign been given at that precise moment? Why was it in the exact era when I was alive that the imminent derogation had been affirmed of all the rules that had directed and maintained the work of the six days for so long. Why was the end of the world so imminent in my lifetime?

---

[25] Although the specific anomalous phenomena cited in the story are fictitious, the author must have had the devastation caused by the August 1883 eruption of Krakatoa in mind.

Then the thought returned to me, more precise and more pressing, with an ineluctable urgency, to which the strange winter, warmer than a summer, had previously given birth in me; and, after long, often painful, meditation, I acquired the certainty that the world was going to end because my shadow no longer had a head.

At present, the evidence for that proposition appears to me to be so perfect, Monsieur Almoner, that I believe I would be insulting the perspicacity of your intelligence by insisting any longer on the reasons that determined me to admit it. A learned man like you ought to understand immediately what I, being simple of mind, took a long time to perceive.

Everything in nature is connected. Nothing there can be disordered without the whole being shaken. The ensemble of existing things can be considered as a gigantic house of cards; the almost infinite prolongation of its duration has enabled belief in its solidity: the illusion of the guests in the ephemeral dwelling. Withdraw a single card, however, and everything collapses and scatters. To speak more directly, a single fact deflected in its normal accomplishment, a single point of support removed from the unique and multiple equilibrium, a single law transgressed in the universal order, might imply—what am I saying? must necessarily imply—the dislocation of the entire enormous edifice. And my headless shadow was the fall of everything into nothing.

As soon as that conviction was established in my mind, I became the prey of a frightful and incessant melancholy, not because I was thinking about my own life soon being precipitated in the common disaster, and not because I was thinking about my wife and my children being destined to the most horrible death. Although I had amity for myself and for them, all the tenderness that the heart of a husband and father can contain, a more general concern, more broadly human, alarmed me.

No, personal interest was only the lesser cause of my dolor. I had pity for the entire earth, so beautiful, for so many beings fortunate to live there. What? It was true, it was certain that the dawn would no longer smile over the sea, so blue and so mild, and the plain, so green and so flowery? There would no longer be any sun there, since there would no longer be any sky? There would be no more stars there, since the night itself would no longer exist? Oh, my God, to think that, after the frightful hour, the birds would no longer sing in the vanished trees, that nowhere, nowhere, would roses any longer bloom. And so many men and women, who loved one another, would cease to love one another. The noblest projects of glorious ambition would no longer even conclude in the putrescence that follows funerals. On the eve of the universal disaster, fiancés, he twenty, she sixteen, were still exchanging promises...

An immense pity for all things and for all living beings seized my heart without release; as I always had eyelashes moist with tears, people around me said that a weakening of my lachrymal glands was the cause of those tears, those slow, growing tears, which trembled...

No, I was weeping because of the end of the world.

I also experienced I know not what remorse. Certainly, it was not my fault if the frightful cataclysm was so imminent; but after all, it was in me, innocent as I was, that the first sign and the cause of the disaster of everything was produced.

Was there a remedy? Was there a remedy for such a menacing evil?

Pity imposed on me the thought that there might perhaps be a remedy...

The world was about to perish because the law that regulated it had been broken in me, because my shadow had no head. I wondered whether there might not be a means of giving my shadow my head. That result attained, everything, necessarily, would be reestablished in its former order, and the universe would continue to live.

I cannot tell you, Monsieur Almoner—for my ideas on that subject are slightly confused—how long I employed in inventing some stratagem appropriate to repair the abnormality of my figuration on the wall. I only remember that, more than once, I masked myself with several very large masks, hoping that more blackness, more opacity might perhaps interrupt the light. Alas, the masks of my face had no more shadow than my face.

God, who had doubtless felt compassion for the earth and human beings, sent me an inspiration, for which I thank him on my knees.

In order for the peril to be averted, at least for the present, for everything to be returned to the state demanded by natural laws, it was not necessary—why had I thought of that?—that my head appear on the wall; it was sufficient for my shadow to be similar to me. Well, if I ceased to have a head; if, in one fashion or another, I ceased to have a head, my image would no longer be in discord with my form, the universal rule would no longer be violated, and the eternity of life, naturally, would follow its course.

I assure you, Monsieur Almoner, that when that idea came to me, I uttered a cry of joy. Humankind was saved! I did not hesitate or a moment to seize my razor, and, standing next to the window before the narrow mirror, without thinking about the despair of my wife and my children in mourning behind the funeral carriage, I got ready to cut my throat...

But no, the separation of the head from the trunk could not be complete, attempted by my inevitably hesitant hand, of which a horrible torture would attenuate the persistence. I could only be decapitated usefully—which is to say, totally—and I could only become entirely similar to my shadow, with the methodical, tranquil, as if mechanical, aid of someone who would act without passion and without dolor. Only the executioner could make me perfectly similar to my image on the wall or on the road; the executioner alone could give me the joy of saving universal life from annihilation. Oh, the admirable hope: my cadaver, if it were stood upright, similar to its shadow!

But only the worst murders are guillotined...

Oh, Monsieur Almoner, I loved them so much, my children, my daughter above all; I loved her so tenderly, so proudly. She was so pretty. When we went out together, the way people looked at her made me swell with pride. She was blonde, with little hairs over her forehead. I had hesitated for a long time to marry her, because I was so happy to have her with me. However, the following month we were to celebrate her wedding. She loved her fiancé. They had sworn to me that they would often come to see me, and that they would not send the children they would soon have to a nurse in the country.

The children would remain in Saint-Remy-sur-Oise. It was agreed that I would go every morning to my son-in-law's home to see whether they were well, and to bring them rattles, and later toys. And my wife, slightly given to teasing but fundamentally good, was very content with that arrangement. We said to one another: "Well, old sport, we won't be all alone. The boys will come back from Paris and marry near here. There will be a family that isn't poor, happy and cheerful. In the evening the drawing room on the first floor will scarcely be large enough to hold all those people, who will laugh, amuse one another, tell stories, and we'll all be very content. All of us..."

Oh, Monsieur Almoner, I don't repent of my useful barbarity, but it's frightful nevertheless that it was necessary, in killing them, to do so much harm to my wife and daughter, in order to be sure that I wouldn't be sent to prison, to be sure that my neck would be severed, that my shadow would finally be right, and that the world wouldn't end, and that, for a long, long time, there will still be fiancés and roses...

Fear on the Island

In literary terms, the inexplicable is blameworthy. Yes, I recognize that a writer does not have the right to relate extra-natural events if he is not in a position to furnish, at some point in his story—Théodore de Banville, by virtue of a horror of surprise that Charles Baudelaire did not share, demands that it should be in the first lines—a plausible explanation, even if it is fantastic. In any case, it seems to be better that they are of a real order. The work, extraordinary but never magical, of the great Edgar Poe triumphs precisely by virtue of the prodigious art of eventually reducing to almost banal humanity—quotidian so to speak—the most prodigious and frightening abnormalities. That there is some analogy between that artistic procedure and the obsolete game of enigmas appears certain; we owe to it so many perfect masterpieces that it is not possible to reprove it. In sum, the reader would be authorized to accuse of puerility, mystificatory impertinence or deplorable ingenuity the writer who, after having attracted, lured, troubled and even exasperated him by an accumulation of miraculous effects, suddenly avoids responsibility for revealing the causes to him, and leaves him, as the saying has it, in suspense.

Such reproaches have been addressed to me with regard to a few pages published here under the title "A Village, Near the Road...", and never would have they been better merited if in writing those pages, I had wanted to produce a work of literature, if I had not taken care to state, several times, that it was not a matter of a work of fiction but a true story, an adventure that, in addition to myself, had seven witnesses; an adventure that, I affirmed, was denied by none of those witnesses, and which, in fact, could not be, since it was veritable and true in every detail.

It would have been easy for me—for the habit of invention, far from sterilizing the imagination, renders it more fecund and more prompt to engenderment—to adapt some fantastic or reasonable termination to the bizarre and burlesque travel anecdote; but I did not want to do that, out of respect for the truth, out of respect, above all, for the mystery that it was given to us to see and touch, and out of respect for my fear. And I did not reread my honest story before it was printed, for fear of being incited to make amendments in which the artist—which is to say, the liar—would have too much part. Numerous incorrections have been noted therein, which, it is said, are not usual to me. I hope that a few faults of language here and here are as many proofs of my sincerity.

What! You did not believe me? Are you, then, one of those people who have never sensed in the inexplicable, grotesque or terrifying aspect of some event the malice or cruelty of an invisible and obscure entourage of beings—are they beings?—attentive to human existence and ever avid to manifest themselves, but always ready to slip away when the curious abruptness of our reason goes to surprise them and draw them into the broad daylight of observation? For myself, I have experienced many a time their ever-closer approach (which never goes as far as explicit presence) and, welcoming it with malaise or joy depending upon whether my soul is momentarily disposed to the fear or hope of the unknown, I have retained amiable or dolorous memories of frissons that I could not have owed to any human adventure...

In those days—I had just reached the age of twenty—I experienced a great dolor. A woman that I loved tenderly had betrayed me. A distress more bitter than that of being betrayed by the woman one loves tenderly does not exist. Later, having grown old, when their hearts are extinct, it is the custom of many men to mock their despairs of old, and even to doubt them. Those men resemble amputees denying the pain that they endured in the limb they no longer have. But the heart of poets survives in the persistence of the dream; we still weep our old tears.

In those days, then, my brand new pain counseled me to forget my ambitions, my pride, and to flee, to exile myself. I had one sole need: some solitude comparable to the void that had been made in my self. That solitude I found, not far from Paris, in a narrow little island between the barely-separated arms of a river. One does not imagine, rubbing shoulders with so many passers-by, how close the desert is to crowds; it is sufficient to walk for a few hours to be entirely isolated.

The islet that was my refuge was too small for a village to be built on it, too infertile—a rock devoid of humus—for anyone to attempt to cultivate it, and too scantly agreeable to the eye, bring deprived of trees and lawns, for a guinguette to install swings and barrel games there. As soon as the boatman had returned, I found myself alone, absolutely alone. I discovered an old abandoned roadman's hut; it was there that I slept; food supplies in tins, a few bottles and packets of tobacco—I had brought all that—were amply sufficient for me in the retreat of sorts that I counted on making in that wild place; and my dolorous soul would perhaps be gradually appeased in the silence and the solitude.

What point would there be in my saying this if it weren't true? Where would be the merit in inventing such a banal exile of a lover rendered misanthropic and misogynistic by betrayal? Those who have known me for a long time will doubtless remember having mocked the morose obstinacy that took me away for an entire month from them and the literary combats of my dearest works. In truth, I am writing, without literature, things as they were; and everything is veritable in my story, even that which will appear truly extraordinary, even that which woke me up in the middle of the twelfth night...

Alone, I did not know boredom, nor regret of multitudes. I rarely turned my head toward either quay of the river that embraced the island with its barely-separated arms; I never experienced any desire to hail the boatman, to reenter the animation of the nearby village, where canoeists sang on Sundays. I pleased myself on my island, talking to my chagrin, interrogating it, and replying to it. We understood one another very well, the two of us. I walked for a long time over the sand and stones, or I sat down, nonchalantly, on a rock projecting into the water.

Far from wanting colors or voices, I was glad that there were no flowers there at all, and no birds. The nights, above all, were pleasant, because of the silence—for the river flowed so slowly, the wind scarcely stirred the leaves of the rare trees, and the sky was so heavy with mute shadow—and because of the immensity: because of the infinite silence. And in the middle of the deserted island, like a cemetery devoid of phantoms, my bed in the hut, my bed of dry grass, which I had surrounded with old plants, was like a cellar or a coffin with which one sleeps well.

Oh, I slept well there. The fatigue of frequent slow walks, with the mass of despair weighed down by melancholy, threw me on to the bed, and I slept, without dreaming, for a long time. For eleven nights I slept, without waking up before dawn, in the perfect silence; but I woke up in the middle of the twelfth night...

I woke up with a start. I was sitting in the dark, my eyes wide, my heart hammering. Why had I woken up in that way, so abruptly? I did not know. I asked myself: "Why, then, did I wake up like that, so suddenly?" but I still did not know. Finally, I had a vague memory of a sound that had suddenly rung out, and had woken me up. But what sound? I did not know. Well, doubtless I had had a nightmare. I lay down, I plunged back into the amiable, dear oblivion of sleep.

I sat up again! This time I knew, yes, I knew, what had snatched me from repose.

It was the sound of a cough. Someone, I was sure of it, had coughed in the silence of the night, in the desert of the island.

An absurd idea.

Since I was alone, absolutely alone, on the desert island, in the silent night.

However, it was certainly a cough that I had heard.

I smiled.

It was probable that I had coughed myself, in my sleep; I must have caught cold, along the water, the day before; it was my own catarrh that had shaken me.

I smiled again. I went back to sleep. The awakening, at dawn, was pleasant, and that day was pleasant, in the good solitude, and the slumber of the evening was pleasant. But toward the middle of the thirteenth night—yes, toward the middle, I think, of the thirteenth night—again I started on my bed of dry leaves, like a soldier waking up to the clarion; and, stupefied, alarmed, with a cold frisson running down my back, I heard someone cough, someone was coughing, someone was still coughing.

Let's see! Was I, sitting up, still dreaming? No, I was no longer asleep, I was sure of no longer being asleep. Was I mad? No, I was not mad. I was sure of not being mad. Since there was no one on the island, since I was alone on the island, since a sound as faint as that of someone coughing could not have come from the villages or along the course of the river, since I, myself, had not coughed, what was that cough, and where did it come from?

Colder, the frisson shook my back. Ice melted on my temples. For that cough was terrible! Sometimes, lightly, the cough of a child afflicted by whooping cough, it sounded in dry bursts, at unequal intervals, and tore the silence like a fingernail scratching a widow; sometimes, heavily, the cough of an asthmatic old man, it persisted in greasy gurgles of bubbles inflating and rising in a bilious mud; it was so distinct that it seemed to me to be very close, oh, yes, very close!

It was in that very hut that someone was coughing, or behind the wall of the hut; and, at the same time, it seemed to me to be very distant, because of the strange sound, the sound of mystery, that was within it. For an instant, I thought that it was below me that someone was coughing! I thought that I was lying on someone, a child or an old man, whom my weight was oppressing to the extent of making them cough. Then I imagined, shivering and sweating, that many leagues way, a little boy prey to the croup was dying, or a centenarian, finally moribund, was gasping.

I leapt out of bed. I went out into the darkness. I had had the suspicion that, during the evening, some old beggar, with one of those poor children that hold their hands, had introduced themselves, unknown to me, on to the island, and that they were coughing, chilly and suffering, one after the other, and together, at the foot of a tree.

No, no one. Solitude in the dark. In any case, as soon as I had quit the hut, the sound of the cough had ceased.

I went back in. I lay down, again. I listened...

Nothing. Nothing, any longer. It was finished...the silence...

Exhausted by fear, I went to sleep.

But every night, thin, like a child's cough, or thick, like an old man's cough, very distant and simultaneously very close, the coughing recommenced: the obstinate, tearing, frightful coughing; and I listened, for entire hours, terrified, a cold sweat forming from my neck to my loins. Sometimes it fell silent. I breathed freely. Perhaps he was dead, the person, child or old man, who was coughing. Oh! He was finally dead!

But soon, more frightening after the silence, the staccato rattle resumed ripping the night and the silence and my frightened soul and my heart and my entire being. And I gasped myself, with fright, in the obsession of that agonizing cough.

Oh, you can easily imagine that, by day, delivered from anguish, my reason recovered, I sought to render account of the nocturnal sound. No, no, nothing could explain it. There was no osprey on the island with its horrible sobbing laugh, there was no hollow from which the wind could emerge in a hoarse plaint, no cleft in the rock in which the water could churn and weep in surges; and the nearest villages, the nearest roads, were too far away for the cough of any living person to reach me therefrom.

However, every night, at the same time, the frightful cough sounded, in the desert silence of the island...

The Reflection, the Odor, the Flame and the Image

One evening when he was very poor—even poorer than the day before, when he had been very poor—Albe Cyrille, maker of verses by vocation and starveling by habitude, began to find the time long. Having been unable to distract himself from his cares even by fervent application to the completion of a sonnet, he made the decision to go for a walk on the boulevard; one hears things and sees things there.

As he turned the corner of a street on to the boulevard, he perceived through the four open second-story windows of a house a very sumptuous apartment in which, under the dazzling crystals of chandeliers, the red silks of curtains and the furniture were quivering, and the gilt of moldings sparkling; drawing rooms were being prepared for some fête. And further away, through the less bright opening of another casement, the pale silks and mysterious lacy veils of a bed were visible.

Expelled three days before from a small lodging-house in the Rue d'Allemagne, in which he occupied had occupied a tiny room at four francs a week, Albe Cyrille judged the luxury of those drawing rooms brutal, mediocre and bourgeois, and the elegant mystery of that bedroom banal. And he was going on his way when he saw the reflection of the whole apartment on the asphalt, which was shiny with recent rain. He found it pretty, bent down, picked it up as if it were a bright extended cloth, folded it up carefully and put it in the right hand pocket of his coat, in order to make use of it if the need arose.

An odor charmed him. Guided by the instinct of his nostrils, he did not take long to find himself in front of a grocery, behind the display window of which turkeys, excessively white and yellow, studded her and there by the black roundels of truffles, developed their enormous swellings between two plates of turbots aureoled by parsley, under a species of arbor in which the branches of cherry-trees were mingled, and from which grapefruit and pineapples hung down, their peel drooling sugar, and, held in the air by pink or green ribbons, the light gold of small mandarin oranges.

After the creamery at the corner of the Rue d'Allemagne and the Passage de l'Epargne refused to give him any more credit, Albe Cyrille had been eating for two or three mornings—he never ate in the evenings—at a little restaurant that sold slices of beef for six sous, because they were horsemeat, and mutton chops for three sous, because they were dog-meat. Cyrille was scornful of turkeys, because they were simple, as if familial, and turbots, fish cherished at wedding feasts and masonic banquets, and ripe fruits, albeit exotic, from southern lands that were too close, still so far away from marvelous sunlit beyonds. Only the meager oranges trembling in mid-air, which resembled tiny breasts stolen from the torsos of gilded children, found grace in his eyes, and they would be acidic.

Only one thing pleased him entirely, and that was the good odor of victuals, the fresh fruity perfume that came from the whole shop. He seized that odor between his hands, quickly closed so that it would not escape, and he put it in the left-hand pocket of his coat; perhaps an opportunity would come along to make use of it.

An enthusiastic crowd of idlers had gathered around a jeweler's display, tightly packed and urgent, in which the heads of young women with dazzled eyes advanced between the necks of men, and the fists of louts, good instruments of violence, were clenched by an instinct of appropriation. Exhibited in the window, in an enormous case of pale blue velvet, were necklaces with triple rows of Brazilian diamonds, bracelets of Cape rubies, brooches opening sapphire petals like roses made of blue splendors: the wedding adornments of the Archduchess of Thessaly.

Albe Cyrille, when he arrived from the province, had brought a little cross of hollow gold, one of those crosses known as "jeannettes," which his grandmother, a old gray-beard woman under a red headscarf, always wrapped up warmly, her aged hands extended toward the embers of vine-branches under the hood of the hearth, had confided it to him in order that it would bring him good luck. At the Mont-de-Piété he had been given three francs for it, and the surcharge was eighty-five centimes. He could not understand how people could take pleasure in modern jewelry made of fine stones that were found everywhere. What he would have liked to see was the diadem that the Dove with the Iron Beak, Chamiram,[26] Queen of Assyria, widow of Menones and widow of Ninus wore in order to marry, in the royal sepulcher, the cadaver of Ara the Handsome.

However, expanded above the heads of the idlers, the splendor of the display-window was radiant and very beautiful. With a raised hand, Albe Cyrille took that flame as one might catch a luminous butterfly, and he put it in one of the pockets of his waistcoat; the slightest things, in certain circumstances, can be useful.

In the Place de l'Opéra, in front of the staircase of abrupt riding steps, he stopped, in order to see beautiful young women descending from carriages. To begin with, many old ones and many ugly ones appeared, for more often than not, it is poor young women who, in compensation for the many things they do not have, possess the glory—even more glorious in dirty dresses and rags—of being twenty years old and pretty.

However, emerging from a coupé lined with mauve satin and luminous in places with mirrors, the perfect princess arrived, in whom the most miraculous splendor triumphed that a woman can have, who had in her open corsage, under a mist of lace, the breasts of Aphrodite, made of marine foam rounded and solidified under the first caress of the palm of a god.

Albe Cyrille remained cold. It was not that he had some friend who deflected his amour from any other amour; his most recent mistress had been the housemaid of a prostitute, almost old and almost dirty, encountered in the creamery on

---

[26] i.e., Semiramis.

the corner of the Rue d'Allemagne and the Passage de l'Epargne; but, only slightly pagan—since Parnassus is no longer, Olympus has been renounced—he was especially inclined to the pale, long and melancholy breasts of virgins, already thinned by the imminent martyrdom; the fervent pity of his dream caressed those breasts that weep.

He drew away. He saw in one of the mirrors of the coupé the reflection of the princess, who had turned back in order to pick up a forgotten fan; and that image, more beautiful than the woman whose image it was, enthused him to such a point that he leapt into the coupé in order to steal it. People hurled themselves upon him, insulted him, threatened to take him to the police station and nearly beat him. He let them speak, and ran away, content because he had taken the image in his prompt hand. He put it in a pocket of his jacket, in the one beneath which his heart beat. That mage, he would certainly be able to employ. When? Perhaps soon.

He followed the boulevard and the Rue Royale, traversed the Place de la Concorde, and went along the Seine. On the sidewalk of the quay he walked very rapidly among the increasingly sparse passers-by. Weary, having not slept in a bed for a long time, his belly dolorous because of the rarity of meals, somber because of the darkness left within him by extinct hope, and also desolate at no longer being loved, even by the maid of the prostitute who sat in a window, he sought a refuge where he could be sad all alone.

He knew that there is a bridge whose first arch straddles a broad paved sidewalk. He had slept there sometimes. He recognized the descending stairway; he found himself alone under the ogive of the arch, and the noisy silence of the water ran alongside the stones.

He dreamed for a long time.

And he smiled.

From the right-hand pocket of his coat he took the reflection of the apartment and the bedroom; he stuck it to the gray stones of the bridge, and all the twilight was in fête. As he was very hungry he took from the left-hand pocket the odor of victuals and fruits, and on a table offered by the reflection of the drawing room he set out a fine feast. But how lugubrious it is eating in the dark! He remembered the flame that he had in his fob-pocket; it illuminated, everywhere, diamonds more luminous than diamonds, sapphires bluer than sapphires and all the marvelous radiance of an ideal jewelry. No, the flashes of the stones in the diadem on the Dove with the Iron Beak were no brighter!

And he began to eat fabulous game, with a silver knife and fork in his hands, and fruits that only ripened beyond the orchard of the Hesperides. He ate furiously, and he ate a lot, stuffing himself. If, at times, he was obliged to close his eyes because of the excess of light around him it did not prevent him from opening his mouth again, again and always, because his appetite was renewed by the unexpected, miraculous dishes.

But it is tedious supping alone! And from the breastpocket of his coat, beneath which his heart was beating, he took out the image, the image more beautiful than the princess, the image resembling a thin, frail martyr, with pale nipples, clad in a desire for paradise. And they supped together, he and the image, in the dream of the apartment, in the dream of the gems. But because one is a man, and the dream, at its extremity, demands to be real, he took her away, the reflection, to the reflection of the bed, more mysterious in the tremulous ideal of silk and lace.

In the same way that he had eaten too much in the lie of excessively bright lights, he loved too much on the illusion of the bed. And he held breasts and kissed a mouth, and without repose, endlessly, he embraced, crying all the joys of amour to the heavens, a dear little supple and quivering body of a goddess, exquisitely attenuated in a little saint, near to breaking in an unexpected martyrdom—so much that in the end, strength and breath failed him, and he fainted, ecstatically.

A few hours after daybreak, a clipper of dogs and castrator of cats, who combined his usual profession with that of shaving the mariners of merchant boats in the open air, saw someone lying dead on the pavement under the arch. Someone went to alert the police commissaire, who hastened to arrive with a physician. A crowd of people, gathering around the dead man, seeing his poor clothing said:

"It's someone who has killed himself because of poverty."

"It's someone who has died of privations, of starvation."

The doctor, kneeling on the pavement, confirmed the death of Albe Cyrille. But everyone was very surprised when, after an attentive examination of the cadaver, he declared that, contrary to all probability, the unknown man had died of an excess of food—indigestion, in a word—and of another excess, that of amour.

And Albe Cyrille's eyes, not yet closed, were dry and calcined, like those of a man who has advanced his head for too long toward a glass-blower's furnace, or has gazed for too long, and too closely, at the sun.

The Portrait on the Empty Wall

In the apartment where I installed myself in the first days of a winter already long ago, a portrait of a woman remained, without a frame, hung on the wall of the room that would be my study. I scarcely glanced at it while the movers were putting my furniture in place: a dull, vague face, a mediocre painting.

The previous tenant, I thought, *has forgotten that portrait; he'll come to look for it soon, or tomorrow.*

I decided to leave it there, and not to touch it; it might be precious to the person who would come to recover it.

But no one came to reclaim it.

Two days later, as I was sitting at my table, it embarrassed my view. I rang; my domestic could take it away and stow it in some corner. In the meantime, I considered it attentively, and when the domestic came in and asked: "What does Monsieur desire?" I replied: "Nothing." For now it seemed to me that I recognized, not the portrait, but the woman whose image it was.

Yes, I recognized her, certainly, quite certainly…but who was she? I could not have said. That hair, a dull chestnut color; that slightly jaundiced forehead, very smooth, traversed by a single crease; those eyes, which had the grayish-blue of shallow lakes; where had I seen them, alive? I didn't know. The sight of them now caused me a melancholy that was not without tenderness, and at the same time, it seemed to me that the odor of an extinct fire, of ash, floated in the air, as if the wind sliding down the chimney, had scattered around me and over me memories of an old hearth…

"What!" I exclaimed.

Alas, yes, there was a resemblance, evidently due to hazard, and spoiled in addition by an awkward painter, to the very tender friend, the almost maternal lover, with a consolatory caress, who, her arms always open to my returns, always clement my faults, had cradled my first fatigues and my first repentances.

Where was she? Where the dead are.

Perhaps it was the perfume of her distant tomb, the odor of ash that had filled the room...

I saw the portrait less clearly through my tears.

From then on, I had a dread, which was that someone might take that portrait from me. But many days went by; I had no news of the previous tenant; I ended up convincing myself that the image was mine. I made a frame for it of black wood, not shiny, in which I put a little bunch of those flowers which, seemingly dead, never fade. It restored the serenity of my anxious hours to have the caressant and consoling friend there, facing me, close at hand.

But once, obliged to work by night, I had lit all my lamps and the candles in four candlesticks in order to surround myself with light, when I raised my eyes to the portrait, I could not retain a cry of surprise. No, no, it did not resemble the maternal lover of my adolescence! What error, what illusion, had made me recognize her in it? Dull as it was, thanks to the lax brushwork, it resembled, I could not doubt it, the resplendent and marvelous creature who, for a whole year of joy and glory, enchanted my eyes and inflamed my mind: the illuminatrix of my triumphant virile years. Dead for a long time, alas, I rediscovered her, ardently beautiful, like a reignited star. And I was sure of it, even though I could only see the portrait poorly through the dazzle.

For several weeks I slept by day and worked by night. Oh, as long as no one took the portrait away from me! I had made a radiant golden frame for it, in which a violent bunch of golden lilies and bloody poppies burned, renewed every evening. And when my genius was extinguished, I reignited it at the flame of the resplendent and marvelous creature.

But once, when, exhausted by the long, sterile effort of the lacerating and breathless climb toward the ideal work, never attained, I had fallen asleep with my head on the table, I was awakened by a roseate radiance of dawn, I had a strange surprise when I looked at the portrait. And I thought that, for a long time, I had been mad.

No, no, it offered no rapport with the beauty of the splendid lover, my luminous inspiration. But there, in the pale light of the nascent day, insufficiently exquisite, in truth, excessively humanized by an artist devoid of reverie, was the delightful child who, so young and so puerile, deigned to love me, already aging, and made her young springtime into the sun of my autumn.

She too was dead, alas, since they had all died. But I saw her again, in the ingenuousness of her imminent blossoming, like everything that will flower, sing and radiate, but has not done so yet. I was certain of it, although the image was scarcely visible to me through the tears that I had in my lashes, like a morning dew.

For long months it was my custom to work in the first light of the morning. Oh, what a disaster it would have been if the former tenant had come to demand the portrait! In a frame of white-painted wood, every dawn, I put a little daisy in it—a single daisy, or a lily-of-the-valley, or an eglantine that was scarcely pink; and under the angelic puerility of the delectable child who had deigned to love me, already growing old, my poems were filled with a breath that went to be a breeze, and a green perfume of a woodland path not yet in flower.

But then, gradually, a disdain took hold of me for works previously realized, and the ennui of future works. I had been installed for a long time in the apartment in which the previous tenant had left the portrait, and that portrait of the dead girl bore less resemblance to the time resuscitated within it.

Had it resumed the features of the triumphant lover, or those of the maternal friend? No, it no longer resembled any of the women I had loved and who had loved me. It no longer resembled anyone. I only saw in it dull chestnut hair, a slightly jaundiced forehead, very smooth, traversed by a single crease, and eyes that had the grayish-blue of shallow lakes. And I no longer paid any attention to it; I would no longer have had any pain if someone had come to take it...

I was astonished, however, albeit without chagrin, one day—how many days had passed since I had lodged there?—when, chancing to raise my eyes, I saw that the portrait was no longer on the wall. I rang for my domestic, who had grown old in my service; like me he had white hair.

I asked him: "Has the former tenant come?"

He seemed surprised. "No, Monsieur," he said. "No one has come."

"In that case," I asked, "who has taken the portrait away?"

He considered me with the expression one has in gazing at a madman. "What portrait?"

"The portrait that was on this wall."

"There has never been a portrait on that wall," he said.

"That's possible," I said. "Leave me."

And I had no sorrow. There is no new abode in which, for those whose heart is still alive, the past does not hang up changing memories; but after the years comes the invisible forgetfulness, which takes away the portraits from the empty wall.

Effects Without Causes

I believe that there are shadows that are not the shadow of anything. I also believe that one can see reflections in mirrors that are not reflections of anything. Why should shadows and reflections not exist by themselves? Because the words by which they are designated imply that they have no original personality and are only the images of beings and things? That is mediocre reasoning. Words can deceive. In the same way that there are poorly-named people, cowards called Achille and whores named Mary, perhaps there are objects that have incomplete or even absurd verbal representations. Vocabularies are not infallible.

Take note, in addition, that if, for the expression of all substances and all qualities, of everything that exists, we have to refer uniquely to written or spoken syllables, what will happen to our reason on the day the some academician, elected sovereign of the world, and slightly troubled by that sudden exaltation, takes it into his head to declare that, prior to the first minute of his omnipotence, human languages were radically mistaken, precisely because they seemed to follow a law, and that henceforth, random chance will be the sole logical correspondence between the meaning and the sound proffered by a voice or represented figuratively by writing? Then, having cut out all the words from the dictionary one by one, on the one hand, and in the other, all the definitions that the dictionary gives for them, having put the former in one bag and the latter in another, the most innocent person in society—perhaps a vaudevillian absolutely ignorant of lexicography and syntax—will draw words from one bag and definitions from the other, as in a lottery, and will decree incontestably the new associations of words and terms. Doubtless, to begin with, we would be a little anxious, like people changing furnished apartments, but we would not take long to install ourselves quite comfortably in our new abode.

Let us admit that, by some encounter antithetical to the lottery, the eternal things, the eternal thoughts, would henceforth be expressed by vocables that once expressed precisely the opposite. That would not change anything in the customary course of reality, in our reveries, or in our passions. If "indigestion" signified "hearty appetite," we would be no less hungry for bread, meat and the various things served at lunch or dinner time, We would still revere if "ordure" were substituted for "ideal", and it would be with an infinite tenderness that, falling to our knees before the one who will be dear to us forever, we would say to her: "I hate you."

It is necessary, therefore, not to attach too great an importance to words themselves. I have already said that there are shadows of nothing, reflections of non-being. I believe so, at least. And I will tell you, in that regard, two stories that are rather singular, and then a third story, which is even stranger.

Once, when I was walking at night along a dark steel-gray river, without the rips of drowned stars between tall poplars like black stakes, I saw a giant on the water with a crown of light gems, as if the rockets of a fairground firework display had fallen in his head. Immediately, I was afraid. I am very inclined to take fright; that is because my mother, when I was small, put me to bed in a room without light; I woke up in the mist of darkness chilled by sweat, in fear…of what? Perhaps of daylight. With the result that I was very frightened.

But I reasoned, as they say. *Let's see*, I thought, *it's impossible that a giant crowned with gems is lying on the water between Bougival and the Île de Croissy. This is some kind of mirage, or else it is the reflection, in the water, of the turret of some villa, with that of the lamps of the table where coffee is being drunk.*

Very meticulous, as I am, I looked behind me, to my left, to my right. I did not discover anything that had a real resemblance to the giant lying on the Seine. In any case, he had vanished. He had been there, however. I have often thought about that vast somber body with the luminous forehead—a kind of enormous and mysterious corpse.

The other story dates from a journey I made to Brittany with Villiers de l'Isle Adam. We had departed together in order to visit a relative he had in a seaside village, a curé whom Villiers called Uncle Victor. The uncle received us very cordially in his presbytery, a vast building near the little church. It was agreed that I would sleep in a room on the first floor, where there was nothing but a bed, chair and a maid's mirror bought at some fair, on a wooden mantelpiece painted with marble variegations.

It is necessary that I say that, on that night, I had a mind somewhat disposed toward the terrors of the marvelous because Villiers, at dessert, had recounted the adventure of a cat in that same presbytery. As Villiers went into the large kitchen after a day spent hunting, he saw, in the dusk, the curé's scrawny little cat, hairless, very small and very thin, a very old cat, quite desolate, a skeleton of a cat, sitting on its rear, in the high, dark fireplace, in front of the black and red of two firebrands in a cross. Villiers had come in slowly, without making any noise; and the cat, the sad cat, was alone, or at least thought that it was alone, before the cross of sad firebrands, with the consequence that, renouncing the mute discretion that, for some unknown reason, for such a long time, animals have given proof before humans, the lamentable cat opened its little mouth, yawned, yawned again, and said: "Oh, how bored I am!" But suddenly, having perceived Villiers, it ran away, as if ashamed of having been caught *in flagrante delicto* speaking.

I was still thinking, almost ironically, but not entirely, about that adventure when I went into my room on the first floor of the presbytery. When I lifted the candle I saw the bed, I saw the chair, and, in the mirror n the mantelpiece I saw a scrawny cat, hairless and wretched.

"Good," I said to myself, in order to reassure myself—for I repeat that no one is more inclined to fear than me—"It's the cat that Villiers told me about. Of course, it isn't going to say 'How bored I am!' firstly, because cats can't talk, and secondly, because it wouldn't be polite before a guest. It must be on some piece of furniture and I'm seeing its reflection in the glass."

But there was no other furniture except the bed and the chair. Having looked, searched and rummaged everywhere, I could not discover any cat. However, there was one in the mirror. The reflection of my body hid the animal, but as soon as I moved to the right or the left, I saw the reflection of the cat—the cat that did not exist!

I was truly sick with fear. But as I am never obstinate in seeking the explanation of mysteries, and I prefer to submit to them, shivering, I went toward the bed and, having reached it, blew out the candle and lay down quickly.

More than once, before going to sleep, I seemed to see in the maid's mirror, above the mantelpiece of marbled wood, the scintillation of an open agate.

I have had insomnias since in thinking about that image of a cat without a cat. But it is necessary for me to hasten to tell you the third story. You will certainly be obliged to recognize, having read it, that the extraordinary often produces itself purely for the pleasure of being extraordinary.

We are now very far from Brittany, a land haunted by legends. After midnight once, I had missed the train for Chatou; I was obliged to spend the night at the station hotel. Scarcely had I lain down between the telephone and the frame in which the conditions for a return journey to London were painted, than I saw a form sitting in the armchair next to the bed—a form simultaneously angular and vague, giving the impression of a specter in the long pleats of a white veil.

Trembling—because of my customary fear—but very expert in things called supernatural, I did not hesitate to divine that it was a revenant; surely, if the form had stood up, I would have heard the sound of trailing chains. It did not stand up.

Alarmed, but polite, I asked: "Who are you?"

"A revenant," said the form.

I would have sworn it! I said: "Doubtless you're the specter of some poor man who was murdered in this room. Far be it from me to disapprove of your returning here in the hope of tormenting your murderer, perhaps unpunished, but I will make the remark to you that I exercise at *Le Journal* the functions of lyric poet and dramatic critic, which ordinarily go poorly with that of cut-throat; I am, therefore, not your murderer, and you ought to recognize that, resolved to pay for my overnight stay, I have the right to sleep peacefully, without a phantom, in this room."

The Form said: "You astonish me! You think that there was once a murder here? Not at all. No crime has ever been committed in the house where you are a guest and I am a ghost. But I am exercising my profession. As in the real world, there are special functions in the supernatural world. I am a Revenant, in the same way that one is employed in a ministry or the third role at the Théâtre de la République. I have no need to have been a victim in order to be an avenger. I tug the sheets of an infinite number of people who have nothing to do with any shroud.

"And to be clear, I'm not coming back, I'm coming. I'm a dead man who has never lived, and, since we're close to the Gare Saint-Lazare, a returnee who never went. That doesn't prevent me from being formidable and agitating sinister sounds, which you'll mistake in a little while for the train to Asnières pulling out—a true revenant, that one! That's our difference. Yes, Monsieur, there are apparitions of the living who have never appeared, Hamlet's fathers who were never poisoned, Banquos dead who were never Banquos alive.

"Providential law, of which you know nothing, employs us to frighten criminals, but when there are no criminals we show ourselves as if there were, like policemen patrolling in quarters where there have not yet been any nocturnal attacks. However, if my presence inconveniences you, I will gladly consent to go and exercise my métier of Revenant in the next room."

I was in accord with that, eagerly. The revenant vanished, and I slept very well. But my awakening retained the certainty that, terrible, charming, and even farcical.. Mystery has no need of Causation.

The Curious Adventure of a Hat

I wake up with a start. The clock, at that moment, chimes three o'clock—three o'clock in the morning. No daylight is sliding as yet through the crack between the shutters. The room is tinted everywhere by the vacillating light of the night-light.

I try to go back to sleep. I cannot. I look around, here and there, intently, in order to fatigue my eyes, to oblige them to close. On the contrary, they widen. Oh, that's singular: my hat is moving in the penumbra, of its own accord, at the approximate height that it would maintain if it coiffed the head of a man of medium stature. But it isn't coiffing any head. Beneath it, there is nothing. And it is moving around the room. It has a dignified, serene air, even ceremonious, being a top hat. And it is very curious, truly very curious, that hat, which no one is wearing, and yet is moving.

Is it the case that, unconsciously, I've gone back to sleep and that I'm dreaming? Not at all. I pinch my arm, I touch the cool marble top of the little table, I think about a book I've read, a novel that I'm writing. I really am awake, in full possessions of the little reason that remains to me. And I can see the top hat coming and going. However, I recall perfectly having hung it up, when I came in, on the hat-stand. In any case, if I hadn't hung it up, if I'd thrown it no matter where instead of hanging it up, that wouldn't explain in any fashion how it is maintaining itself in the air, and how it is moving around

To tell the truth, I am extraordinarily cowardly; but so many strange things have happened to me since I started taking notice of the things that happen to me that I have finally acquired the habit of the inexplicable. I succeed, therefore, in not shivering with terror, and, having got out of bed, I walk toward my hat, in order to observe its bizarre conduct at closer range.

Now, far from fleeing from me, like someone or something that one has surprised *in flagrante delicto* in the miraculous, my top hat advances toward me; yes, truly, it comes to meet me, and it salutes me. I mean that it inclines forward, as if it were moved by an invisible, very polite, hand that is saluting me. Utterly surprised, I confess, I fall into a armchair.

My hat descends at the same time as I do, and there it is, in front of me, at the height of my head, only a little higher. I don't know whether I'm mistaken, but it seems to me that, for a visitor entering without having been warned, this would be a spectacle liable to cause some astonishment: that of a man almost naked sitting in an armchair facing a top hat, isolated from everything, in semi-darkness.

However, that situation, passably ridiculous, cannot last for long. I want to clarify matters. I speak to my hat. I ask it: "Come on, let's be serious. How can it be that you're there, between the floor and the ceiling, without visible support, instead of being on the hat-stand, where I hung you up when I came in? For I have a clear memory of having hung you up."

Then my hat agitates, lifted up in front, as if hair beneath it were standing on end. It's evident that my question appears out of place to it, that it has irritated it. Very courteous by nature, I prepare to apologize for a perhaps-indiscreet interrogation, but it does not leave me the time. It has risen up again to the height, or very nearly, where it would be sustained if it coiffed a man of medium height. I stand up in my turn. It heads toward the door. I follow it, as one does in escorting a guest.

It stops. It salutes me, taking its leave. But after a backward movement, as if to go out, it approaches abruptly, and I feel it on my head. I see myself in a mirror, and I burst out laughing. And there was reason, I assure you, for it is entirely comical, a man in a chemise, beneath a black silk top hat.

The Gratitude of a Trumpet

It is necessary to recognize that, whether by virtue of a personal singularity of the eternal design that presides over Adamic destinies, or a diminution of human value that only obliges the Unknown to lesser efforts, and even authorizes mockery, the manifestations of Mystery are losing their sublimity every day, and sometimes go as far as to don puerile and silly exteriorities. They are no less extraordinary, but it seems that they are no longer worth the trouble of being so. Without ceasing to be inexplicable, prodigy is becoming ludicrous. One might say that in the drama of the incomprehensible, the great leading role is being understudied by some fairground clown.

Personally, I have frequently been witness to droll miracles, well made to amuse, not without causing cold sweat and fear. I want to tell you the story of a trumpet that certainly never had its peer. It is necessary to tell you that in a small town in the north of France, I had been a member of the jury for a contest of brass bands, and I had admired an instrument that emitted notes of a quite exceptional force and charm. I insisted ardently that the prize be given to the brass band of which it was a part, and several times, I said to my colleagues on the jury: "Did you notice? There was a trumpet, especially!"

After the banquet, where more than one toast was proposed to the Union of Choral and Instrumental Societies, I was heading on my own from street-light to street-light toward a small brasserie whose beer had been praised to me, when I felt something hard slide under my arm. I looked down. It was a trumpet. I did not marvel at all. I understood immediately, and I was quite touched.

Evidently, in order to thank me for my favorable judgment, the trumpet-player had wanted to make me a gift of his instrument, and, after having pushed it under my arm, he had fled modestly. Worthy fellow! Tomorrow, I would send the trumpet back to him via the hotel messenger-boy.

I sat down in the deserted garden of the brasserie, the brass instrument posed on the table.

As I emptied a third glass of beer, it began to play—the trumpet, I mean. It played a triumphal march, in my honor, evidently: more thanks. But I was obliged to be surprised. Lyres can sing on their own when the wind traverses them, but I had never heard mention of an Aeolian trumpet. And this one, to entertain me, was playing the tunes most delightful to me; it knew all the themes with which musicians ornament the mediocrity of the verses I write for them.

I was standing up, with my hair raised, flattered, undoubtedly, but frightened. Suddenly, there was a quack. It was the end of the prodigy. On the table, there was no longer a trumpet.

I have never told this story, for fear that people would mock me. At least mouths blew into the trumpets of Jericho.

Official Record of an Interrogation

The two guards pushed the man into the examining magistrate's office.

"Hey!" he said. "Look out; you nearly stepped on my dress."

On his dress? He was dressed in a gray and green check suit. When he came in he made the gesture with his left hand of lifting up a skirt, and with his right hand, that of lowering a veil over his face.

The magistrate, his face white and pink, rather fat, with side-whiskers like snowy chrysanthemums, looked at the man who had been brought to him, almost a child, thin, puny, pale and pretty, with short blond hair, curling over a low, narrow forehead, and demanded, with his shoulders on the back of his armchair: "Your name, age, profession and domicile?"

In the voice of a little girl reciting a fable, the accused stammered very rapidly: "Anne-Louise-Chrétienne Doucelet, eighteen years, milliner, Rue de l'Abbaye, 14."

The judge shrugged his shoulders. "Your name is Lucien-Raymond-Renaud Maulurier; you're twenty-two years old; you're a student of law; you reside at Rue des Écoles, 226,"

"No, Monsieur, my name…"

"Enough. Write, clerk." The magistrate went on "You know of what you're accused? Four weeks ago, on the twenty-sixth of June, at approximately eight o'clock in the evening, you threw the girl Doucelet, your mistress, from the Pont du Rueil into the Seine. Her cadaver was found in the grass under a tree on the Île de Croissy."

The accused could not help laughing; they were little light and muffled giggles, like a schoolgirl tickled in class by her neighbor on the bench.

"Pardon, Monsieur, pardon. But it's too funny, though, you saying that. You think that I, Chrétienne, threw

Chrétienne in the water, where she drowned? The world must be mad to imagine such things." Then, seriously: "It's true that I've committed a crime, but not the one you think. My fault was not to have been good to Renaud, and if I'm guillotined, it will serve me right. But they don't cut off the heads of people who are already dead, do they? I need to tell you the whole story."

While the magistrate, irritated at first, and then surprised, considered him intently, not without some anxiety, the accused went on:

"It was two years ago that I met Renaud. I was very pretty before having died in the water. Not a regular beauty, no, but amusing in the eyes, the lips, the cheeks, and a little turned-up nose, such that someone at the Café Voltaire made up a song that said:

> *On her little pink face*
> *Flutter wings of flesh,*
> *Her nose as pert as a bird,*
> *With its tail in the air.*

"As soon as we had talked at the Medicis, Renaud and me, it was agreed immediately that we'd live together. I wasn't an honest girl, of course; it wasn't only because my mother as a laundress that I was familiar with men's underclothes, but after all, since I'm a milliner, I worked sometimes before going to the café; I was what they used to call a grisette. Renaud understood that I was better than the whores at the Medicis, and it was charming, our honeymoon, that spring, in the little room of the fifth floor of a chic house, from which you could see the trees and the whiteness of swans on the green lakes of lawns."

He spoke more slowly and gravely, in a voice that was less shrill: "How we loved one another! How good it was to hold one another tightly, in the evenings, at the window, higher than all the city, closer to the sky than any other living beings!"

He seemed astonished by the words he had spoken. He resumed smiling, and he spoke again, his voice light and clear:

"To be sure, it wasn't boring, in the beginning. Everything I wanted—pretty dresses, jewelry, and dinners in places where one eats well, and boxes in theaters—Renaud gave it to me. He was from a rich family, in Brittany, who sent him lots of money, and all that he wanted—all that he wanted was me!—I gave it to him, and gave it to him again and again. That happiness would have lasted a long time if Renaud had been reasonable, but he had the stupidity of being jealous.

"Look, if I gave you my word, you wouldn't believe, Monsieur le juge, that I'd stay at home for three weeks without going out even once on my own, not even at night! However, true is true, it's the pure truth. Then it began to be boring, being so happy. It isn't amusing only to have one bed, when one has the habit of having several.

"I ended up making arrangements in a manner to pull strokes on Renaud without him noticing. Often, when he went to lunch with his correspondent, who was a curé—a canon, as he put it—I'd rejoin the little comrades of a dressmaking workshop who walked along the Boulevard Michel at midday, munching a croissant, and we'd go to bars with young men who made us laugh or old ones who made us laugh even more, and gave us their card to go and see them. 'You'll see, you'll be content, I'll only tell you that!' But it was necessary to go home, because of the time that Renaud would return.

"In sum, well, he was wrong; if he'd wanted an honest woman, he only had to marry one from his homeland, or his canon's daughter, if canons have children. Then, there were evenings when he was utterly tiresome, and terrible. It appeared that he was born and brought up out there in Brittany in a big château where there are ghosts, with noises of chains in corridors and voices that came through the shutters, from the wall in the courtyard. And often, after dinner, when I said to him: 'Hey, chéri, what if we were to go to the Bullier,' he replied: 'No, no, not this evening, there's a storm, let's go home. We won't light the lamp. I'll talk to you very quietly, in the dark, I'll tell you things…things that don't happen to people who are alive...things that happen to people who are dead…let's go home, let's go home, in order to be frightened!'

"Well, that was quite a party, that! And it was true that, all alone, at home, we were frightened. There were nights when, both lying down, him half-dressed, one of his hands on each of my shoulders, pale, lips trembling, hair standing in end, he stammered such frightful adventures of specters that love one another, skeletons that break their bones by hugging one another so hard, that I started howling with fear like a beaten whore.

"Once, after snatching me from the bed, and sticking me against the wall, he shouted almost in my mouth: 'And you know, it's necessary that you don't believe that we can ever be separated from one another, when we've been united as we are!'

"I said, trying to make a joke: 'All the same, what if I left you?'

"He howled: 'Imbecile, I know full well that you're an abominable slut and that you lie down, day or night, with anyone who opens his bed to you. But if you can steal your body from me for an hour, I defy you to take your soul away, which belongs to me forever! Know one thing! Know one thing! And this is what all the old women of my homeland say, who sing songs on the road: there's an indissoluble hymen beyond the hole where the flesh rots, from which the spirit escapes. If there are ruptures before death, there's no divorce after life. Better than that, my child, the union continued won't be enough. Death isn't limited to keeping couples together; it substitutes one personality for another; with the consequence that, if I died tomorrow, I'd live on in you, and if you died, I'd become you!'

"The concierge often told me that some mornings—those after the nights when he'd been so frightful, Renaud went to church to hear mass. I have religion; it's good to go to mass. All the same, you'll admit, Monsieur le juge, that hearing things like those he said to me isn't amusing, every night."

He drew breath, and then continued:

"All the same, I loved him, my Renaud. I could have left him, yes. There were old ladies who sent me telegrams to tell me that a very respectable monsieur would be glad to meet with me...I even went to those rendezvous, because a woman always has a heap of little things to buy, doesn't she, that she can't ask her lover for. But it goes without saying that I loved him, Renaud, because he was so good, such a pretty boy, too, and because in between all that, he gave me 'everything I needed.'"

After a pause:

"But there was the adventure of the bridge, the adventure for which I'll be guillotined, if I'm not dead. I said to him: 'No, I don't want to be frightened this evening.' and we set off for Rueil, After dinner at Maison Fournaise, it happened that a monsieur at another table, who was alone, said a heap of things to me with his eyes, moving a watch-chain in which he had diamonds mingled with bits of gold. Because of the brightness of the diamonds I understood immediately that he wanted me to go and chat with him, just for a moment—to arrange something—at the back of the alleyway beside the restaurant. I said to Renaud: 'I'll be back in a minute, my love.'

"The monsieur with the gold chain hadn't joined me yet when, in the darkness of the alley, Renaud grabbed me by the wrist. He dragged me away, made me climb the stairway of the bridge, pushed me on to the bridge, bent me over the parapet and shouted in my ear: 'Slut! Slut! That's enough! You're going to die! You can be sure you're going to die. The only thing, filthy creature, that could stop me killing you is the thought that, dead, you'll become me, you'll become me with all your dirtiness, all your treasons, all your clowning, all your depravity! But no matter: to have you in me, after your death, will be the just punishment for having loved and possessed you alive.'

"And he threw me over the parapet. I fell into the water, where I drowned. Since then, I no longer remember anything, except that I'm dead—so that it's nothing to me to be guillotined. And Renaud, it will be necessary to guillotine him too. He'll be dead for the first time. That will be a superiority for me, which I already had, since he loved me more than I loved him. And we'll be together. I won't be any prouder for that, and I'd rather go, even as a phantom, to the bars of the Boulevard Michel. But I know that's impossible. He has me. He wants me always to be frightened with him. And I obey him, who has become me."

The Tears That Do Not Know What To Mourn

Once, in an unknown country to which chance, if not destiny, had guided me, I felt a great desire to weep. That day, I did not have any motive for despair, except for the insipidity of everything. That is so quotidian that I had long since lost the habit of being moved by it. Why, then, did I experience such a desire to weep? It was extreme, urgent and torturing. It seemed to me that I was going to die if I did not weep. It seemed to me that I would be infinitely happy if I wept. But at the same time, I took account of the fact that it would be impossible for me to shed tears unless a truly determining occasion was offered to me. My tears, amassed behind my eyelids, were like water behind a sluice-gate, water that wants to flow, but will only flow if the sluice is opened. A circumstance was required for the dear effusion.

I said to myself: *It would be extraordinary if there were nothing better or worse than coincidence between my need to weep and my arrival in this unknown country to which the hazard, if not the destiny, of the voyage has brought me. Certainly, I shall find here what is needed to satisfy the desire that I have conceived.*

I walked though the poor quarters of the city; I saw through windows devoid of curtains or glass, the destitution of beds, the tremulous labor of old women setting aside the least ignoble rags, the meager and green nudity of children on bare tiles. I gave alms, but I did not weep.

As I traversed a square, a tram crushed a woman who had thrown herself on to the rails; I helped to carry her as far as a nearby pharmacy but I did not weep.

I read in a newspaper that a mother, in order to remove them from misery, had poisoned her two children; I saw, in a theater where there as a matinee, the adventure of two little orphans that a wicked old woman, by beating them, constrained to beg; I felt deeply touched, but I did not weep.

I would do well, I thought, *to go to the cemetery. Cemeteries are places that offer occasions for sobs; between the tombs I shall probably find the opportunity to satisfy this desire to weep, which is augmenting, augmenting incessantly.*

The cemetery was charming because of the wind that stirred the willows, in which perching doves swayed, because of the rays of evening sunlight that leapt from tombstone to tombstone like roseate wagtails. But the epitaphs spoke of separating deaths, of unconsoled widowhoods; tombs deplored cradles; and here and there, a name reminded me of some dear departed—friend, relative, and father and mother, alas—over whom I had thrown the first spadeful of earth in the cemetery of my homeland.

However, I was not weeping, with such a great desire to weep, when my gaze fell upon a small elevation of gray earth, whitening, as if chalky, over which a very low cross planted, in old unpainted wood, cracked, rotten and crumbling; and there was no inscription on the wood. I had stopped; I considered the gray and chalky earth. Who, then, as underneath it? I had a kind of tender curiosity to know. I could not have explained why I had that curiosity.

I asked a gardener of the cemetery, who was going past with a spade over his shoulder: "Can you tell me, Monsieur, who is buried here?"

He shrugged his shoulders. "Who knows?" he replied. "It's a whole story. Ten years ago, a little girl who was dead was found on the other side of the city. She wasn't wounded, she was dead, that's all. She wasn't a beggar; she was well-dressed, like a demoiselle, and pretty. But nobody recognized her. All the same, it was necessary to bury her, with the permission of the Maire. She was put there. She's been there for ten years. She has no crypt, no marble slab, no wreaths, as you see. She ought not to find herself any worse off than the others."

The gardener went away.

I thought: *She died on the road. Who knows whether she didn't leave home in order to come to meet me? Who knows whether she might not have been the person that I always believed I would see appear at every turning in the road? Perhaps we would have recognized one another? But that's the way it is; souls that are destined for one another aren't informed of the direction in which it's necessary to go. This one turns right, that one turns left; and the weaker dies first, on the road.*

Then I fell to my knees beside the pale funereal earth, and I wept delectably for a long, long time, forever.

www.ingramcontent.com/pod-product-compliance
Ingram Content Group UK Ltd.
Pitfield, Milton Keynes, MK11 3LW, UK
UKHW041410180426
11947UKWH00007B/38